DR.'S SURPRISE TRIPLETS WIFE NEEDED

A MEDICAL ROMANCE

Carol Hutchens

DEDICATION

To my husband Larry
and our sons for believing in me.
And to the new blessings in our family; our daughter-
in-law and grandson.

ACKNOWLEDGMENTS

My parents started me on my journey to becoming a writer. Both were readers, but especially my mother. My dad read and never stopped trying to master new things. They insisted we study and do our best. They gave us wings...all we needed to do was learn to fly. I miss them every day.

CHAPTER 1

"What do we have?" Dr. Daniel Prince demanded as he rushed to scrub for the emergency caesarean. As Raleigh's largest hospital, Capitol General had the most advanced neonatal unit in the area so cases varied.

"DOA on oxygen. Severe head trauma. Late stage pregnancy." A nurse read from the chart as another tied his surgical gown. The odor of antiseptic and disinfectant drifted around him. Adrenaline raced through his veins. His need to protect was why he became a doctor.

Childhood experiences made him watch over others, but he couldn't convince his younger brother to focus on a career. Greg's enjoyment of life made Daniel feel every one of his thirty-five years. Because of his protective instinct, he'd never been carefree as his brother.

That was part of Greg's complaint. He didn't want to be like Daniel. Greg wanted to have fun.

Hands extended, Daniel paused for a nurse to snap surgical gloves on his hands. Shoving worries about Greg's irresponsibility aside, he entered the operating room. Blood surged through his veins as he approached the operating table. "Fetal heartbeat?"

"Steady. But there's an echo."

"Echo?" Daniel frowned at the body on the gurney. "Are you hearing a second heartbeat? Do we have twins? Have you notified NICU?" He turned toward the nurse at his side. "Do we have a sonogram?"

"There wasn't time. Patient just arrived." Glancing down at her chart, she reported the expected information. "Mid-twenties. Over-all appearance suggests good health. No signs of needle marks. No skin discoloration to suggest excessive drinking. Fingers not stained from smoking."

Daniel nodded to the anesthesiologist, then his glance dropped to the body on the table. It was normal to see a patient's skin look white as the sheets covering their body. But this patient's face looked different. Her face looked cold and distant as a marble statue. The only difference seemed to be the blonde curls escaping the bandage around her head.

Daniel tore his glance away. No matter how hard he tried, he couldn't save this patient. His only hope was to focus on saving her unborn child. Turning toward his staff nurse, keeping his voice business like, he spoke in his usual no nonsense tone. "Is she an organ donor?"

"Not mentioned on the chart."

Surprise held Daniel's hand frozen over the patient's abdomen. The uninformed response was not what he expected. Words ringing with tension, he snapped. "Check her driver's license."

He regretted the sharpness of his tone instantly. He was good at controlling situations, and taking risks to save lives, but delivering an infant when the mother was DOA, hammered at the shield around his heart. A quick glance told him his team felt the tension as well. They understood the implications of this situation. A child needed parents.

He understood the importance of a parent in a child's life more than most people. That factor shaped his life just as it would this infant's. "Is there a father?"

"I don't have that information." The slight tremble in the nurse's voice leveled off as she read from the chart. "The

EMT's put the patient on oxygen as soon as they arrived at the scene. They lost her on the ride to the hospital, but continued with the oxygen."

On the other side of the table, a nurse dropped a surgical instrument on a metal tray. The clanging chime blended with the murmurs of the surgical staff as they prepared for the surgery.

The noise of the room and the hum of equipment added to Daniel's sense of urgency. He shared a bond with this team's commitment to make things right for their patients. And this patient was no different. Even with though the mother was dead, they would fight to save her fetus. The infant deserved a chance at life.

"Has Dr. Morgan been called?"

"Yes, Doctor. NICU has been alerted. Dr. Morgan is on the way."

Glancing at the clock of the far wall, Daniel frowned. He wouldn't wait for a neonatologist. Delivering this fetus was his job. His body snapped to autopilot. "Give me the patient's stats?"

Silence dropped over the room.

His words echoed off the walls, causing the cold truth to slam him in the face. He usually asked that question before making an incision. But this patient was DOA.

Silently, Daniel cursed his mistake. "Is the fetus getting enough oxygen? Do we have a steady heartbeat?"

Rustling movements told him the team had recovered from his blunder. But he stole a quick glance at the patient's face to confirm the situation. From where he stood, the damage to her head didn't show. All he saw was an angelic expression on a face too young to die. Too young to leave an infant motherless.

Gritting his teeth, fighting thoughts of the unfairness of a life lost so young, of a child cheated of its mother, he focused on her exposed abdomen. After a quick examination of the bulging mound, he realized the situation had escalated to a new urgency.

"We have more than one fetus." Daniel pressed the abdomen with gentle fingers to confirm his suspicions. "Check the heart beat, again."

"I detect a second heartbeat." The nurse said from the other side of the table.

"I'm here, Dr. Prince." Dr. Morgan appeared at his side.

Daniel sent her a quick nod and pressed his fingers against the abdomen again. Brow arched, he turned to the neonatologist at his elbow. "You'll need extra staff. We have three babies."

After a stunned moment of silence, a frenzy of activity started behind him as the surgical staff prepared more instruments for the additional infants.

Dr. Morgan rushed to the phone on the wall to call in two extra teams from the neonatal intensive care unit. Three infants meant they were probably dealing with preemies.

Daniel met the anesthesiologist's eyes over the mask covering his face. Their questions went unspoken, but they shared concern for the condition of the infants. "Ready?"

If he hadn't seen the deathly white face and blue lips of the mother, Daniel wouldn't have suspected anything unusual about this C-section. But this delivery was definitely different. He had to save infants facing the world without a mother.

Lifting the scalpel, he made an incision down the mother's abdomen. "What's the update on organ donor status?"

He reached in the layers of skin and muscle and noted the missing barrier of the amniotic sac. *Not good.* How long since the water broke? With a skilled flick of his wrist, he pulled the first infant from the mother's body and said over the slurping sound of muscle and tissue. "It's a boy."

The infant was small, less than five pounds, by his guess, but the skin was pink tinted and looked healthy except from one thing. Murky green fluid dripped from the baby's body. Daniel did a quick suction of the mouth and nostrils and put an encouraging hand on the small chest. The infant responded with a cry.

Daniel made quick work of clamping off the umbilical cord and passed the baby to waiting hands. "Dr. Morgan, alert your team. We have signs of fecal matter."

Reaching his hand inside the abdominal cavity for another fetus, he heard nurses rushing the first infant to the warming table to clean him and run the Apgar scale. When his fingers found a second fetus, Daniel pulled gently. Remains of the amniotic sac hooked on the infant's shoulder as he worked the body free. More green fluid dripped from the second infant's body.

Daniel sighed. One sac. Two same sex babies. Identical twins. A quick inspection showed the second infant's color was good.

He made a mental note to thank the EMTs for their swift action in supplying oxygen to the mother. The second twin was smaller, but the oxygen given the mother made all the difference in the infant's chances of survival.

Dr. Morgan leaned close. "With the amino fluid being this green there was definitely an early bowel excretion."

Daniel nodded. "I suspect pressure on the mother's abdomen during the accident caused it."

"Infant number one is four pounds, ten ounces." A nurse called from the far side of the room.

Daniel cleaned the second infant's mouth and nostrils. He'd guess baby number two weighed less than the first. Infants had a much better chance of full recovery if they were close to five pounds at birth.

Infant number two cried. The staff cheered.

Daniel spared a twitch of his lips and reached into the mother's abdomen to search for another fetus. His fingers bounced off a balloon like object. They had twins and a single. No identical triplets for this mother.

His heart gave a thud as he remembered the mother would never know one way or another. Sighing at the thought, he carefully pulled the third fetus out of the mother's abdominal cavity. The tiny girl's skin was bluer, but she didn't have green fluid covering her body. A good sign. Her chances were compromised enough by her need for oxygen.

A hollow sensation twisted Daniel's gut, but the baby

squalled almost before he suctioned her mouth properly. He allowed a smile behind the shield of his mask. This little lady might be tiny, but she was a fighter.

"We have a female. Can you tell she's complaining by her demanding cry?" Relief that he had saved the tiny infants from dying with their mother filled his voice. Laughter sounded from the staff in the room. Daniel clamped the umbilical cord and passed the infant to Dr. Morgan's waiting hands.

Reaching in to the mother's abdomen, he searched for another infant, just in case. Working on a DOA mother was hard on the team, but saving three infants was encouraging. He didn't find any additional infants. They had three live births. The tightness in his shoulders eased.

Three motherless infants were three too many, but they were alive and the NICU teams would work to keep them that way.

"Do we close?" His voice lifted over the chatter in the room as the nurses from NICU took charge of the three infants. "Do we know about organ donation?"

"Number two infant is four pounds five ounces."

"Doctor Prince?"

Daniel turned his head toward the urgency in the voice of the nurse standing in the doorway. She held up an object, he immediately identified as a driver's license. "Not an organ donor. But you need to take a look at this."

Daniel turned to his resident. "Clark, close up. And don't make one stitch that will leave a scar."

All eyes turned in his direction and stared. But he'd made his point. Honor the dead. He turned toward the nurse at the door. "What is it?"

"We have a problem." A nurse called from the isolettes where the infants were being checked.

In two long strides, Daniel was beside the cart holding the baby girl. The nurse passed him a stethoscope. "I'm getting an irregular heartbeat."

Daniel's hand was wider than the tiny chest as he positioned the stethoscope. "Have you double checked?"

"Three times. All with rapid, weak beats."

Daniel listened again and frowned. "Dr. Morgan, any suggestions?"

The neonatologist left the twin she was checking and stepped to his side, "Could be the heart, PDA, RDS, or Apnea. It's too soon to tell."

"We need a cardiac monitor on this one." Daniel put the stethoscope on the tiny chest and listened again. "Call in a heart specialist, stat." He glanced toward the nurse. "Get an oximeter on this infant. Keep close check on the blood levels until the heart specialist gets here."

"Good idea to monitor the oxygen in the blood. It may only be respiratory stress disorder, but it's too soon to tell." Dr. Morgan looked over her mask. "Don't worry. My NICU team will take it from here."

Daniel nodded, conceding he had stepped on her turf. Reluctantly, he moved to make room for the NICU team to get closer to the tiny infant. "How are the male infants checking out?"

"Good numbers. Color is good. We'll keep close check for fever. That green fluid usually means trouble." Dr. Morgan stepped close to Daniel's side. "The NICU teams have the isolettes ready to move when the infants are stable."

Daniel stared over his mask at the three tiny survivors and nodded. Remembering the way his hands tingled when he touched their skin, unsettled him. He hadn't wanted to let go of them. He didn't want the triplets out of his sight. But Dr. Morgan's quick response reminded him she was the expert and she was ready to take over.

Behind her, at least a dozen people dressed in the pastel colors of the NICU, gathered around the three infants to take charge of their care.

"Dr. Morgan, keep close check on baby number three." Daniel tried to shake off this feeling of attachment making his cautious. He didn't usually feel this tug of connection. The mother being deceased must have activated his protective instinct.

"Will do." Dr. Morgan put her stethoscope against the infant girl's tiny chest. "Where is that heart specialist?"

"I'm here," Dr. Casey said as he rushed through the door and joined Dr. Morgan at the infant girl's side.

Daniel stepped back to wait with the rest of his team. Their part in the delivery had ended.

"Dr. Prince?"

Daniel turned to find the nurse who called him before the panic over the baby girl erupted at his side. Eyebrow raised, he angled his chin indicating she should continue.

"The patient's name is Sigourney Eller. This paper was taped to her driver's license." The nurse held up a folded piece of paper. "Your name is listed as her emergency contact. Is she one of your patients?"

Daniel grabbed the paper. He had never heard the name Sigourney Eller, or seen the woman pictured on the license before she arrived his surgical table. So why had she carried his name and telephone number?

A flash of realization sliced through him. *Greg.*

Lead settled in his chest. Perspiration formed beads on his forehead. This could only mean one thing. His brother was involved with the mother. Quick on the heels of that point, came a thought that knocked all the air from his lungs. *Where was Greg? Had he been in the car accident?*

Daniel rushed out of the operating room. "I need a phone." *He. Had. To. Talk. To. Greg.*

⚙

"Come in," Cydney Eller answered the knock on her office door as she looked up from the file of her latest advertising client. Her assistant entered. With the tiered skirt flouncing around pencil thin hips and fuzzy pink sweater clinging to her shoulders, Tamera looked more like a model than a secretary.

"Got a minute?"

Smiling, Cydney leaned back in her chair. "Sure. What's up?"

"I'm bummed out." With a grace as natural to her as breathing, Tamera arranged herself in the chair in front of

Cydney's desk. "My yearly physical is today."

That comment sounded so much like her sister, Cydney clenched her fists to control the swift jab of pain. "Which is worse, do you think, trying to pee in a cup or that paper gown that leaves your backside naked?"

"I always miss the cup." Tamera giggled.

"Putting your feet in those stirrups is always fun," Cydney said rolling her eyes.

Another laugh escaped Tamera. "You hate them too?"

Cydney nodded. "I get to do it twice a year. I have to go with Ziggy to make sure she keeps her appointment." She blinked back the moisture in her eyes.

Tamera peeped through the long curling locks swishing around her face. "How long since you heard from her this time?"

Cydney focused on rearranging the files on her desk. "Not a word in six months."

"That's good. She usually calls to borrow money if she's in trouble, right?"

Tamera's sympathetic tone forced Cydney to answer. "I wish she would call to say she's okay."

Tamera stood up. "Try not to worry." She flounced to the door and turned. "These yearly physicals put me off having kids. How about you?"

"I'll pass on kids." Cydney expelled a sigh. "I didn't do very good job raising my sister. I'm afraid to risk taking care of a baby."

"Ziggy is twenty-seven years old. You can't blame yourself for her actions."

"Thanks, Tam. You're the perfect assistant and good for my ego, too."

"I want an advertising job, like you. So guard your back, boss."

A smile twitched Cydney's lips as the door closed on Tamera's laughter. Why couldn't Ziggy be like Tamera and settle into a job for more than a two months?

But Ziggy always did things her way, and the world had better wait. Cydney stared at the folder of one of the firm's biggest clients. The major drug company was located near Raleigh in the Research Triangle Park. This project was the one she had longed for. It was her chance to earn the promotion she'd worked hard for, but her mind filled with thoughts of her sister instead of advertising slogans.

Their father had called Ziggy his little Angel. With blonde curls and big blue eyes, she looked angelic. That was part of the problem. Everyone expected things to work out for Ziggy, and that the way her sister liked it.

Cydney closed her eyes and mouthed a silent plea. *Please call. Tell me you're okay. Please, Ziggy. Please.* For the next hour, Cydney worked without interruption, until a buzz broke her concentration.

"Cydney?" The intercom on desk crackled static. "Uh, Miss Eller? There's a police officer here to see you."

Staring at the black box emitting the strained sound of Tamera's voice, nerves clenching with dread, Cydney said. "Send him in."

Not another one of Ziggy's fender benders. Gripping the arms of her chair, Cydney stared at the door as if expecting a two-headed monster, but a clean cut young man in a dark navy uniform appeared, instead. "Come in, Officer."

"Ms. Cydney Eller?"

Cydney swallowed the boulder in her throat. "How can I help you, officer?"

"I'm sorry to deliver bad news, ma'am. But your sister has been in an accident. You need to go to the hospital, immediately."

"How bad is she?"

"Sorry, ma'ma. I'm not at liberty to say."

"I'll take you, Cydney." Tamera peeped out from behind the officer's shoulder.

But old habits flared up and Cydney shook her head. She needed to take care of herself. Standing, Cydney straightened her shoulders and headed for the door. "I'll drive. You have that doctor's appointment."

Daniel shrugged out of the long surgical gown and flung it aside as he ran toward the nurses' station, the folded paper clutched in his hand. "I need a phone."

When the flustered nurse at the desk didn't respond fast enough, he leaned over the counter and grabbed the phone. Ignoring the nurse's exclamation, he dialed the familiar number and pressed the phone to his ear. Ten rings later, there was still no answer. Daniel slammed the phone down, then jerked it off the cradle and tried the call again.

Nothing.

Greg! Answer the damn phone.

After a third try, he forced his brain to switch off big brother mode and return to duty. His gut twisted in knots as he headed toward the family waiting room. He hated delivering bad news to families needing updates on the condition of their loved ones. This time the news was especially poignant. Three infants were alive, but the mother had died.

Greg? Call, damn it. Taking a deep breath, Daniel stepped to the waiting room door and said in a firm tone. "The Sigourney Eller family?"

A slender young woman in a navy suit stood shakily and walked toward him. Her green eyes glowed in a face void of color. Short sable-brown hair framed her face as she looked at him with a silent plea in those expressive eyes. "I'm Cydney Eller. Sigourney is my sister."

Daniel's chest tightened with sympathy and other emotions as he offered his hand. This part of his job was never easy and the woman staring back at him was as pale as her deceased sister had been. "Daniel Price. I'm very sorry, Ms. Eller."

"My sister isn't—"

"She suffered extensive head trauma in the accident. EMTs rushed to her aid, but pronounced her brain dead on arrival. I'm sorry I don't have better news."

Any color left now drained from the woman's face, and Daniel had thought she was pale to start with. Her fingers clutched the strap of her shoulder bag until her knuckles glowed white against the black leather. He wished he could offer more sympathy for her loss, but they were strangers and she held her body stiff as a marble column.

At the mention of marble, a hollow feeling filled his chest. Dread almost choked the air from his lungs. Loosing a sibling would be like losing part of your life.

❦

Cydney tried to swallow as she stared at the stern faced doctor. If she kept her body rigid and concentrated on his green surgical scrubs, maybe she could ignore the pain his words inflicted.

Ziggy couldn't be dead.

Wouldn't she feel some shock to her universe if Ziggy had died? She had practically raised her. Ziggy was more like her child than her sister. But the buzz of conversations continued around her and her skin tingled under the doctor's watchful stare. His eyes were the color of dark chocolate. She even noticed his brown hair looked alive with curl. And still she felt numb.

Alive. That's how she wanted Ziggy. Alive.

The doctor's alert gaze should have reassured her, but the confidence he wore like a second skin made her tremble with denial. A man like this didn't make mistakes. His confident manner and years of training forced her to believe his words were true.

"It can't be…" she denied the message ringing in her head. Swallowing the tears filling the back of her throat, she whispered, "Ziggy usually survives her escapades unscathed."

"She didn't suffer, if that's any comfort. She died instantly."

Her gaze clung to his face to keep her anchored in reality. Muscles bunched along the doctor's strong jaw. His eyes darkened with compassion. She inhaled a shuddering breath, then wished she hadn't. Medicinal odors filled her lungs and made her head swim.

Until her last breath, she would associate that odor with the man in front of her. She could tell by the warmth in his eyes that he didn't like delivering this news anymore than she liked receiving it. Pain twisted in her chest, but she wouldn't burden this doctor with her emotions. She learned early in life to take care of things herself. It was time to face facts. She had to wake each morning for the rest of her life with the knowledge that she had failed her only relative. *But...Ziggy couldn't be dead. She was too young to die.*

"I…t-thank you, Doctor." She turned to walk away, needing to escape and hide her pain, but the doctor called her back.

"Ms. Eller?"

She turned to face him on legs so stiff they felt frozen. He stared at her from eyes so deep she could get lost in them. "Yes?"

"Do you know why your sister carried my name as her emergency contact?"

Ziggy hadn't even listed her as her emergency contact. How had she failed so badly that Ziggy would list a stranger instead of her own sister? When had things gone so wrong between them? Had she made a mistake when she insisted Ziggy should find a job?

"I-I…w-what was your name again?" Cydney fought against emotions clouding her brain. *Why had Ziggy trusted this man more than her own sister? Who was he? How had Ziggy known him?*

"Daniel Prince." His tone hardened as he returned her stare. "Dr. Daniel Prince."

Feeling her legs wobble, Cydney dropped to the nearest chair. "I…I-I'm sorry. I haven't seen my sister in several months." She swallowed a mound of regret. How could she know Ziggy would die? Was it wrong to expect a person her sister's age to hold down a job? "We had a disagreement. She walked out. I don't know why she carried your name in her purse."

A sense of failure robbed her lungs of air. Nerves pounded behind her eyes. First, her dad deserted them when she was six. Her mother fell to pieces. She and Ziggy nearly starved before a neighbor called social services. Now, this doctor oozing life and good looks was telling her that her precious sister was dead.

A deep loss washed over her, made even stronger by the sense of failure eating at her insides. *What now? What did she do now?*

Since she was old enough to notice her mother's response to disappointment, she had vowed to concentrate on a career. She wanted to have choices about her future, unlike her mother who needed to depend on a man. But what did choices matter if Ziggy was dead?

Chills raced along her limbs. She shivered. *Why, Ziggy? Why?*

"About your sister—"

"Doctor Prince?" A police officer approached, Daniel.

"Yes?"

"Is Gregory Prince your brother?"

Squaring his shoulders, preparing to receive the news he had feared since the nurse handed him the folded paper from the woman's wallet, Daniel nodded. "Yes."

"Sir, your brother was in the accident with Ms. Eller's sister. I'm sorry, Dr. Prince. He died, instantly."

Daniel ran a hand over his head, knocking off the surgical cap he had forgotten he still wore. Blood pounded in his ears. His skin turned icy. So, this was how families felt when he told them a loved one had died. The news hit like a blow to the back of the knees even though he had feared it was coming. *Greg was dead.*

Twenty-nine was too young to die. Greg…was too full of life to be on a cold slab in the morgue. Why hadn't Greg listened? Why hadn't he slowed down when Daniel warned him to stop driving at break-neck speed?

A soft hand touched Daniel's. Tingles pierced his skin, alerting his numb senses he was still breathing. But this woman's touch only added to the pain attacking every inch of his body. He was supposed to protect his younger brother. Set a good example for him since their father hadn't. Be a loving uncle to Greg's kids. Spoil them.

Kids! *Greg didn't have kids.* Unless. A second blow almost

brought him to his knees. *The triplets! Could it be?*

Sigourney Eller had carried his name in case of emergency. What if the triplets were his brother's children? It was a small measure of comfort, but Daniel relished the knowledge that Greg had known he could count on Daniel no matter what. *Now, his name in the woman's wallet made sense.*

"Was Greg driving the vehicle?"

"Yes, sir," the officer sent a troubled glance toward the woman at Daniel's side. "Ms. Eller's sister was the passenger."

Cydney Eller's gasp drew Daniel's glance. Color drained from her face. He saw the depth of his pain reflected in her eyes. She removed her comforting touch from his arm and stepped away from him.

Time stopped. Reality kicked him in the gut. Had he lost Greg only to gain nephews and a niece? Daniel met Cydney Eller's wide-eyed stare. His silent gaze begged her to forgive his brother's life ending mistake. Should he tell her of his suspicions? Could she take another shock this soon?

What if he was wrong?

Their siblings could have no connection beyond a casual encounter. Maybe neighbors? But his gut told him different. He'd felt a jolt of energy when he touched those infants. How could he explain such a fanciful response to a woman who had just learned her sister was dead?

But he couldn't walk away from her either.

If those infants were Greg's, he would do everything in his power to protect them just as he tried to protect their father. *If they were Greg's.* He had to find out.

"Officer, are there any legal issues I need to take care of regarding the accident?" What were you supposed to say to the police officer who told you your only brother was dead? *You're a good man, officer. Did my brother cause the accident? Was the passenger to blame?* None of that worked. *Greg was dead.*

"I need your address, Dr. Prince. There will be charges for towing and storage of the vehicle in the impound lot."

Daniel recited his address. *Greg had gone out with a bang, just as he lived.* "Anything else, Officer?"

"The rest will wait. Please accept my condolences, Ms. Eller, Dr. Prince."

"Thank you, Officer." Cydney Eller's voice was soft as she acknowledged the words.

Daniel held his hand out, and fought the urge to ask for proof. Could they have made a mistake? Made the wrong ID? Could there be another Gregory Prince? Hands on his hips, he stood staring at the doors closing behind the officer. Was it true, then? Things like this really happened?

"I'm sorry for your loss."

Cydney Eller's kind words pierced the fog filling Daniel's brain and brought him back to alert. Shaking his head, he turned to face her. He opened his mouth...but no words came.

This was all new to him. He faced life and death situations daily. But this time his younger brother was the deceased. His only sibling died, leaving three infants needing his protection. "I guess we both need to plan a funeral."

Cydney dropped to one of the chairs and looked at him from glazed eyes. "I can't believe Ziggy is dead. She was always so full of life. People loved her."

She talked fast to hide her emotions and put some distance between her and this doctor. The pain in his dark eyes touched a soft spot in her that wanted to offer comfort. He was suffering just as she was. But his brother may have caused the pain ripping her world apart. But even if this doctor's brother had been driving the vehicle in the accident, he hadn't caused the lack of contact with her sister.

She had to live with the blame of that.

Pulling in a shuddering breath, she blinked moisture from her eyes. She was the one to blame for that last argument. She insisted Ziggy should get a job. Pain clawed at her chest. Spots danced before her eyes. Her words forced Ziggy to leave.

"Put your head between your knees." He wrapped a hand around the back of her neck and pushed her head down. His hand felt warm and strong. *A healing hand. Sturdy. Caring.*

This man took care of people. She inhaled deeply and pushed away from his touch. She couldn't remain connected to him. The brush of his hand sent tingles racing through her nerve endings and made her long for the safety his presence offered. But she couldn't give in to the urge. This doctor had his own grief to deal with and she couldn't expect comfort when he needed the same in return.

Yet, his mask like expression made her suspect he didn't accept unwanted emotions. Well, neither did she. If she accepted his offer of comfort, she might weaken, and she couldn't let that happen. *Not now.*

"Greg's laugh made people smile."

Lost in misery, she almost didn't hear his low words, but she recognized the pain in his voice. He was staring at the floor. She doubted he realized he'd spoken the words aloud. But needing to ease her pain, she responded.

"Ziggy twisted everyone around her little finger and left them thinking what she wanted was their idea." Cydney tried to shake the confusion filling her head, but despite her need to remain aloof, her words continued. "I hated the last six months without her. H-how can I face a lifetime without her?"

"I haven't thought that far ahead." Air whooshed past his lips.

Cydney heard the echo of her pain in his voice and squared her chin. His shoulders were broad enough to carry her troubles and his, but making another mistake was unthinkable. Look how her dealings with Ziggy ended.

"I...saying thank you seems strange in the circumstances." She saw his dazed expression and her heart softened. "I appreciate your kindness, Dr. Prince." Her knees wobbled as she stood. "I'm going to see Ziggy. Take care of yourself."

He held a hand up and blinked the dazed look from his eyes. "Wait. We need to talk. Was Greg dating your sister?"

Cydney fell back in the chair before her knees dumped her on the floor at his feet. "I don't know."

Eyes boring into her, he lifted a shoulder. "They were together in the crash."

"That doesn't mean they were dating. They could just be friends, or work together."

"Was your sister pregnant when you saw her last?"

"Why do you ask?" Cydney demanded and clenched her fists. "She would have told me if she was pregnant."

"You were estranged."

Heat filled her cheeks. The bitter taste of guilt rose in her throat and almost choked her. The room spun around her. *But. She. Must. Remain. Strong.*

"For six months, not eight or nine months. Ziggy would have asked for money if she was pregnant." Her head jerked toward him. A harsh sound, intended for a laugh, escaped past her numb lips. "She wouldn't go to her yearly physical without me. She would have called me."

"I'm sorry to add to your pain, but your sister was pregnant at the time of the accident."

"Pregnant? Her baby died too?" Pain from her sister's betrayal almost consumed Cydney. *She could have had a niece or nephew to love.*

How could Ziggy have been that angry with her? As much as Ziggy loved babies, she wouldn't have kept news of her pregnancy a secret just because they argued, would she? But everything about Ziggy's absence seemed strange this time. Unlike previous times when she stormed out in a temper, Ziggy hadn't called. No asking for money or promising to get a job.

"It's been six months." Confusion sounded in her voice. "Ziggy would have called. She would have told me if she was pregnant. We don't have any other family."

⚅

Forgetting his own grief, Daniel reached out a hand to soothe Cydney Eller's distress. Tingles shot up his arm as he copied her offered comfort from minutes earlier.

Comfort.

That's all he felt. They were two people dealing with the shock of losing a sibling. He couldn't feel protective of a woman he met ten minutes ago. *Could he?* Why would a woman as competent as Cydney Eller appeared to be, arouse his protective instincts? He avoided emotional relationships. His parents' marriage seared that message in his brain long ago.

Take care of the weak, but remain heart whole, was his plan.

But this woman made him question that decision.

Mother...He hadn't thought of her until now. He needed to call the cruise ship and alert his mother. But first he had to give Cydney Eller the details on her sister's arrival at the hospital. He had been so worried about Greg's whereabouts he hadn't explained the situation properly when they first met. "Ms. Eller, your sister left you a niece and twin nephews to love."

Cydney's eyes widened. "Ziggy d-didn't have children."

"EMTs put her on life support for the trip to the hospital because she was pregnant."

"I…I don't understand."

"I did a C-section after she was declared brain dead. One baby turned out to be three."

Cydney stared at him. "Ziggy's baby survived? Three? She had triplets?"

"They're in the neonatal intensive care unit, being evaluated as we speak. They're small but they have a fighting chance." He took a deep breath, then added. "If my suspicions are correct, we are the aunt and uncle of three newborn triplets."

"I-I can't believe it? What…who—"

"I assure you, I intend to see they get the best treatment this hospital can offer."

"Were they injured in the accident?"

"They appear to be fine, other than being premature."

Cydney jumped out of her seat and started for the elevator. "Where are they? I want to see them."

"Give the medical team time to assess their condition." Daniel followed her, offering words similar to many he had uttered in the past. But this time each word stabbed him with the painful awareness of Greg's absence.

"What floor are they on? I need to tell the doctors to spare no expense for Ziggy's babies." She rushed toward the elevators.

"I assure you they are receiving the best care available."

"Do I need to sign papers," she paced back toward him as

she waited for the elevator to open, "to show I'm their guardian?"

Daniel frowned. She wasn't going to let this go. In her professional suit, with a purse the size of a briefcase, Cydney Eller didn't look like the mothering type. But she seemed concerned about the welfare of the babies. Did she really plan to take care of those infants?

"We need results from DNA tests before you sign anything." If those were Greg's babies, he wouldn't allow anyone to take charge but him.

"Why? You said they were my sister's babies. You delivered them with your own hands. What more proof do I need? I'm their aunt. I intend to take care of them."

"Just like that," Daniel snapped his fingers. He felt a moment of regret as pain flashed in her eyes. She wanted to make-up for the guilt she felt over arguing with her sister. He understood that but he couldn't allow her to take charge of his brother's babies because she felt guilty. "What if your sister was a surrogate? What if the father's family wants custody?"

"Do you want babies, Doctor?"Cydney stared at him.

"I hadn't planned to have children, but if Greg's the father. I will take care of his babies."

"The father could be...anyone. You delivered those infants. You know I'm their aunt. My sister loved babies. She would never give her child away. If she was pregnant, and I have your word she was, those babies are my family."

"And I strongly suspect Greg was the father. That means they are the next generation of my family and I intend to make sure they are safe."

"Then we have a problem."

Watching her mouth pinch tight, Daniel believed her. Everything about Cydney Eller spelled trouble because of his awareness of her, and it wasn't just his peace of mind

CHAPTER 2

Three babies!

Since childhood, Cydney had vowed she would never have children. She loved babies as much as Ziggy, but her mother's lapse in caring for them had scared her. She had tried to protect Ziggy, but if she couldn't keep her sister out of trouble, how could she raise kids of her own?

That's when Cydney worked out a plan. She needed to focus on a career and forget having a family. But Ziggy's infants needed a mother. There was only one option Cydney could live with. She had to take care of her sister's infants, and Daniel Prince would not change her mind.

Rushing forward on tiptoes, to keep her heels from clacking on the hospital floor, she ran down the corridor to keep up with his long stride. This doctor was tall, broad shouldered, and as determined as he was good-looking, but she wouldn't back down.

Had his brother been the triplets' father? Did the brothers look alike? Her sister's eyes were sky blue. Daniel Prince had eyes dark as chocolate and so sharp his stares pierced her skin. Who would the infants look like?

Pain slashed through her chest. It didn't matter who the infants resembled. She was avoiding the most important question. *Would the triplets survive?*

"Are they healthy?" She gulped air in her lungs and tried to keep pace as Daniel Prince whipped around another corner.

He glanced over his shoulder, revealing a profile half the female population of Raleigh would drool over. "They have a fighting chance."

"I can't believe you didn't tell me about the babies."

"Sorry." He caught the elevator before the door closed and motioned her to enter. "I was distracted."

By news of his brother's death. He didn't have to say the words. Cydney understood. Moisture pooled in her eyes. Trying to fight against the pain, she leaned against the back wall of the elevator, and inhaled in a deep breath. She sister had died, but she had to hold herself together. Three tiny infants needed her, and this doctor wanted to claim them as his family. She couldn't let him take the babies away from her.

She had guessed his intentions the instant Daniel Prince voiced his connection aloud. Chin angled, he sent her a look intense enough to sizzle bacon. She had seen that look before when Ziggy spotted something she was determined to have. Except, this time she was facing a stranger who wanted to take charge of Ziggy's babies.

"I'm just thankful they survived the accident." Cydney forced her body away from the wall of the elevator and straightened her shoulders. No matter what happened, she owed Daniel Prince. He delivered the infants alive. "Thank you."

His lips pinched in a tight line, but he gave a curt nod and stared from under lowered brows. She sensed his disapproval, but couldn't find the energy to dispute his obvious opinion of her sister. How could she? She didn't know if Ziggy had done everything in her power to make sure her babies were healthy.

Doubt filled Cydney's head as she recalled her sister's habits, but she clamped her lips shut and kept her worry to herself. Giving Daniel Prince reasons to take the infants was not a good idea. His professional contacts could assist him in keeping the infants safe. All she had to offer was her love.

Her love hadn't been good enough for Ziggy. Would love save the triplets?

"We missed visiting hours." Daniel announced as the elevator rocked to a stop. "But I know the doctor in charge of this unit. They will let us in if the infants are stable."

He turned down a hall to the right of the elevators. Instantly, their surroundings changed. Soft blue and green replaced the intuitional beige color on the walls. Bright colored graphics added a cheerful note to the hallway.

Daniel paused in front of double metal doors strong enough to bar a prison. Cydney was so close on his heels she bumped into him when he stopped. His height and strength cushioned her. The warmth radiating off his body pulled at her battered senses. She felt the urge to rest her cheek against his shoulder and soak up his warmth.

Ziggy's body would be cold and stiff when she went to see her. Just for a moment, Cydney needed this man's warmth to sooth her pain. But she had learned from her mother, leaning on a man caused trouble. Thoughts of depending on Daniel Prince brought her to alert. She sprang back a step, before she made a mistake and showed any sign of weakness to the man wanting to take her family. Her face burning with heat, she lifted her chin. "Sorry, I wasn't watching where I was going."

He grunted acknowledgment as the massive doors clanged open.

A nurse appeared in the doorway to block their entry. Her gaze roamed over Daniel's green scrubs and her brows arched in a silent question.

"We're here to see the Eller triplets I delivered about an hour ago."

"Of course, Dr. Prince. We just finished hooking them up." The nurse eyed Cydney over his shoulder. "Ma'am, I'm afraid you missed visiting hours."

Cydney opened her mouth to issue a desperate plea, but Daniel spoke before she formed the words.

"She's with me." He lowered his voice. "The mother of the

triplets was DOA. This is her sister. She needs to see that the infants are okay."

Doubt raced through the nurse's eyes, followed by sympathy. Finally, she gave a reluctant nod. "This is highly unusual, but considering the circumstances," her tone was kind, despite the exhaustion lining her face. "I'll give you ten minutes."

After putting on protective covering from head to foot, Cydney and Daniel followed the nurse into a room alive with noise from machines.

Phish. Beep. Clunk. Hiss.

The sounds mingled with the nurse's voice. "We labeled them Big Brother, Little Brother and Baby Girl."

"Why are the triplets in intensive care?" Cydney's tone was tense as she caught sight of the name of the unit for the first time. All the noise from so many machines was frightening. If the infants needed intensive care, they must be in danger.

She couldn't lose them now. Not so soon after losing Ziggy.

"They're in NICU because they're premature and low weight. We don't know the gestational age, but we're prepared for any problems that occur." The nurse's inquiring glance bored into Cydney as if asking her to enlighten the staff as to the length of her sister's pregnancy.

Waves of guilt washed over Cydney making her heartsick on top of the shock of this event. *If she hadn't expected so much from Ziggy, and been more forgiving of her party loving ways...maybe.* Chin high, shoulders squared, Cydney met the nurse's stare. "I don't know when my sister got pregnant."

"How are their stats?" Daniel's tone blended with the noise of the machines and staff caring for the infants. His question distracted the nurse and prevented more questions.

Appreciating the reprieve and sensing a kindred spirit behind his abrupt tone, Cydney stepped closer to him. They were two wounded spirits needing comfort, and for reasons of their own, neither dared to show their emotions.

"The babies are doing as well as can be expected, all things considered." The nurse walked past row after row of incubators. "With fecal matter showing in the amniotic fluid, we're keeping a close check on the twins for sepsis. Both boys have a slightly elevated temperature which alerts us to possible problems."

"What problems?" The nurse's words almost flattened Cydney. All she could think about was the infants needed someone to protect them. Daniel Prince had knowledge she lacked.

She glanced at some of the tiny infants they passed and forced back a cry. Many of the babies were so small they looked more like tiny birds stretched out on boards, than human infants. Breath shuttering, she clenched her fists. Medicinal odors filled her nostrils. Tension blocked the gasps of fear trying to escape her lips.

She would carry the guilt of knowing she let Ziggy down, with her for the rest of her life, but she could not fail Ziggy's infants. Shuddering at the sights around her, she tried to focus on the nurse's explanations.

"Are you okay?" Daniel leaned close and asked in a low voice.

Cydney straightened her shoulders and managed to nod her head. Ziggy was dead and three infants were motherless. How could she be okay?

Beeps, pings, whooshing noises mingled with the squeak of their paper shoes against the floor. But noise didn't seem to matter to the tiny patients. None of the infants in NICU cried.

At least, not the kind of crying she expected. In this unit, infants clung to life by a tiny grasp, and made little mewling noises like wounded animals. Images of tiny bodies too small to be human swam before Cydney's eyes as the nurse stopped beside three incubators lined up, side by side, on the end of the row.

Cydney tried to prepare, after seeing the infants they passed, she tried to steel her nerves, but her first sight of the triplets sent shock racing through her body. A wave of protectiveness filled her heart as she stared at Ziggy's infants.

The triplets were so tiny they looked like dolls. Yet, they were nothing near the bird like appearance of some infants in the unit. She said a prayer of thanks and focused on the new members of her family.

Ziggy's triplets.

Amazement and disbelief battled with her understanding of what she was seeing. IVs were sticking out of every inch of the babies' bodies. Tape held needles in heels, hands, and on top of three tiny heads. The sight of so many needles and machines hooked up to the triplets sent chills racing down her spine.

The babies looked perfect, but so frighteningly small she couldn't imagine holding them. All she could think of was *Ziggy would have loved them on sight.*

"The boys are identical twins. The larger twin weighs four pounds ten ounces. The smaller one weighs five ounces less. But this little girl is a different story." The nurse turned to the incubator with the pink nametag, *Baby Girl.* "She has more is-sues, and more IVs. Sensors for the cardiac monitor are what you see taped to her chest. Doctors want to keep close check on her."

"What's wrong with her?" Fear clutched at Cydney's in-sides. To have this baby survive the accident…and then lose the tiny girl was unthinkable.

"Are the problems serious?" Daniel placed a hand on Cydney's arm as she swayed.

"Dr. Morgan is checking for respiratory distress syndrome. As you know, RDS is common in premature infants." The nurse explained. "Baby girl is more fragile than her brothers. She has more trouble breathing as well as the heart issues. This lighted monitor on her ankle is the oximeter to measure the oxygen in her blood."

The nurse glanced at the chart. "At this stage, there's noth-ing unusual to worry about. All three infants are in incubators to keep their body temperature up and give them oxygen. We're keeping constant check on blood levels. Dr. Morgan ordered additional tests to make sure Baby Girl doesn't have other problems."

"What problems?" Cydney couldn't hide her reaction, but she didn't care. She had already fallen under the spell of these infants.

"Just the usual problems for premature infants."

"C-can I touch them?" Cydney motioned to the small openings in the incubators.

"Of course, but don't rub them skin. Just keep a steady pressure with your touch. Hold their hands or feet, but be careful of the IVs." The nurse glanced around. "Things are quiet for now so I'll give you a few minutes."

Fingers trembling, Cydney reached to touch a tiny hand no larger than a penny. Baby Girl's fingers, slim as toothpicks covered with skin, moved under her touch and Cydney's heart thumped against her ribs. A sense of awe almost overwhelmed her. Love and a protective instinct stronger than the urge to breathe took hold of her. Lifting her gaze for the baby girl, Cydney met Daniel's intense stare. "She's so small."

He looked pale.

She tore her attention away from his mask like expression. She wasn't sure she wanted to know what he was thinking. If he shared her sense of amazement and fierce protectiveness, she understood. But if he wanted to take these babies away from her, he'd have a fight on his hands. Her vow to remain childless disappeared with her first glance at her niece and nephews. Trying to hide worry over Daniel's intentions, she examined every inch of the little girl.

She could see Ziggy's pointed chin and button nose in the tiny face. Tiny wisps of blonde hair curled against the doll-size head. Pink dresses and ruffles, that's what Ziggy would want, and Cydney vowed to see that Baby Girl had a chance to wear them.

It almost ripped her heart out to turn away, but she needed to check on the boys. Slowly, she moved to the next incubator and went through the same process of counting fingers and toes, and looking for familiar features, two more times.

Little Brother was heavier than his sister, but his limbs were just a spindly. Big Brother was slightly larger, but his limbs looked like twigs covered with skin. A Styrofoam cup taped over a needle in his scalp looked like a party-hat gone mad.

The sad image brought tears to Cydney's eyes.

Would these infants survive to celebrate their first birthday? She tried to hide her distress as the nurse ushered them out the door. Showing weakness wouldn't convince Daniel that she could care for these babies.

"You can come back for regular visiting time in two hours." The heavy metal doors clanged shut, closing them out of the NICU.

Cydney walked to the viewing window, not wanting to lose sight of the infants. *Triplets. Ziggy would have loved having three babies.*

"They're so small. I can't believe they survived." She breathed as Daniel stopped beside her.

"I never imagined it was like this. I never gave a thought beyond the birth." He paused.

A nurse in NICU approached one of the boys. She reached in the incubator, lifted the small infant by an arm and a leg, and flipped the baby over as if he were a pancake.

Cydney gasped her outrage. "I thought you were supposed to be careful about holding a newborn. That nurse handled Little Brother as if he were a-a…football."

A noisy breath escaped Daniel's lips. "Everything looks different from this side of the glass."

Cydney tore her gaze away from the living, breathing, infants, and glanced at the large clock hanging on the wall. It was two hours before they could see the babies again. She needed to view Ziggy's body. "I have to go."

Daniel checked the clock. "You don't have enough time to go to the funeral home and get back for visiting hours. We need to talk to the doctor. Call the funeral home. Tell them you will come later."

Cydney opened her mouth to tell him she needed to view her sister's body so she could accept the reality. But she couldn't find the words.

"The dead can wait." Daniel's glance swept over her.

Shivers shook her from head to toe. His suggestion made sense she argued silently. What other excuse could she have for agreeing to go along with his plan?

♣

"Let's get some coffee while we wait." Daniel argued with himself all the way to the hospital cafeteria. He kept assuring himself his medical training was behind his suggestion and nothing else. He didn't want Cydney Eller to collapse at his feet. At one point, she turned so pale he guessed she had nearly fainted. He suspected she was in shock. But one thing was clear. Cydney Eller didn't measure up to his first impression. Seeing her in the no nonsense business suit, he expected someone hardhearted. Considering his brother's past history with women, he could excuse thoughts that Cydney Eller might be a social butterfly. But she'd proved she was neither.

She focused on events, even when her skin turned the color of clotted cream. She checked each infant as close as a mother pregnant for nine months would have, not as a person only learning about the triplets, minutes earlier. And she cared what happened to the babies. Had he been wrong about her? Was she more than a business suit chasing a career? Could she turn away from work and take care of three premature infants?

If she could, then he had a problem. His brother's children were his responsibility. He would do what he had to, to keep those infants safe.

What if that included allowing Cydney Eller in his life?

He had noticed the spark in her green eyes and the slender curves under her dark suit, but he wasn't interested in a relationship. Giving the elevator button a jab, he watched for the ground floor button to light up as his past flashed through his head. His politician father chased skirts openly, leaving his mother to seek solace in her social life as a powerful senator's wife and leaving him and Greg to fend for themselves. Was it any wonder his protective streak was a mile wide?

He had sworn he would never have children. He wouldn't expose a child to fears of being unwanted. Showing the child off in public, then ignoring him in private. He wouldn't risk that kind of existence for his child. He survived that life once. Greg hadn't been so lucky.

Greg never outgrew his need to be center of attention, and Daniel promised himself Greg's children would never feel unloved and unwanted. But how was he going to get around Cydney Eller so he could do his duty? She had staked her claim to the triplets.

Now what was he going to do?

Daniel waited until they were seated at a table in the corner. Coffee cups in hand, black for him and two creams for her. She needed something on her stomach before she passed out. After a few sips her color turned to normal and he pulled the cell phone he retrieved on the way to NICU, out of his pocket. "I'm going to call my lawyer."

Her face turned the color of the cream in her coffee. Her eyes searched his face as if she were trying to read his mind. After long seconds, she gave a nod and reached for her purse. "I'll call mine, too."

With her face the chalky color of death, Daniel could see the resemblance between the two sisters and quickly held up his hand. "Not necessary. I just need to check our options. The hospital will demand a guardian's name for insurance coverage. We need to know where we stand."

"So, I should call mine—"

"One lawyer should be enough. Drink your coffee," Daniel urged as he pushed a button.

That his attorney was on speed dial could mean several things, Cydney knew. He could have many lawsuits, or his attorney was a close friend. The tone of his voice as he left a message told her the attorney was a friend.

"Phil, this is Daniel. I have an urgent legal issue. Call me as soon as you can." Daniel closed the phone and trained his attention on the woman across the table. "Tell me about yourself, Ms. Eller."

Her brows arched to her hair. "So you can save your attorney some time, Dr. Prince? I assure you I can take care of the triplets."

"One baby is a responsibility and expense. Are you ready to

take on three preemies? That's a large chunk of change. You're assuming eighteen years of demands and expenses." He should be proud of his casual tone, but her fluctuating color made him ashamed. He hadn't intended their conversation to sound like a background check. But she so quick to turn defensive, he wondered why. "I wasn't looking for personal information. Just trying to take our minds off our worries and get acquainted. Most parents know something about their partner."

"But we aren't parents." Her gaze bored into him, showing her business training.

"We are now." Daniel's coffee mixed with the odor of hospital disinfectants. And he knew after tonight, he would associate the scent of coffee with Cydney Eller and green eyes.

Finally, she gave a nod and sipped the steaming coffee. "Sorry. It's been...a...long day." Her voice wobbled. "Actually, you sound as if we were conducting a job interview. I noticed because I'm up for a promotion at Gibbs and Associates Advertising here in Raleigh. Do you know the firm?"

"Sorry," Daniel shrugged, "I don't advertise. Baby business is always good."

One corner of her mouth tilted and she saluted him with her cup. "I'm sure you recognize our jingles."

Daniel tried to ignore his reaction to her first smile, but her eyes held a glint of humor that pulled at him. Her half smile distracted him from the sadness hanging over them like thick fog. He sensed trouble if he let down his guard and sharpened his tone. "I don't watch much TV."

Her clear gaze met his over the edge of her cup. "Do you have any interests outside your work at the hospital?"

"Now you're investigating me?" He managed a light tone, but his gut tightened. Why was he aware of every move this woman made? "I'm invested in my career. And yes, three infants will require major adjustments to my schedule. But I have the resources to make things work."

"So, you can question me, but I can't probe into your life?"

Daniel barked a laugh. His whole body jerked in response to the spark in her eyes. "I assure you my brother's infants will lack for nothing."

"Except a mother figure. Unless you're married?"

"I am not. Are you?"

"No."

"I guess I spoke too soon." Daniel stared in his cup. "No matter what we decide, the triplets will lack one parent at least."

She frowned. "I haven't ruled marriage out of my life."

"Too busy with work and a career? Nothing wrong with that."

"No, but being single could cause problems when I apply for custody of the triplets." Cydney leaned toward him to emphasis her point. "But I will do anything to keep those babies safe. They are my last living relatives."

"Then we shouldn't have a problem." Daniel forced the words past the obstruction in his throat. Hearing Cydney Eller voice the same words echoing inside his head hit hard. *Blood kin.* He couldn't walk away from those infants if he wanted to. Even if he had to battle for custody of infants he believed were Greg's children, he wouldn't stop. He had to protect members of his family.

"It's time to go."

Her determined tone snapped Daniel to attention. He stared in her eyes, willing her to believe him. "I won't let anything happen to those infants. You understand that, don't you?"

"Is that a threat, Dr. Prince?"

"I wanted to reassure you, nothing more." Daniel held her gaze, and flinched mentally. Did she think so little of him? Why, when she didn't even know him. They were strangers, possibly stuck together for life because of their siblings. They should try to get along. "Don't you trust me?"

"I believe your intentions are good. But you intend to hand those babies over to a nanny's care. I can take care of my sister's babies myself." She pushed her chair under the table, and met his stare. And just that quick, standing in the near empty hospital cafeteria, new battle lines affecting both their lives were drawn.

He wanted custody of the infants because they were Greg's. She wanted to take care of her sister's babies.

Neither of them had a 'legal' leg to stand on. Until DNA results returned, neither knew for sure if their siblings were actually the parents of those infants.

⚏

On the way back to NICU silence hung over them, like a dark cloud. Cydney tried to think of a way to stop Daniel Prince from claiming custody of the infants. Testing for DNA was the obvious choice, but getting results from a lab took time. She needed to make plans now.

Wishing Daniel had no connection to the infants seemed useless. Someday when the triplets were old enough, she wanted to be able to say their parents had been a couple. Memory of her lonely childhood made her determine to provide them with a family that loved them, and not just one parent, but two. But her reaction to this man set her teeth on edge. If she considered her family history, any relationship with Daniel meant disaster. Her mother had changed men faster than hairstyles.

Her mother would have loved Daniel Prince.

That fact alone warned Cydney of trouble. After her parents' divorce, her mother fell for one handsome man after the other. A man was perfect in her mother's eyes if he had a warm smile, good looks, smooth charm.

Except for the charm, Daniel Prince fit the description perfectly and he was successful, which was an added bonus to her mother. But Cydney wasn't looking for a man to take care of her. Yet, tension twisted in her stomach at thoughts of taking care of the triplets on her own. She might need Daniel's help. But she rejected that possibility as soon as it flashed through her head. Daniel Prince had a protective streak a mile wide. She figured that out from the note in his voice when he told her about the triplets.

Because of his protective nature, Daniel would try to take charge of the babies. But if she was going to care for the triplets, she wanted to do it right. She wanted the babies to feel

33

loved and safe. She wanted them to have the security she and Ziggy had missed. Disagreeing with Daniel over parenting issues would steal any sense of security from the infants' lives.

But...could she take care of three preemies...alone?

Could she work and take care of their needs? Could she spend nights caring for infants and create bright, alluring jingles during the day? How could she juggle the demands of being both mother and father, and do good work on her job?

When they reached the waiting room outside NICU, people were watching the clock, eager for their few minutes to visit. Grandparents, parents, and children waited with varying degrees of patience. Thoughts of how much Ziggy would love the triplets, tugged at Cydney's heart, but she couldn't break down in front of Daniel Prince. He had his own grief to deal with. She couldn't show weakness.

"Dr. Prince?"

Cydney turned to see a woman in a white coat approach Daniel.

"Dr. Morgan, this is Miss Eller," Daniel motioned toward Cydney. "the triplets' mother was her sister."

"Please accept my condolences, Ms. Eller." Dr. Morgan turned to Daniel. "It seems odd to see you on this side of the glass." She indicated the viewing window. "The news isn't all bad. The infant boys scored high on the Apgar, but we are concerned about their risk of sepsis. Their temperatures are elevated."

"Is sepsis serious?" Cydney asked.

"It can be for premature infants. If we find it fast enough, antibiotics usually take care of the problem." Dr. Morgan looked at her clipboard. "Baby girl's Apgar wasn't as good, but her color is improving with aid of oxygen. She is more active than the boys are. She's definitely a fighter. But there are signs of respiratory distress syndrome. It could take care of its self with time, but the team is watching for any sign of trouble, and we have her hooked up to monitors."

"What if it doesn't get better?" Cydney asked.

Dr. Morgan winced. "She needs time. If she doesn't show signs of improvement soon, we may face surgery." She studied the baby's chart. "We really need to pin point gestational age. When did your sister get pregnant?"

"I don't know." Feeling her face flame, Cydney met the doctor's gaze. "Why is that important?"

"Knowing the gestational age helps us to gage organ maturity and assess any risk factors involved." Dr. Morgan turned to Daniel. "We logged the first part of The Dubowitz/Ballard Examination today." She glanced at Cydney. "That's the first step of determining the gestational age. The neuromuscular testing is done at twenty-four hours after birth. Once we determine age, we know better what we are dealing with. My guess is thirty plus weeks."

"How did you reach that conclusion?" The caring tone of Daniel's voice gained Cydney's admiration. He cared about the tiny patients and it showed.

"We found meconium in the sac," Dr. Morgan turned to Cydney. "That's the baby's first bowel movement."

Cydney winced. Baby poop times three. *Help*.

"Knowing the gestational age can help us rule out chances of surfactant deficiency. The infant female seems susceptible to breathing difficulty, so I suspect she is deficient. We need healthy lungs."

Cydney focused on Dr. Morgan. "Is Baby Girl the only infant in danger?"

"There's no easy answer to that question." Dr. Morgan explained. "If a baby is low birth weight, there are many things that can go wrong."

"I'm worried about the heart monitor." Cydney confessed.

"The first twenty-four hours are critical. We are keeping a close watch on all three infants. Once we have results of the Dubowitz/Ballard Exam we'll know more. At this point, things look good. The cardiac monitor is her safety net." Dr. Morgan glanced at her chart. "We'll start watching for signs of jaundice at two days. Any questions?" When they shook their heads, she gave a wave and walked away.

Turning to Daniel, Cydney asked the question she didn't dare ask Dr. Morgan. She hadn't known Daniel Prince long, but she knew him better than she knew the doctor she just met. "What do you think their chances are?"

"They have good color which means good oxygen supply. Respiration is good except for the infant girl. BP and pulse rates are good. I'd say they're holding their own."

Cydney's shoulders slumped in relief as woman with a clipboard approached. "Dr. Prince? I'm Susan Ballard from the business office. I have some forms you need to fill out."

"I've been expecting a representative from your office, Ms. Ballard."

"Are you the guardian of the Eller triplets?"

"I am."

"So am I." Cydney stared at the woman.

Ms. Ballard frowned. "The hospital needs one guardian with custody rights to sign permission forms." Her glance darted between them. "I can have a court appointed guardian—"

"No!"

"That isn't necessary, Ms. Ballard. Ms. Eller and I will work this out and let you know by tomorrow morning."

"I need these forms signed now. Someone needs to be on record for the financial office to call in an emergency."

"Put my name down."

"Mine, too," Cydney chimed in, "I can pay the hospital bills."

"If that's true, advertising executives make too much money these days." Daniel cut his eyes at her and picked up the pen to sign the form.

Ignoring his attempt at humor, Cydney filled in the form Ms. Ballard reluctantly passed to her. Obviously, the woman decided two signed forms were better than none. But Cydney gulped as she passed back the form. Massive medical bills would empty her savings account. But she couldn't let Daniel Prince take charge of Ziggy's babies.

Ziggy!

Pain shot through Cydney's chest. She needed to view the body and arrange a funeral. Then what? How could she work for a promotion and keep check on the triplets? How could she stop Daniel Prince from taking charge of her sister's babies?

"Daniel," the attorney's voice sounded when Daniel checked his voice mail. Phil had called earlier and brought up to date on the custody issue. "I checked on your situation. Things don't look good. You and the sister need to appear in front of the judge at eight sharp tomorrow morning. See you at the courthouse."

Daniel bit back a curse and turned to Cydney Eller. She insisted on remaining in the NICU as long as there was a chance of seeing the triplets through the viewing window. Nurses had closed the drapes ten minutes ago, but Cydney hadn't moved away from the glass. She focused on the infants as if willing them to improve. He expected her to twitch her nose or start chanting any second. He understood her desperation. He shared that feeling.

They were two strangers at odds over their siblings' children as well, but if the babies were Greg's, they were his last link to his brother. It was his duty to his family, his responsibility as the older brother, to care for the infants. *He had to honor Greg's memory.*

"Listen to this message from my attorney." Daniel stepped to her side and held the phone toward Cydney. His focused on her expressions as she listened to the tinny sounding words of the recording. *Who was this woman? She couldn't be anything like her sister. She was too rigid. Greg picked the fun loving females.*

Color drained from Cydney's face, but her eyes blazed a burning green and Daniel couldn't tear his gaze from her pale features. She changed from a business professional to an avenging angel right before his eyes. Anger radiated from her with a beauty he couldn't deny and his pulse quickened. He wanted to learn more about this woman.

"What does this mean?" Her voice quivered, but she held

her chin high.

Admiring her determination, Daniel met the panic in her gaze. "Best guess, I'd say we have a fight on our hands if we want custody."

"But the triplets are our family. At least, they're my family." Her eyes glowed with the resolve of a fighter. He couldn't walk over Cydney Eller without consequences, and that intrigued him.

"I expect the judge will order DNA tests since the triplets don't have a parent to act as guardian."

"But that's the whole point. I'm willing to be their guardian."

Daniel's jaw clenched as he returned her stare. "You know it's futile for us to take opposite sides on this issue. If we disagree now, what will the judge decide in court?" Air whooshed out his lungs as he raked fingers through his hair. "We need to stick together to keep these babies out of the state system. Agreed?"

Her throat worked, drawing his attention to her long slim neck. She looked graceful and feminine, yet strong. She had been pale, before, but now the last hint of color drained from her skin, leaving her face as colorless as a marble statue. He suspected she could be as hard as marble if she needed to be, and that gave him reason to pause. Cydney Eller was no pushover. He would have to fight to gain custody of those infants.

Finally, Cydney gave a nod and short, sable colored hair bounced around her face. Eyes, green as traffic lights, sliced through him. Challenged him. Dared him. Then her lips moved, emitting a voice hoarse with emotion. "Agreed."

CHAPTER 3

WhathaveIdone! What have I done? What. Have. I. Done?

Cydney took a stumbling step away from Daniel Prince. She couldn't escape the hospital odors or the sense of dread squeezing her chest, but her resolve strengthened with distance from him, though her knees still trembled. Willing her backbone to remain stiff, she squared her shoulders and held her head high as she walked to the elevator. *Time to leave.* Time to escape the weakness she felt when she was near this man. Being close to Daniel Prince drained her power of will right out of her body.

Her defensive shield back in place, she stopped at the elevator and turned to look back at him. "I'll be at the courthouse at eight o'clock."

What have I done?

Those words whirled through her brain as she met with the funeral director and again, as she viewed her sister's body. For an instant, when she caught the first glimpse of her sister's alabaster skin and the rigid form of her body, she wished she had accepted Daniel's offer to accompany her to this ordeal.

But she refused his offer. She couldn't rely on his strength for fear of ending up like her mother. *Dependent. Needy.* That's why she pushed Ziggy to get a job and avoid being helpless. She didn't want either of them to repeat their mother's mistakes. But look at Ziggy, now.

Her beautiful sister.

Ziggy's sparkling life force had drained from her cold body, leaving nothing of her joy and natural warmth behind. *Except the tiny triplets.*

The image of those infants blurred Cydney's vision as she reached out to touch her sister's smooth, cold cheek. Finally, she couldn't hold her pain any longer and tears rolled down her cheeks. Pressing a fist to her lips to keep back sobs, she fought the grief shaking her body.

How did I fail you Ziggy?

Sometime later, when she didn't have a tear left in her, Cydney stared down at her sister's rigid shape and made a promise. Drained by the sorrow of her loss, and worry about doing the right thing for the triplets, she made a final pledge to the sister she loved so dearly.

"Ziggy, I promise to do whatever it takes to keep your babies safe."

Ten minutes before eight the next morning, Cydney approached the door of the courtroom where Daniel Prince and another man stood waiting. With her lack of sleep, the day already seemed long. Thoughts of Ziggy and worry over the babies filled her head all night. Up early, she arrived at NICU for visiting hours at six, only to learn Daniel Prince had already been in NICU to check on the triplets and departed.

Head high, Cydney drew a shuddering breath and concentrated on hiding her reaction to his appearance, but it wasn't easy. He looked as professional as the attorney at his side and much as she hated to admit, clean shaven and wearing a dark suit, Daniel Prince looked stunning enough to bring a statue to life. *Too bad, he couldn't work magic on her sister…and his brother.*

But it was time she faced reality. The nurse had told her Daniel could come and go in the NICU because he was on staff. His efforts to check on the triplets earned her respect. He was a good ally for the babies and she admitted as she held each infant's hand and touched their tiny bodies. Daniel cared about the babies even without being certain they were related to him. In her mind that made him a kind person.

And that was part of her problem. She couldn't ignore Daniel's good qualities any more than she could ignore the tiny infants belonging to her sister. The fact that the triplets had survived their mother's death was a miracle. If she had to share this miracle of life with Daniel, she would.

Early reports from the nurse said the triplets' condition remained the same. The baby boys had elevated temperatures, and the baby girl still needed heart monitors and oxygen. The medical team would complete the remainder of the gestational testing today.

Ignoring the hum of activity as people rushed to find the right courtroom, Cydney thought back to yesterday's events as she moved toward the two men. Daniel could have spent more time with the infants she realized now, but he went with her to get coffee and stayed by her side. His support and kindness melted some of the loneliness around her heart.

She admitted her growing respect for him just as he turned in her direction. The quick slice of his gaze over her face left her feeling she had stepped through a security scanner. Her breath caught and she lifted her chin, waiting. Wanting his prognosis of her appearance to be positive, she realized, and that fact filled her cheeks with heat.

"Good morning, Ms. Eller."

"Dr. Prince," her words sounded stiff as she tried to hide her reaction to him. Her planned greeting dried on her tongue as his brown eyes chased across her face like melted chocolate. He had kind eyes. Caring, compassionate, interested, eyes…all the things she longed for in a man. But not from this man.

This near stranger could take Ziggy's babies away from her.

Heat washed over her, chased by chills racing through her blood. Even considering the risk to her career, she couldn't give up now. Not with Ziggy's babies depending on her. She couldn't crumble under the weight of her loss and the ache in her heart as her mother had when her dad left.

She refused to allow any man to have that power over her.

But…if she refused to cooperate with Daniel…how was she going to save the triplets? The hospital demanded one guardian or social services could take charge.

If she joined Daniel, to fight for joint custody, how was she going to gain custody after they left court?

She kept reminding herself this was about the welfare of the triplets. Her need to do the right thing didn't matter. If she repeated those words a hundred times a day, she might get through this and keep Ziggy's babies safe.

Brow arched, Daniel's gaze bored into her when she remained silent. Then he turned to the man at his side. "Cydney Eller, my attorney, Phillip Lawrence. Phil, Cydney's sister is the mother of the triplets."

"Ms. Eller, please accept my condolences for your loss." Kindness filled the attorney's blue eyes as he shook her hand. "It's a sad event, but we must act to protect the infants. As Daniel's attorney, I suggest you present the judge with a united front. I know the two of you just met, but if the judge thinks you are willing to work together for the welfare of the babies, we may be able to keep custody. Are you agreeable?"

"I am willing to do whatever it takes to protect my sister's triplets." Cydney sent Daniel a warning glare. *Whatever it takes.*

"Any issues? Any dirty laundry I need to know before we go in? We have five minutes. Bring me up to speed." The attorney's glance bounced between them, as they remained silent. "Right. Then let's go get custody of those babies." He pulled the door open and motioned them inside.

Cydney's legs trembled as she walked toward the table in front of the courtroom. Knowing Daniel was following close behind turned her knees to jelly. Was she doing the right thing by agreeing to work with him? What did she know about him? He might not even be the triplets' uncle. What if Ziggy hadn't been dating his brother?

On the other hand, suppose he was the triplets' uncle. What then? Would he want full custody of the infants? Then what? If she went along with his attorney's suggestions now, was she asking for problems in the future? What if she backed away?

Daniel put a hand on her elbow to guide her to a table in front of the judge's bench. She gasped as pricks of awareness tickled her skin. Because of the humid July weather, she was wearing short sleeves today, and she felt the heat from Daniel's touch all the way to her toes.

This was not good. Her reaction to him spelled trouble. Maybe she should…

As if sensing her doubts, Daniel leaned close and whispered in her ear. "It's the right thing to do, Ms. Eller. You know that."

His warm breath brushed her cheek. Chills chased along her limbs. His words and the attention he focused on her made her shiver. Could he read her mind? Did he know she reacted to his nearness? Could he tell she had lain awake half the night crying, and spent the other half wondering what she should do?

She glanced at him out of the corner of her eye and gave a slight tilt of her head. He was right. Much as she wanted to argue, or wail and complain about the situation, it was fruitless. Ziggy's triplets came first. They agreed on that one point, at least. Sighing, she kept her back rigid. Her life had changed forever when her sister died in that accident. She had to adapt.

The triplets were only part of the story.

Grieving for her sister, dealing with guilt over their last meeting and working out how she could care for the babies and continue her job, were just a few of the things crashing through her head. Daniel Prince was another big part of her concern. Until DNA tests proved otherwise…he was part of her new existence.

Suddenly, the noise around her changed. A door at the side of the room opened. A bailiff appeared and in a loud voice, ordered all present to stand. The judge entered the courtroom.

Cydney stood on knees trembling so much she was not sure she could stay upright. Then her mind went blank. Fear of how these proceedings would end and lack of sleep numbed her brain. She stood. She sat. She listened. At one point, Daniel put his hand on her arm when the judge stalled in making a decision. The judge wanted to get social services involved.

Phillip Lawrence jumped to his feet. His voice rang with a firm tone as he addressed the bench. "Your Honor, we have family members willing to take custody of these premature infants. Dr. Prince is their uncle. Considering how burdened we know social services to be, why drain state resources when family members are willing to take charge in this case?"

"Good points, Mr. Lawrence. Do we have proof your clients are actually related to the infants?"

"Your Honor, Ms. Eller is the deceased mother's sister. That's our only proof."

"Ummm, normally, I would agree. But in this age of advanced fertility techniques, we can't be certain the deceased was actually the biological mother of the triplets, can we?"

"My point, exactly, your Honor," replied the attorney representing the state.

Mr. Lawrence objected, loudly.

Voices erupted.

Noise and camera flashes filled the courtroom. For the first time, Cydney realized there were reporters present. She should have guessed. Her job in advertising made news exposure a good thing, but not this event. Seeing all the cameras and the hungry looking reporters lean toward the bench to catch every word said in the proceedings, she cringed.

She shouldn't be surprised. Raleigh was the largest city in North Carolina, but even in a town this size, a woman listed as DOA and giving birth to live triplets, was news.

The judge slammed his gavel, repeatedly. "I am ordering DNA tests. Until the results return, since I doubt anyone unrelated to three premature infants would volunteer to take custody, I am awarding temporary joint custody to Ms. Eller and Dr. Prince. Next case."

Cydney let out the breath she hadn't realized she was holding. In a voice barely over a whisper, she asked. "Is it over?"

"Afraid not," Phillip Lawrence cast them a glance, grabbed

his briefcase, and headed toward the exit. "We pulled off a stalling tactic, not a win."

"What happens now?" Cydney rushed to keep up with him.

When they reached the hallway outside the courtroom, the attorney stopped and turned to Daniel. Angling his elbows to block reporters crowding close to get a statement, he said. "You get DNA tests done. The judge will send written orders for the triplets to be tested. Then we wait."

Then he stalked off, leaving Daniel and Cydney standing in the crowd of reporters.

"Let's get out of here." Daniel elbowed his way past when a reporter shoved a microphone in his face. Holding her arm, he guided Cydney toward the door. "It's almost time for visiting hours."

⁂

"I don't understand." Cydney said a short time later as she turned a stunned gaze on Dr. Morgan. "Baby girl has RDS and jaundice, and some other deficiency?"

"Surfactant deficiency. Surfactant helps to keep the lungs inflated. When it's missing, infants have RDS. Most infants outgrow the problem with the help of medication and maturity," Dr. Morgan repeated patiently. "Jaundice is common in eighty percent of premature infants. The boys have a yellow tint to their skin as well."

"Even Little Brother? He looks so sad with his poor, bloated little abdomen." Cydney moved to the infant's incubator.

"Lethargy and extended belly are signs of sepsis." Dr. Morgan checked the infant's chart. "His temp hasn't changed. That's good news."

"He looks so pitiful. I wish I could hold him."

"Good. As soon as their condition levels off, we want to start kangaroo care." Dr. Morgan smiled at Cydney's blank look. "We encourage parents to snuggle the infants against their bare skin."

"I-I can do that." Cydney swallowed. The image of Daniel holding an infant against his bare chest made her heart flutter.

"With three infants, it will take a lot of your time." Dr.

Morgan cautioned.

"I'll make time." Cydney replied. *Ziggy would have dropped everything to snuggle her babies*. She couldn't fail the infants like she did Ziggy.

"I can help." Daniel spoke up, earning a glance from Cydney.

"We aren't ready, yet." Dr. Morgan turned to Big Brother's incubator. "This infant has a higher fever and vomiting."

"What's in his stomach to throw up?" Cydney sent Dr. Morgan a questioning look. "I didn't know they were getting bottles."

"They're getting IV fluids that provide total prenatal nutrition, TPN. Big Brother is vomiting up the fluids in his stomach because of the fever. Much like an adult does with a stomach virus."

"H-how bad is he?" Unconsciously, Cydney stepped closer to Daniel. When she realized she had moved, she turned to the incubator and touched the infant's warm skin.

"We need to be realistic." Dr. Morgan's gaze rested on the incubators for long seconds. "These infants are sick, make no mistake about that, but for now, all their symptoms are curable with time and medication." She put Big Brother's chart back in place. "If I sound blunt, it's because we have to deal with facts. We need time. Each day gives the infants an edge. By the way, we have confirmed they are at thirty-two weeks development. That's a start."

Thirty-two weeks.

Cydney's breath caught. Her head swirled. Ziggy had been two months pregnant when she stormed out of the apartment. *Ziggy knew she was pregnant and she didn't tell me.* Cydney swayed and a warm arm circled her shoulders.

For a second, she welcomed Daniel's support and absorbed his strength. But a beat later, she straightened her spine so only his arm on her shoulders touched her. She couldn't be dependent like her mother. Or be irresponsible like Ziggy!

How can I think that when Ziggy isn't even buried yet? What's wrong with me?

But she made an effort to be a stronger person than her mother, and more responsible than Ziggy. She worked to be the perfect daughter and sister so she do the right things for her family. Until now, if she failed, she tried harder. Leaning on someone else made her weak.

Forcing air in her lungs, she fought to stop the whirling in her head. Daniel's warmth and strength were appealing. Standing close to him, breathing in the clean scent of his soap, revived her flagging spirits. But she could not show weakness.

His arm tightened around her shoulders. She inhaled deeply and focused on keeping her body stiff. Daniel's reassuring presence sent strength to her weakening limbs and this time, she didn't pull away. She needed the warmth of another human just for a second. Just until the shock of Ziggy's betrayal faded.

◆◆

Three hours later, Cydney left her office building in a daze. After explaining her situation to the senior partner in the advertising firm, she was officially on compassionate leave. The length of her absence was dependent on condition of the triplets and the court ruling on final custody.

She released a shuddering breath as she drove back to the hospital. Her brain kept telling her, she should be relieved. But she had worked so hard to earn a promotion, and despite the crisis she found herself in, she refused to lose sight of her goals.

Staying focused on a career gave her options she could explore and work out logically. She fought to control of her life. But Ziggy's death and arrival of the triplets changed everything.

Having choices meant adapting to change. Facing problems and choosing the best solution. For the time being, that meant taking compassionate leave, which left her with one less demand on her time.

But what did she do now? How could she cope without work to focus on day and night? All this time, she had centered all her energy on her career. Now, she needed to change her priorities and make new plans for her future.

She had to face reality. And she wasn't prepared. Other than caring for Ziggy when they were kids, and babysitting for Donna, she hadn't been around many babies. She voided kids. Now, Ziggy's triplets were her responsibility. At least, they would be if she had any say in the matter.

Had her lack of parenting skills failed Ziggy?

Taking her eyes off traffic, she glanced at her watch. It was nearly time for visiting hours.

She eased her foot off the gas, resisting the urge to speed. *Had rushing to get somewhere caused Ziggy's death?*

⁂

How long would reporters remain interested in the triplets?

Dodging microphones reporters shoved in her face, Cydney escaped into the safety of the hospital lobby and passed through security, arriving in the NICU as visiting hours started. Fear washed over her as she stood beside an incubator and held a tiny hand. Dr. Morgan said the triplets needed time and maturity to survive.

Would these tiny infants get better?

Cydney moved her hand to touch Big Brother's ankle. The baby's skin was wrinkled and soft. All three infants showed a yellow tint to their skin. The baby boys still had fever. Baby girl still needed help breathing. Cydney fought back tears and tried to control the anger threatening to consume her.

Ziggy should be here.

"We think the mother received a blow in the crash, causing fecal matter to be excreted by one of the twins." The nurse's voice broke through the emotions whirling in Cydney's head. "We caught the sepsis early, thanks to Dr. Prince and Dr. Morgan." She pointed to a needle in Big Brother's head. "This IV is for the antibiotic."

"When will we know if the treatment is working?" Cydney forced words past the fear building inside her. After losing Ziggy, she couldn't face losing the infants as well. *Please. Please let them survive.*

"Try not to worry. This is what we do in NICU. Sick babies get our total attention. Each infants has a nurse who reports directly to me. The babies need medication and time to grow."

There was that word, again. *Time.* Looking at all the needles, tubes and beeping machines connected to the triplets, Cydney knew the babies needed something else, as well.

They needed a miracle.

Her insides twisted as she stared at the infants. The tiny girl's lips were not as pink as the twin boys' lips, but maybe that was because she didn't have a fever. "How did Baby Girl escape the sepsis?"

"She was in a different amniotic sac from the twins. Be glad of that. She is fighting enough battles, without adding sepsis to her issues. We ran more tests on her blood, today."

The tiny infant in the incubator looked like an octopus with all the IVs and tubes springing from the taped objects on her tiny body. Cydney squeezed her eyes tight, refusing to give in to the urge to cry. This baby needed her to think positive. She had to ignore thoughts that she had not been the perfect big sister. Taking charge of Ziggy's babies was the only way of correcting the mistakes she had made.

❦

Daniel returned to the hospital twenty minutes after receiving the call that his patient was in labor. Rush hour traffic in Raleigh was a nightmare but he made the trip in record time. Shoving through metal doors, he rushed down corridors, thinking about all the things his brother had missed with the birth of the triplets. In his bones, he knew those babies were Greg's.

He recalled the buzz tingling along his arms when he removed the infants from the mother's lifeless womb. Nothing explained that feeling, except the miracle of delivering his own nephews and niece. That wasn't a birth he would trust to any other physician. Nothing about the arrival of the triplets was normal and Greg missed it all.

Thankfully, his current patient's pregnancy was going according to plan. She was expecting twins. The Warrens were ecstatic. In their mid-thirties, and settled in careers, they very much wanted their first baby. When they discovered they were expecting twins, their joy doubled.

Greg would have loved having triplets.

"Mr. Warren, how are you?" Daniel said as he entered the room.

"Good to see you, Doctor." Mr. Warren's concern eased into a smile. This father-to-be accompanied his wife to every appointment and worried about the strain on his wife.

Greg would have been in frenzy until he held his child.

Daniel turned to Mrs. Warren. "And how is our expectant mother doing? Are you excited? Ready for your new life or do you want to change your mind?" Daniel teased as he examined the patient's bulging abdomen.

If only Greg could go back, slow his speed. Focus on his driving. He felt he had to comfort Cydney Eller. He couldn't let go the fear that Greg had made a mistake.

Candace Warren managed a weary smile, though strain lined her face. "I'm ready to get this pregnancy over with."

"So am I, Doc. We haven't slept in weeks."

"Don't count on sleeping after your twins arrive." Daniel laughed as he checked the mother. Replacing the sheet over her lower body, he sent her an encouraging smile. "Won't be long, now, Candace. You're at four centimeters, already."

"How long?" The Warrens said at the same time. They exchanged looks and laughed.

Tim Warren's face wrinkled in a sheepish grin as he shrugged. "Guess we're impatient."

Daniel gave a sympathetic smile. *Greg would have started ranting at the delay.* "Not as impatient as these little guys."

Candace gasped. Her face twisted in a pain. She gripped the bedclothes in tight fists and panted. When her breathing slowed, Daniel dropped the chart on the side of the bed and lifted the sheet to check her again.

"Wow, that wasn't hard." Candace fell back against the pillows. "I'm ready. Let's get this show started."

"Things are moving along. You dilated two more centimeters." Daniel checked his chart. "Are you planning on breastfeeding?"

"Yes, I want to give my babies the best start in life that I can."

"I'll have the nurse instruct you on techniques." Daniel paused, brow wrinkled. "You might want to try to deliver without any medications if you think you can."

"Will it hurt the babies if I need medication? We took the natural childbirth classes, and that's what I want. But with twins, I'm worried I can't make it through the whole birth process without help from medication."

"It's always the mother's choice as long as everything looks normal. The babies might be sluggish at birth from the medication, but that's to be expected." Daniel put a hand on her arm. "This is your show. Your choice. You know how much pain you can take. If the pain gets too bad, all you have to do is ask for medication. My team will be there to take care of your babies no matter what you decide."

"Thank you for explaining that, Doc. The instructor of the birthing classes made it sound like the mother was a failure if she asked for medication. But Candace is having twins and I don't want her to suffer." Tim held his wife's hand and gave her an encouraging smile.

Greg would have said something like that. Make it easy on her, Doc. That's how his brother wanted life to be. Easy.

"Thank you, Dr. Prince. You've been so much help these past few months." The smile on Candace's face would put the Mona Lisa to shame.

Ah, the joys of parenthood. Something Greg would never know.

Daniel nodded to the couple and left the room before the couple noticed the expression on his face. This couple's experience was how pregnancy and birth should be. Two people sharing their love and supporting each other. Two parents anticipating the birth of their baby.

Not a father dead on at the scene of an accident and the mother listed as DOA, leaving orphaned triplets alone to fight for their lives.

But he would not leave the triplets to fight alone. He would protect them every way he could no matter what choices he had made in the past. Delivering babies was his life, but he had denied wanting to be a father. Memories of his childhood and the mistakes his parents made had put him off fatherhood. Then he delivered the triplets, felt connected to them, and things changed. Still, major obstacles blocked his way to protecting the infants. Legal issues were at the top of the list, even if Cydney Eller wasn't trying to stake her claim to the babies.

What if the triplets weren't Greg's? His hopes of still having a connection to his brother would end in disappointment. But he couldn't get the babies out of his mind. He'd delivered preemies before, and knew the strain of multiple births on new parents. And even with his medical training he couldn't stop worries about the triplets' chances of survival.

What if the tiny infants didn't make it? Much as he trusted Dr. Morgan and the medical training of her staff, he couldn't deny his fear that medical skills might not be enough.

And worries over the triplets' medical condition were just the start. Cydney Eller's presence loomed large on his list. Did she have more legal claim to the babies than he did? Even if DNA tests proved the triples were Greg's, would a judge decide in favor of a female wanting custody of the babies?

※

Hours later when Daniel prepared to deliver the Warren twins, those thoughts were still rattling around in his head. But nothing about this couple resembled Greg's situation.

The Warrens planned for the birth of their baby. Learning they were expecting twins surprised them, but Candace was in her mid-thirties. She understood her reproductive system was past its peak and knew the chances of a multiple birth. The Warrens were prepared.

Had Greg made certain his babies were healthy during pregnancy? Why didn't he ask me to guard his babies during pregnancy?

Daniel delivered the first twin, a boy, and sighed. Good birth weight, about six pounds, good color, and a healthy infant.

Had Greg given any thought to the responsibilities of being a father?

Greg had lived for the moment. If he was bored, he looked for excitement. When that activity grew old, he tried something new. How would Greg handle three premature infants? He wouldn't have walked away...would he?

The second twin was a girl. Fraternal twins were common to a woman in her mid thirties. Her body released two ova during her monthly cycle. It meant double joy for this couple wanting children so bad. Two perfect infants. Both over five pounds and healthy. No NICU stay for these infants.

Why had Greg kept the news of his impending fatherhood a secret?

He had always been gregarious, sharing news about his life. But he hadn't mentioned one word about his girlfriend's pregnancy. Had Greg been dating Sigourney Eller? Was Greg the father or had he been in the wrong place at the wrong time?

Daniel checked the Apgar scores for both of the Warren infants. Perfect. With ruddy skin, squalling lungs and weighing in at six pounds one ounces and six pounds even, both twins received excellent marks.

"Congratulations, Mr. Warren, they're perfect." Daniel's words were wasted. Tim Warren was white as a sheet, his gaze locked on his newborn infants. Daniel turned to the exhausted mother. "The babies are almost as beautiful as their mother."

Candace rolled her eyes, but her face glowed as she smiled. "I told Tim you should write a book on bedside manner. Thank you for everything, Dr. Prince. We're so grateful."

"You did all the work, Candace. We'll deliver the afterbirth in a few minutes, then you need get some rest. Nurses will bring the infants in for a feeding before you know it. Call if you have any questions."

Ten minutes later, Daniel walked down the hall, but the image of the Warrens' shinning faces reminded him of the death mask on the face of the triplets' mother when he delivered her babies. What a cruel twist of fate. Had Sigourney Eller wanted her babies? Would she have loved and cared for them as Candace Warren would her infants?

Of course, not, Daniel stabbed the elevator button. Age made a difference. Sigourney Eller was ten years younger than Mrs. Warren was and unsettled. According to Cydney, Sigourney couldn't hold down a job. Candace Warren held a secure position and that fact alone defined the difference in the two women's attitudes in his opinion.

Daniel sighed as he stepped on the elevator. If the triplet's mother couldn't hold down a job, what kind of life would she have provided for her children? If they had his brother's blood in their veins, the babies would have faced a double risk. Would Greg have settled down to take care of the triplets and their mother? Or would he have left when changing diapers got old?

The elevator jerked to a stop. When the doors opened, Daniel stepped out. Answers to those questions kept him awake at night. But one thing he knew for certain. If the infants were Greg's, he would make they were safe.

And if they weren't Greg's?

Daniel missed his step, but caught his balance before he stumbled.

What if the triplets weren't Greg's babies?

Cydney Eller's image flashed in his head. She had been on his mind since the moment they met. Something about her reminded him of Candace Warren. Both career oriented, but over the months of her pregnancy, Candace convinced him that her expected infants meant the world to her.

He had figured Cydney for a no nonsense business type at their first meeting, but that was before he watched her react to the triplets. She had the same look of awe on her face that he had seen on Candace Warren's face. When Cydney caught her first glimpse of the triplets in NICU, it had been love at first sight.

There was no doubt in his mind that Cydney would take good care of the triplets. But he couldn't let go the connection he felt with the infants. That feeling hadn't happened when he delivered the Warren twins. He wasn't going through some identity crisis or reacting to the shock of his brother's death. The connection was real.

Even if the triplets were not Greg's, they had touched him as no delivery ever had. He couldn't shake off the feeling that the triplets needed him. Was it because the mother had been

DOA when he delivered her babies? He considered that possibility, but he couldn't ignore his need to make sure the triplets were safe.

So what was he going to do about Cydney Eller?

After checking on the triplets, Daniel headed for the parking garage and pulled out his phone to call his attorney. "Phil, I need answers."

"Did you do the DNA test?"

"First thing when I got back to the hospital," Daniel said. "But getting the results back takes too long. Can you have someone check on Greg's routine for the last few months? I'd like to know what he was doing even without the complication of the triplets."

"Will do, might take some time, though."

"Try to find out if there's a connection between Greg and Sigourney Eller. It shouldn't be difficult to do if they were dating."

"If they weren't?"

"Might be harder," Daniel blew an impatient breath, "but I need to know about her, too. If Greg is the father of those babies, I want to know what sort of person she was."

"Can't you judge from the sister?"

"Was Greg anything like me?" Daniel barked into the phone. He held it away from his ear and stared at it as if Phil could see his glare. Then he sighed and held the cell to his ear. "Sorry. I'm on edge."

"Understandable. I'll put someone on Greg's trail right away."

"Phil," Daniel paused. Reluctant but determined, he forced the words out. "While you're at it, check on Cydney Eller, as well."

"Daniel—"

"She's trying to claim custody of the triplets. I need to know who I'm dealing with."

"If you're sure—"

" I am." Daniel heard the doubt in his friend's words. Phil

was advising caution. But Daniel's gut was twisting in knots. "I need to know about the woman claiming custody Greg's babies."

"It's your call, buddy."

"And Phil, I need to make a new will. Leave everything to the triplets and make it fast. I want all bases covered, just in case."

"Daniel, think this through. I'd advise caution before you make a decision like that."

"I am being cautious."

"What if the triplets aren't even Greg's children?"

Silence filled the pause.

Finally, raking a hand through his hair, Daniel blew air past his lips and responded. "See, that's the thing, Phil. Without Greg, I don't have anyone."

"Your mother."

Daniel clapped his lips on a curse. "Mother has millions. Those babies lost their mother, maybe their father. They don't have anyone. I can change that."

"Daniel, ole buddy, they have their aunt. Cydney Eller strikes me as the responsible type."

"And maybe they have an uncle." Daniel expelled a noisy breath. "Replace Greg's name with the triplets' in my will."

"How? Last I heard they don't even have names."

"Can't you list them as the Eller triplets for now?"

"I can. But should I?"

"Put. The. Triplets. In. My. Will. And, Phil. Call me when you have that I asked for information."

Two days later, Cydney stood beside her sister's grave and tried to concentrate on taking regular breaths. The July sun beat down on her head, but goose bumps covered her arms and moisture beaded her upper lip. Or was it tears streaming down her face?

Ziggy...

Only a few people attended the graveside service. Cydney caught movement out of the corner of her eye as more people arrived, but she didn't turn her head.

Ziggy would have been so disappointed.

Ziggy liked crowds and loved the energy from them. This handful of mourners would have saddened her. But Cydney didn't know her sister's new friends. She suspected the few people present were her acquaintances, not her sister's, and that would have angered Ziggy even more. She always wanted to be the center of attention.

Oh, Ziggy.

A tall solid body stepped to Cydney's side. Her heart gave a little skip. It was the first sign of joy she had felt since arriving at the cemetery. She didn't need to look. The way her nerves vibrated when an arm brushed hers told her it was Daniel Prince.

What was he doing here? Why had he come? Was he checking to see if her sister's friends were up to his standards? Didn't he realize this was hard enough, without his presence? His offer of kindness only made things worse. His brother had been driving where her sister was killed.

The minister began speaking.

Cydney's knees wobbled.

This was the end. After this service, her sister would disappear in the hard cold ground, never to be seen again. How could she bear the loss? Why Ziggy?

Her legs trembled, shaking her body. A strong hand took hold of her arm, but she couldn't stop shaking. Daniel put his arm around her and pulled her against his body for support. Her breath shuddered.

She would lean on him just for a minute. Just this one time...

Daniel understood. They were both mourning the loss of their only sibling. It was okay to accept his support for the funeral service. It didn't mean she was weak.

The minister's voice rose. "Let us pray."

Air shuddered out of Cydney's lungs. In a trance like motion, she closed her fingers around the red rose Daniel put in her hand. Leaning forward, she placed the rose on the polished surface of the casket. Her knees wobbled, and she swayed.

Daniel pulled her arm close and kept her from falling.

Overcome by the pain of her loss, Cydney turned away from the dark hole waiting for her sister's casket and looked at Daniel through the tears filling her eyes. "I'm surprised you came."

Daniel lifted one black clad shoulder. Warmth and comfort filled his gaze. "I came to pay my respect."

"You didn't even know her."

Daniel glanced around the graveyard. "I delivered her triplets. They might be members of my family. I owe her respect for that." His soft words blended with bird songs filling the air

"But…I didn't attend you brother's—"

"No need. You didn't know him." Daniel glanced at the people approaching her and asked in a low voice. "Will you be okay?"

Would she ever be okay again without her sister?

"Yes. Thank you for coming." She repeated those same words to everyone who came to shake her hand until Tamera reached her side. Her assistant's friendly face warmed the cold ache in her chest and she reached out both hands. "I'm so glad to see you."

"Are you okay?" Tamera shuffled from one four-inch heel to the other as she examined Cydney's face.

Pain almost bubbled over at the familiar sound of her assistant's voice, but Cydney grabbed hold of her self-control and met Tamera's concerned gaze. "I'm fine. Just surprised you could get away from work."

"Things are crazy at the office." Tamera bit her lip, obviously wanting to say more. "It's tense, but exciting, you know? I wanted to take you to lunch but I'm afraid to stay gone that long." She glanced over her shoulder. "Donna's here. You'll be okay with her, won't you?"

"Don't worry, Tamera. I'll be fine. Thank you for coming. Don't work too hard."

"I miss you, Cydney."

"I'll be back soon. Take care of yourself."

"But you won't, will you?" A new voice said as Tamera

walked away.

"Won't what?" Cydney turned to find her best friend at her side. Donna had worked at Gibbs and Associates until her marriage, and quickly had three kids. So she hadn't returned to work.

"Go back to work. You're going to take care of those babies aren't you?"

"I have to go. It's almost visiting hours." Cydney turned toward the street, afraid to answer, dreading admitting to the truth of Donna's words. "Thank you for coming."

"Not so fast, girlfriend." Donna caught Cydney's arm and matched her steps. "I'm going with you. Then I'm taking you to lunch."

Cydney opened her mouth to refuse, but worry and a sense of loss swept over her. She needed to talk and Donna was her closest friend. Even if they didn't spend as much time together as they had when Donna worked in the office, they kept in touch.

Donna was offering a short break from reality and Cydney always enjoyed the lunches they had shared in the past. Spending an hour with Donna would take her mind off her worries and help her sort her thoughts.

CHAPTER 4

"Thanks for coming today, Donna." Cydney looked up from stirring her glass of iced tea. Watching the familiar liquid swirl in the glass, listening to the clink of ice cubs against the spoon, hypnotized her and dulled her pain. "It's good to see you and Tamera. I feel so closed off in the hospital."

"Umm," Donna took a sip of her tea, "you shouldn't be by yourself at a time like this. You should have called me, you know."

"I wanted to, but I couldn't. You have your hands full with three kids." Cydney gazed vacantly past Donna's shoulder. "I can't get the image of Ziggy's lifeless body out of my head." She shivered and shook her head. "Her skin was so pale and cold. Her hair was limp. You know how much time Ziggy spent fixing her curls. She wouldn't want anyone to see her looking like a slab of marble."

"Try not to think about it, hon. Remember the good times. Her tinkling laugh and all the fun she had. Ziggy got more out of life than most people twice her age do."

"It's hard to imagine that Ziggy and Tamera are about the same age." Cydney sighed and played with her silverware to avoid Donna's piercing gaze. "Tamera has a job and her own apartment—"

"And you feel guilty for wishing Ziggy had been more like Tamera? Let it go, Cyd. You were doing what you thought was best for her."

"Does wishing she'd been different make me awful? I just wanted her to be—"

"Happy?"

Cydney exhaled a shuddering breath and gave an energetic nod.

"But she was happy, don't you think? I mean, everything you ever mentioned about Ziggy included one good time after the other."

"I know you're right. And she did have fun…did you notice how blue the sky was at the cemetery?" Cydney's voice quivered and her eyes had a far away look. "It was almost the same shade of blue as Ziggy's eyes."

"Yes, well…who was the hunk that grabbed your arm and kept you from falling?"

Cydney smothered a gasp and felt the sudden urge to giggle. "You think he's good looking?"

"And you don't? Are you dead?" Eyes wide with distress, Donna covered her mouth. "I am so sorry, hon. I stay home with the kids so much I've forgotten how to make polite conversation with another adult."

"No, you're fine. I do think it's funny you should say it," Cydney shrugged and met Donna's gaze, "because the instant I saw him I thought of my mother. And how much she would have loved him."

"Your mother had good taste."

Cydney looked up from tracing a ring on the tablecloth. "You would say that." She forced a teasing tone to her voice. "You fell hard and fast for Charlie."

Shadows darkened Donna's eyes. "We're all entitled to one mistake I guess."

The muscles in Cydney's shoulders stiffened, much as they did when she prepared to hear bad news. Was instinct alerting her to trouble? Donna sounded different, unlike her usual gregarious self. Now that she was feeling more alert, she noticed new lines of strain around Donna's eyes. "What are you saying? What's going on, Donna?"

"Things aren't too…peachy at home just now." Donna's stared around the room at other customers in the restaurant. Finally, she brought her gaze back to Cydney and shrugged. She attempt a normal tone fell flat as she admitted. "But hey, they say bad things happen in three's, so I guess we're coming out ahead so far today."

"If you mean Ziggy and your trouble with Charlie, don't forget Tamera's grandmother."

"Is she sick again?"

Cydney nodded. "I feel sorry for Tamera. She is so close to her grandmother. She only moved out on her own a few months ago."

"Girlfriend, you think you are so clever." Donna pointed her fork at Cydney, "You're trying to distract me. And it almost worked. But I know your tricks. Now, spill it out and I want to hear the long version. Who is he?"

Cydney laughed. It was so good to feel normal, even if only for a short time. "I can't believe you think he's a hunk."

"Tall, dark curls and eyes deep enough to get lost in…and so aloof…yum. Just thinking about warming him up gives me the shivers. Now, tell all."

"Aloof? Cold fish appeals to you?" Guilt brought a rush of heat to Cydney's cheeks. She knew Daniel's emotions were sincere. Why pretend he was distant and uncaring, unless she was trying to protect herself

"I think he's yummy. Aloof, maybe, but all that energy sparkling in his eyes is alluring! And sexy…who is he?"

"His brother died in the accident with Ziggy." Cydney paused as the server arrived with their salads. "How are the kids?"

For a moment, Donna looked as if she wouldn't allow a change of topic, but finally she shrugged. "Fine, growing like weeds and full of life…sorry. Sorry! There I go again. I can't keep my foot out of my mouth today."

"It's okay." Cydney tightened the grip on her fork. One of the hardest parts about spending so much time at the hospital was knowing death hung over the place like a dark shadow. "How do you like the salad?"

"Fine…stop stalling." With the bluntness only close friends dare use, Donna pierced Cydney with a glare. "You have to face the situation sooner or later, so talk to me. How much do you know?"

Cydney swallowed. Donna was right. She couldn't hide from reality. Ziggy was dead and she had to continue for the sake of the triplets. "You mean other than the fact that my sister is dead. The man who we think fathered the triplets is dead. And they left three babies fighting for life in NICU. Ummm, not much, really."

"This is so like Ziggy. Not telling you she was pregnant until it was too late. Are the babies hers, do you think?"

Air whooshed past Cydney's lips. "I think so, but you know Ziggy. She loved babies so much she might have signed a surrogacy agreement to make some cash. I just don't know."

"But you feel responsible because you told her to find a job and she stormed out. You're beating yourself up, thinking this is all your fault."

"How do you know it isn't? Maybe Ziggy needed more love than—"

"You loved her to bits." Donna pointed her fork at Cydney. "I can't count the times I watched her twist you around to get her way. You didn't cheat your sister, Cyd. You worked hard to provide a home for her and support her. You had to. She wouldn't work."

"But, maybe—"

Donna leaned across the table. "You're thinking about keeping those babies aren't you?" Watching the expressions chase across Cydney's face, Donna huffed and slammed her fork down on the table. "You are. I see it in your eyes."

"I don't know what's going to happen." Cydney dropped her gaze to her food, and scattered salad greens with her fork. "Daniel wants joint custody."

Donna heaved a noisy sigh. "Good for him. After all, his brother started this mess in the first place."

"Maybe, but, if the babies are Ziggy's—"

"You need to think about your career. Your life. How can you take care of three babies and handle a job in advertising? I know the demands of that job, remember."

"It's fine for you to warn me off, but you have Charlie and the kids. Someone to love. Without Ziggy, I don't have anyone."

"Taking care of someone else's triplets isn't the answer." Donna stabbed her salad. "You always said you wanted a career instead of kids."

Cydney shuddered at the familiar words. "I know but…it's hard. And…they're so tiny."

Donna gave a snort. "They outgrow the cute stage real quick, girlfriend. Then the trouble starts and it's not pretty." Donna forked salad in her mouth. "You can't throw your future away because of Ziggy's choices. This is your life, and your future we're talking about."

"You keep saying that, but what if they are her babies? That makes them my family, and my responsibility." Cydney swallowed a sob. "I can't turn my back—"

"What if they aren't her babies? What is she was a surrogate? What if you pass up this opportunity at work…let the promotion go to someone else…then learn those babies aren't even related to you? What will you do then?" Donna leaned across the table. "Use your head, Cyd. This double dose of responsibility you use as a shield will get you in trouble."

"I do not—"

"Don't say it." Donna pointed her fork. "Every time something goes wrong, you try to fix it…well, guess what, girlfriend? You cannot make the world a perfect place. Now, stop playing in your food and eat. And tell me everything you know about that gorgeous hunk."

"I can't believe you think Daniel Prince is a hunk."

❧

"Still here?"

Startled by his voice, Cydney turned away from the viewing window. Her gaze landed on Daniel's tired face. She knew the feeling. It was past mid-night, and she was still in the NICU waiting room with a few other parents. Visiting hours were long over, but she couldn't leave the triplets alone. "I wanted to check on them one last time."

"Is everything okay?" Daniel turned a worried look toward the window.

"The boys' have maintained the same temperature for the last four hours, and they're receiving phototherapy treatment for jaundice. Baby Girl is still on all the monitors." Cydney moved a step away from the glass. "I wish we didn't have to wait for visiting hours to see them."

Muscles bunched along the line of his jaw as he stared through the glass. "At least we got custody."

"Temporary custody," Cydney's brittle words reminded him the battle wasn't over. Her custody, his custody or the state's custody, they had a fight ahead of them. And everything depended on results of the DNA tests. She glanced at his face, noting the brackets etched around his mouth. Dark stubble covered his jaw. "I'm sorry. I know you were hoping for custody."

In the days since the accident, they had slipped into an uneasy companionship. She saw him several times every day. And often stumbled over him here in the waiting room, late at night as he kept watch over the infants.

The triplets were lucky to have this proud honorable defender looking out for them. Her impression of Daniel had changed from their first meeting. With his career, she'd thought he would avoid more responsibility.

Daniel's actions proved he was different from her impression when she learned his brother was driving when her sister died. Daniel hadn't turned his back. He cared for the helpless infants same as she did. But she tried to keep her distance. Daniel was the take-charge type. He rushed to protect. It would be so easy to allow him take the lead and shoulder the responsibility.

Tears clogged her throat when she thought of all the triplets would miss in life. Both parents were dead before they had taken their first breath. She prayed they would survive this rocky start, and vowed to give them a normal life. But she didn't know what the next session in court would bring. The judge might grant Daniel full custody. His medical training and the triplets' health issues made that a sensible solution.

Fearing her time with the triplets was near an end, Cydney turned back to watch the NICU staff on the other side of the glass. The triplets and other babies depended on the professional ability of doctors and nurses. How could she fight the decision if the judge decided in Daniel's favor?

She still couldn't believe Ziggy would never see her babies. For the hundredth time, she wondered what her sister had been thinking. How had Ziggy expected to take care of a baby when she didn't have a job. And then she didn't have one infant, she had three.

Had Ziggy known she was having triplets?

From that first night, Cydney had fallen in love with the tiny babies. Now, she faced reality. Demands of the legal system hung over her head like a hammer, ready to drop and end her connection with the infants. Still questions whirled in her head. How could she take care of three premature infants? What should she do about her job? Would Daniel pursue his claim to the babies? What if the triplets weren't related to her or to Daniel?

The jumbled thoughts churned through her head day and night, making her attempts to sleep difficult. She probably looked as exhausted as Daniel did. As if reading her mind, Daniel moved closer. Hair on her neck vibrated a warning. She had tried to control her reaction to him over the past few days, and failed.

"I wish there were more visiting hours." He peered in the window.

Cydney gave a nod, forcing her mind off the way his low voice vibrated along her nerves. She understood the need to limit visiting time in an area where infants were critically ill, but she needed to keep close to the triplets. "I feel so helpless when I'm out here."

Daniel turned to her, but her glance skipped past his shoulder as a sudden cry escaped from one of the new mothers in the waiting room. The woman collapsed in a chair and sobbed as a doctor walked away. Her family gathered around in a protective circle. Grief radiated from their slumped posture in a powerful wave.

Lifting a tortured gaze to meet Daniel's dark stare Cydney whispered, "We are so lucky. Except for the infection the boys have and Baby Girl's breathing issues, all three babies are improving."

"Have you seen the doctor since the five o'clock rounds?"

"No." Cydney shook her head. Five o'clock seemed like days ago. But she hadn't seen a doctor since then, and Daniel arrived in time to hear that report. Since this started, he had been a rock, always around when she least expected.

Like Ziggy's funeral.

She had held on to her emotions until near the end...then in the heat, combined with her pain, everything got fuzzy. The minister's words had echoed through the trees surrounding the graveyard. Spots exploded in front of her eyes, but Daniel wrapped a strong arm around her shoulders, and pulled her back to reality.

In the past five days, she had seen more of Daniel Prince than she had seen of her sister in months, which explained why her opinion of him had warmed considerably.

"You won't see the doctor again tonight." Daniel looked toward the clock. "You should get some rest before you drop."

The corner of her mouth lifted as she eyed the dark circles under his eyes. "You should talk. Some doctor you are, not practicing your own advice." She pointedly stared at the beard on his chin. "You're beginning to look ragged."

Daniel shrugged. "Had a late delivery. Babies can't tell time. Have you had anything to eat?"

Cydney shook her head. With the mix of medicinal odors and disinfectant filling her senses, food was the last thing on her mind. "I'm not hungry."

"You should eat something and go home to rest."

Cydney ignored him, pressing her fingers against the glass as she tried to drown out the sounds of the woman sobbing behind them. "I want to stay a little longer."

"It's late. The nurses won't let you in again tonight, unless there's an emergency." Daniel nodded toward the nurses working in the unit. "Let's get a cup of coffee and let them do their job."

With one last glance, Cydney turned away from the window. This late at night, she didn't trust her resistance to his rugged appeal. She tried to remain distant, but he looked so dependable she wanted to curl against his chest and cry her eyes out.

Part of her reaction to him was because she knew he would understand her grief at losing a sibling. They had that much in common. His kindness touched her. Would it hurt anything if she accepted his comfort for a few minutes? *Did she dare?*

No. Even with their truce over the last few days, and sharing their concern for the infants, they wanted different things. And the same thing.

She admired Daniel's wish to take care of his family. To her secret shame, she even toyed with the idea of stepping away and letting him take charge. He had a housekeeper to run things. He was much better equipped to increase his family by three than she was.

But since she was six years old, she had always trying to do right. First, to please her father so he wouldn't leave them. But he left despite her efforts to be perfect, and her mother fell to pieces. She even tried to make things easy for her mother and sister. But her efforts hadn't reached through her mother's broken heart. Ziggy alone had benefitted from her actions.

Now, Ziggy was gone.

Spending time with Daniel wouldn't change who she was, surely. Later, when she had time to analyze her moment of weakness, she would regret letting her guard down. But for now, she needed the comfort he offered. "Thanks, but I—"

"We need to talk." Daniel's tone left no room for disagreement. Taking hold of her arm, he urged her toward the bank of elevators.

"We talk every day." Cydney fought the fluttering in her chest as her skin absorbed the warmth of his touch. A whiff of his aftershave made her nerves tingle. *This had to stop.* She had to fight against her attraction to this man. He could undo all she had accomplished. Spending time with Daniel made her want to accept the strength he offered. Truth was, part of her already relied on him.

He was the only adult she had any contact with for the last few days. Staying cooped up in the hospital most of the day was starting to play tricks with her mind, and make her want to connect with this man she hardly knew.

Her response to Daniel meant she reacted exactly like her mother...and Ziggy did to a man's charm. Yet she vowed she would be different, be stronger, and have more options than they had. Now she was following the same path.

"We have to stop meeting like this." Attempting a teasing tone, Cydney turned, preparing to refuse his offer. "I feel as if you're my new best friend or something." She managed a grin as he stabbed the elevator button for the main floor. She couldn't let him suspect how much she looked forward to seeing him each day. Or how much she trusted his opinions on the triplets' condition.

The glare in Daniel's red-rimmed eyes showed he wasn't in the mood for jokes. "That's good, because being friends may be the only thing that gets us out of this situation."

About to ask what he meant, Cydney snapped her mouth shut when a hand stopped the elevator doors from closing. More passengers entered the car and their conversation didn't need an audience. But she wanted answers. What did he mean?

As soon as they settled at a small table in front of the night black windows, she blurted the words whirling in her head. "What are you talking about?"

Daniel took a bite of the club sandwich he'd picked from the few choices offered this time of night. "My attorney has been doing a little research."

Her coffee cup clattered as she set it on the table. She didn't trust the grim look in Daniel's eyes or the thin line of his mouth. "What kind of research?"

Swallowing the bite of sandwich, he pointed the triangular ends in her direction. "Remember the judge said he didn't think one person could take care of three babies? That he only granted temporary custody because the infants would be in the hospital until results of the DNA tests came back?"

"So?" Cydney struggled to hide the shivers shaking her limbs. Fear raced through her body. His words reminded her that the judge controlling the triplets' wasn't on their side.

"This judge is dedicated to promoting family values."

"Isn't that good news? Doesn't that mean the judge will agree with us because we're related to the infants?"

Daniel shrugged. "Depends which side you're on. We want the best for the triplets. But we have to be prepared. This judge might decide foster care is the best place for three premature infants."

"Foster care? What are you saying?" Cydney struggled for air as fear squeezed her lungs tight. "You think he'll take the triplets away from us?"

Daniel's dark gaze scanned her face. "I think we're going to lose. I wanted to warn you ahead of time." He expelled a frustrated breath as his intense gaze locked with hers. "That's why I'm going to petition for full custody."

Accepting the reality of his words, Cydney responded with a trance like nod. She had expected as much. After getting to know Daniel over the past week, she wouldn't expect anything less from this man. He would protect his brother's children at all cost. If…if the triplets were his brother's children. "But—"

"It's just a precaution," Daniel held up a hand causing her to swallow the rest of her protest, "just in case things go wrong."

"Sorry, I don't follow—"

"I'm not a lawyer, okay? I depend on my attorney to be the expert in law issues. But I have a gut feeling about this judge. I think he might place the triplets in different homes—"

"No!" Every nerve in her body jerked to attention. "Separate Big Brother from Little Brother? Send Baby Girl out to a different home, alone?" Her words ended in a wail just short of a sob. Dropping her barely touched sandwich, she grabbed her handbag, preparing to rush to the defense of the three infants.

Daniel slammed his hand on the table. Their cups rattled. She stopped in mid dash, and staring at him, fell back in her seat. "What—"

"This is ridiculous. And it ends right now. Tonight." His words vibrated with emotions she couldn't identify. The table shook and coffee sloshed out of their cups.

She stared at him, escape forgotten in the face of his powerful emotions. Daniel always seemed in control. "What—"

"It's time to give those babies a name." His glare bored into her for long seconds, then his gaze dropped and he ran fingers through his hair leaving it standing on end.

Seeing his distress, her breath hitched in her chest. The next instant a rush of sympathy replaced her angry reaction to his words. Daniel's mussed hair and pinched mouth, gave her a sudden glimpse of how Big Brother would look in a few years. Her heart melted.

Daniel and the largest twin had the same square chin with a dimple in the middle. She struggled to control the tenderness bubbling inside her. No matter how much Daniel resembled the baby, she had to maintain her guard. This man and the tiny newborns had become her world over the past few days. In the dimness of the near empty cafeteria, Daniel resembled a tired, grumpy little boy needing comfort, but she had to keep her distance.

She struggled to conceal her emotions with an innocent expression. Knowing there were two volumes of baby name books in her shoulder bag, she cleared her throat. "Names?"

"Yes! They need—"

"Names like a mother would choose?"

Brow arched, Daniel sent her a cautious look. "Exactly—"

"Okay," she tried not to laugh at the confused expression

in his eyes. "Ziggy always wanted to name her first daughter Sigourney Raven." She paused, to allow him time to absorb her words. "What do you think? Do you like that name for Baby Girl?"

"How did your sister end up with a name like Ziggy?"

"I was four when she was born and I couldn't say Sigourney." Cydney bit the inside of her lip to keep from laughing. His disgruntled expression distracted her from painful memories of her sister. "So, do you like Ziggy's choice?"

The lines around his eyes deepened into wrinkles as he stared at her, silently willing her to bend to his will.

Determined to hold her small advantage, she rushed to add, "For boy names Ziggy wanted Regis Dalton and Albert Wolfgang. What do you think?"

"This isn't a joking matter." Daniel met her wide innocence look and wished he hadn't. The fleeting moments of humor ended, leaving her eyes dull. "I'm serious. Those babies are five days old."

He flinched as a hurt look flashed across her face at his careless reminder of her sister's death. He hadn't intended to cause her pain, but the court gave Cydney Eller joint custody of the triplets. It was past time to give the infants real names. If she didn't agree with the decision, he would name them himself. Even if her sister wasn't the biological mother, for the time being, Cydney was the closest thing the infants had to a mother figure. It was time she agreed to give them an identity.

Suddenly, he recalled his own mother. He could guess what names she would pick. It was a miracle he and Greg hadn't been tagged Zachary the second or some other hideous family name. Images of his mother dressed in her finest to attend some function at the country club with his father, flashed before his eyes. But he knew Cydney dealt in reality, despite her creative training in advertising. He wanted her to choose the names.

Social status was the last thing he wanted for these infants. If he had his way, he would choose a normal family life for his niece and nephews. "It's time to give them real names."

Cydney met his gaze, knowing he was right. Babies needed an identity. Despite him hinting she had ignored her duty, she understood his feelings. Turning to stare out the dark window, she fought to control the tears edging her eyes.

Choosing the right name was a big responsibility. Expectant mothers had nine months to select the perfect name. She hadn't had the luxury of months to decide and she needed three names. She had spent half her life denying she wanted children. That changed the instant she saw Ziggy's triplets. But acknowledging a change of heart didn't add to her skills as a mother. What did she know about choosing the right name for babies?

But she wasn't going to reveal her indecision. Daniel could take the triplets away from her if she showed the slightest hesitation or lack of caring. The joint custody agreement was temporary and he had the advantage of having an attorney.

Sitting there in the dimness of the deserted room, she felt like Cinderella without the excitement of the big dance, but with the disappointment of knowing the clock was ready to strike midnight and end her dreams.

Instead of three stepsisters, she had three infants needing her help. She couldn't let them down. Daniel could challenge her right to custody. She needed to prove she was up for the task and ready to do the right thing for the triplets. This was a battle to keep three infants safe and out of foster care. She could not loose.

Lifting a brow, she met Daniel's tired glance. "I suppose you want something dignified? Maybe a family name?" Visions of the fragile baby with wrinkled skin and wisps of blonde fuzz on her tiny head filled Cydney with sadness for the mother who would never hold the precious little girl.

"Precisely" Shadows flickered in his eyes. "Mother's name is Dawn…Father was Zachary."

Cydney noticed his reluctant tone as he mentioned his father. It was hard to ignore her memories, but sensing his pain, she spoke past the tightening in her chest. "How do you like Cecilia Dawn, after the grandmothers for Baby Girl?"

"That's a mouthful. She...isn't very...big."

Cydney's heart lunged in her chest. For long seconds, all she could hear was the sound of blood pounding in her ears. Didn't he think Baby Girl would survive? Is that why he hesitated? She would not allow doubts to curb her hopes. "We can call her Cece."

After long seconds, Daniel nodded and swiped a hand across his jaw. "And the boys?"

Cydney tried to ignore the way his hand shook when he lifted the coffee cup and focused on his question. Over the past few days, she had learned family was very important to Daniel. Yet, that tiny bit of insight scared more than reassured her. She didn't want to know what Daniel cared about, or understand what he was feeling. She wanted to make her own decisions. This wasn't a game. Taking responsibility for the triplets was a lifetime commitment. Could she make the right choice?

Shifting her weight, to find a more comfortable position on the hard plastic chair, she tried to focus. Long hours in the NICU made her brain fuzzy, but doing her best to protect the babies came first, no matter how tired she was. Inhaling a deep breath, she blurted. "How about naming the boys Zachary Daniel and Gregory Max?"

An hour later, she closed the door of her apartment, slumped against the flat surface, and sighed. Even with her eyes closed, she could still see the determined look on Daniel's face when he insisted they decide on names.

Didn't he realize how hard it was to take that step? Choosing names put her a step closer to accepting a role she had vowed she would avoid. Naming babies staked your claim on them. Showed your attachment to them, and filled her with terror.

Everyone she had ever cared about had died. Her dad left, so he was the same as dead to the family. He never called or came to visit before his death. Her mother's way of dealing with a broken heart was finding a new man to fill her life. Even before she died, she was the same as dead to her daughters. Now she had lost Ziggy.

What if...she lost the triplets, too?

Daniel's attitude tonight didn't ease her worries. He had been at her side at the hospital for days. He waited hours for news from specialists, and treatment for the triplets, just as she had. All that time his actions had been admirable. He even came to Ziggy's funeral. So why was she upset with him now?

Because he made it clear he wanted custody of the triplets, and she felt guilty.

Ziggy's death, leaving motherless triplets in need of care, sent her life whirling in confusion. She wanted to do the right thing. But what was right for the three motherless infants, and what was right for her, might not be the same thing.

In fact, the choices were in direct conflict.

She had set goals to reach the level in her career where she had security. She was almost there. She had almost reached the point where she could ease off the pressure and enjoy her position. But taking custody of three infants would change everything.

Yet, the triplets were her only family. They needed her. They needed a mother, a home, a father, and security. How could she give them what they deserved and keep them secure?

Daniel could do that, and not even change his life. Maybe not the mothering part, but what did she really know about his personal life? He could have someone special in his life already, some woman who could act as mother to the infants.

Cydney slid down the door until her butt landed on carpet. She had to make a decision. Her choices were simple. Let Daniel have custody of the triplets and try for her promotion, or challenge him for custody. In her heart, she knew her sister was the biological mother of these children. How could she turn her back on them?

How could she walk away from the years she had invested in her career? Heaving a loud sigh, she pushed up from the floor and walked through the white carpeted living room. The plush white sofa welcomed her tired body as she stretched out with another sigh.

Her thoughts quickly returned to the issue of Daniel and the triplets. The infants needed a mother's care. She was the logical choice. They needed a father figure, too, and Daniel was claiming them as members of his family.

But she couldn't base her future on this man. Everything she had ever believed about relationships, warned her away. Daniel was handsome, like her father, but the similarities ended there. Unlike her artist father and his many affairs with his models, Daniel was a man she could trust.

And that was a big part of her problem. Trusting Daniel, even for the sake of the triplets, went against all she believed.

CHAPTER 5

The next morning when Cydney rushed into the NICU for the first visit of the day, the nurse greeted her. "Morning, Ms. Eller. We're still waiting on the DNA results."

Cydney nodded. "How are the triplets this morning?"

"We had a restless night. Little Brother almost choked."

"On what?"

"Vomit. It happens with newborns. I'm sure his fever is causing the problem. His belly is still swollen from the sepsis. Oh, by the way, I scheduled you and Dr. Prince for new parents' CPR class tonight."

Cydney's heart thudded at thoughts of spending more time with Daniel, but she focused on the reason she was in NICU at six a.m. "Is the baby okay?"

"Yes, but this incident is a reminder of what can happen. You need to be prepared. The babies might choke after you take them home. We encourage all new parents to take the classes offered." The nurse studied Cydney's face. "Are you all right with that?"

"Of course," Cydney said, her gaze darting toward the infants. *How could she object?* The nurse was right. Children choked. She should take classes. But could she spend more time with Daniel and keep her head?

After the time they spent in the darkened cafeteria last night, she wasn't so sure. Even in those depressing surroundings, her heart fluttered in reaction to him. But her doubts would wait until later. She wanted to concentrate on her visit with the triplets. Machines beeped and pinged all around her. Monitors flashed lights. The odor of antiseptics mingled with the sickly sweet stench of formula and soiled baby diapers making her stomach slosh.

Take CPR classes with Daniel?

That thought sent her stomach tumbling. How could she appear in public with him as if they really were the triplets' parents? Could she face people's interest? Could she spend more time with Daniel and not reveal her awareness of his every move?

Could she keep her head?

The low murmurs of the nursing staff competed with whooshing sounds of machines and the mewling cries of infants. The early morning shift in the nursery was the loudest and the busiest of the day.

Fewer people visited at six in the morning, but those who did quickly learned to stay out of the staff's way. The tiny patients had to be checked before the staff changed shifts. Charts needed updating, along with all the routine chores required.

Cydney stepped as close to the incubator as she could and stared down at Little Brother. Gregory Max was a mouthful for such a little boy. Her chest tightened as she noticed his wrinkled face and hands were still yellowish pink. His spindly little legs looked fleshier. Was it possible he had gained ounces in such a short time? She would have to ask about the babies' weight at the next visit when things weren't so busy.

Touching the baby's tiny hand, she waited for the grasping reflex that would make him squeeze her finger. That instinctive motion warmed new parents' hearts. Except...she wasn't a parent. She was...What was she?

Panic seized her. Her nerves clenched. Doubt filled her. What was she thinking? No way could she take care of triplets.

After her childhood, why had she imagined she could take care of one new born, much less three? She and Ziggy barely survived. Their mother wasn't exactly a good role model for mothering.

Except for what she learned when Ziggy was little, she didn't know squat about being a mother. Ziggy's long silence and keeping her pregnancy a secret proved that.

If she were the real mother of the triplets, she would have spent her pregnancy getting prepared. She would have nine months of doctor visits to learn what was happening. Nine months to read and study information on being a parent.

But fate landed her with three premature infants. And just like always, she had said, *I can do this on my own.*

Would she ever forget about needing a parent that wasn't there for her? Would she ever learn she could be part of a team? She insisted she could do things on her own, but now she had doubts. Clinging to the incubator as her knees buckled, one question whirled in her head. If she failed her sister, how could she manage three infants?

"Are you trying to hold up the incubator all by yourself?" Daniel's warm hand gripped her arm, holding her upright.

Cydney shivered under his touch. Heat rushed to her face. The scent of his aftershave and soap brought welcomed relief from the hospital odors overpowering her senses. Inhaling a deep breath, she forced a smile. It was kind of him to pretend she hadn't almost fainted.

"I was trying to get a good look at Little Brother. The nurse said he almost choked last night."

Daniel's brow arched. One corner of his mouth tilted upward. Even this early in the morning, his eyes had a distinctly wicked twinkle that he aimed on her. "A normal occurrence, considering his condition, I'm afraid."

"Is it normal to take CPR classes with a stranger as your partner?" Cydney heard her snarled words and bit hard on her lip.

"I'd venture to guess it's not that unusual." Daniel gave her a deadpan look revealing none of his thoughts, "Most people who sign up for classes are strangers to the other participants."

Cydney rolled her eyes. "That's not what I meant, and you know it." She realized he was still holding her arm and pulled away. "I mean for us to take classes. The nurse said we needed the CPR class before we take the triplets home. Everyone will think we're...we...that we're ...together."

"Would it choke you to say married?" Daniel walked over to Big Brother's incubator and checked the infant with a gentle touch. "Are you ashamed to be seen with me, Ms. Eller?"

"No," Cydney whirled toward Baby Girl's incubator to hide her expression. Unlike the boys, the little girl still had taped tubes everywhere. But the tiny hand grasped Cydney's finger and her heart. *So tiny. So perfect. So alone.*

"I'm worried about giving your associates the wrong impression, that's all." She managed to sound convincing, even to her own ears, but a new thought occurred to her. "You're a doctor. You already know CPR. You're probably exempt from the requirement."

Why did regret grab her heart and give it a shake? Two minutes earlier, she had flushed at thoughts of taking a class as Daniel's partner. Why couldn't she make up her mind? Either she liked him, or she didn't. He could be trusted, or she needed to guard her every move. What was bothering her? Was it Daniel? Or was it her unease over making the wrong decision? Was she afraid she would make the wrong choice? Or wouldn't measure up?

"Everyone needs a refresher course." His attention focused on the baby girl, "I wouldn't want to take the risk of forgetting something. I'll take the class. When is it?"

"We're signed up for tonight."

"Good. You don't have much time to panic." Daniel turned away. "I suggest we fill out the forms for the birth certificates since we decided on their names."

"Can we do that? I mean, we only have temporary custody. Should we wait for a permanent decision?"

Daniel pinched his lip and frowned. "You have a point. I would hate to label a child with a family name if he wasn't related to me." He reached for her arm. "Let's grab some coffee before I get called to deliver more babies."

"Don't you have to make rounds," Cydney tried to step away from his touch, "or some other doctoring things to do?"

"Doctoring?" Daniel laughed as he guided her toward the elevator. "You think my work is like exercising or teaching?"

Her face feeling hot as a campfire, Cydney tossed her head and sniffed. Let him make fun of her. At least he hadn't noticed the way her heart was racing or that she suddenly developed two left feet when he was near.

"I guess I could drink a cup of coffee." Never mind that she had been dying for a hot cup of coffee since she got out of bed at five this morning. But she had been running late. Visiting hours did not wait.

Daniel's cell phone rang as he headed down the corridor to do his rounds after their coffee break. He checked the caller ID and greeted his friend. "Phil. You're up early."

"I've got that information you asked for."

"Talk to me." Daniel's hand tightened on the phone.

"Your brother and the sister were hard to track. They were seen at the same clubs, but no positive proof they were a couple."

"I...see." Daniel's breath shuddered as he inhaled. For the first time, he admitted he had hoped for different news. News that Greg had committed to the triplet's mother.

"Have you checked Greg's apartment?"

Daniel stopped in his tracks and leaned against the wall. *Go through Greg's things? Pack his life away?* "I...uh...I haven't had time."

"You might find something there."

The scent of disinfectant and medications hit Daniel as if he had never been in a hospital before. Nausea tilted his stomach contents.

"I'll check." Use his power as executor of Greg's will to enter the apartment? He had put that chore off, not wanting to loose the last pretense that his brother was alive. "What about that other matter?"

"Cydney Eller?" Phil's voice demanded Daniel admit his interest. "Squeaky clean. Parents divorced. Took charge of the sister early on. Up for a promotion at the advertising firm. Not even a traffic ticket."

"I see." Daniel pinched his forehead. "She's what she seems, then."

"What do you want me to do now? Keep digging?"

Daniel blew out a sigh. He had pried enough. But he needed to know. He couldn't risk exposing the triplets to someone he didn't trust. Still, he was reluctant to go forward. Cydney Eller deserved privacy. "We've done enough. Thanks, Phil."

Who was he kidding? He had invaded Cydney's privacy already. His intentions were honorable, but his tactics were not. He would tell her, and when he did, he deserved her wrath.

⁂

Cydney approached her office with mixed feelings. She wanted to pursue the career she had worked hard to achieve, but all she could think about were the three infants in NICU. But she couldn't see the triplets until visiting hours, and she needed to check in with her office.

What would she do when they were discharged?

Women juggled children and careers all the time and still managed to succeed. But her job in the advertising firm demanded long hours, dedication to clients, and total commitment to the current ad campaign. Was she cheating the triplets if she tried to keep her job and take care of them? Things would be different if she had planned on having a baby. She would have tackled these decisions before the baby arrived.

Like Donna had. Her best friend left her job to concentrate on her family. Did Donna have regrets? From hints dropped at their recent lunch, Cydney suspected she did, and Donna had one baby at a time. Cydney was facing responsibility for three infants.

Of course, she didn't have custody of them yet. Would Daniel try to take custody of the triplets because she wasn't the perfect candidate for a mother?

She settled behind her desk with a sigh, and gazed around the familiar room. She recalled the excitement of learning she had been promoted to her own office. But enough wool gathering. It was an hour before regular office hours, and she had come here for a reason. Honesty forced her to admit that Daniel wasn't the real problem. Her conscience questioned her decision to put in a few hours at work between visiting times.

The perfect mother wouldn't leave the NIC unit. The perfect mother would read medical books to learn all the terms concerning the medical complications the triplets faced. But she wasn't perfect, and it was time she faced facts. Ziggy had taunted her about being so uptight. Could she bend enough to handle three babies?

Could she live up to Daniel's expectations? Could she work at her job and still take care for three babies? Being around Daniel's medical associates made her feel…incompetent. The nurses and doctors Daniel worked with understood medical terminology. They knew what all those machines did and how to run them. Names of medical equipment tumbled off their tongues as easy as…advertising slogans came to her. But it wasn't the same.

Daniel showed respect to his medical contacts. With her, she sensed his restraint. She didn't blame him for not trusting her. A few days ago, they had been total strangers. Now they had to act like family.

But whose family?

Her dysfunctional family or his? From his manner, she would guess he came from a traditional upbringing. But what tidbits she had picked up, Daniel's childhood showed a different story. From the few comments he let drop, his childhood hadn't been any happier than her own. The reasons were probably different, of course.

His father had been a senator and wealthy by most standards. Her dad lived on the sale of one painting until he finished another. But had their focus on family been any different? Would Daniel be a good father figure? Everything about him indicated he would. His caring touch of the triplets and his medical training were points in his favor. But she knew how it felt to be deserted by the father she loved with all her heart.

Divorce taught kids lessons adults didn't notice. Lessons like, no matter how much you loved your parents, or how hard you tried to please, they left you behind when the marriage ended. Even if they said they loved you, their actions left scars.

She and Daniel didn't even have a marriage agreement to base a relationship on. How could they act as parents to three new babies demanding bottles or needing diapers changed at the same time? How could they handle the pressure when they didn't have a foundation of love to start with?

Love Daniel?

That thought sent chills down her spine. Loving Daniel meant giving in to his need to protect those he loved. She had been on her own for so long, could she make the adjustments needed and work with him? She wanted to try for the triplets. It wasn't as if they were trying to hold a marriage together. They didn't have a personal relationship that would self de-struct if she failed. *Again.*

She had tried to work for success, but Ziggy proved the ef-fort hadn't worked with her. How could she be certain she could work with Daniel? Releasing a sigh, she pulled folders across the desk and faced the nagging truth that wouldn't let go. Daniel's opinion mattered to her.

And she didn't expect him to give up his job if DNA results showed he was the triplets' uncle. Why would he judge her as lacking if she tried to continue her career? Why had that thought even entered her head?

Daniel hadn't said a word about her work. It was all in her head. It was her fear of not measuring up that made her se-cond guess every move she made. From the time her parents divorced, she had taken charge of her sister. Now, she needed to take care of Ziggy's triplets.

And she wasn't certain she could do that single handedly, even if she didn't try to work. Could one person take care of three new infants and do a good job? If she answered no, she had to accept help from Daniel, but where did help with the triplets end, and involvement in her personal life begin?

It didn't.

Once they agreed to joint custody, she would be tied to Daniel. Their lives would entwine over the care of the triplets. Her bad days would affect Daniel. His success would reflect on her efforts to care for the infants. Whether they liked it or not, they would become emotionally dependent on one another.

And that was her greatest fear…needing another person to make her life complete made her fear being weak.

All her life, loving someone had meant losing him or her. How could she go into a partnership with Daniel when she knew from the start he did not care for her?

Was it enough that they both loved the triplets?

❧

"Cydney! You're here." Tamera bounced through the office door and stopped. "Want me to bring in your messages?"

Cydney groaned as the door closed behind her assistant. She spent half her time on things other than clients' ad campaigns. Had it always been this way? Had she spent the last ten years of her life with a phone glued to her ear?

Tamera rushed back in the office. "Oh, did you hear, they're going to announce the candidate of the promotion today?"

Bile rose in Cydney's throat. Why had she decided to come to the office today of all days? The one day guaranteed to make her feel like a failure. "Really?"

"It should be you." Tamera sorted through the messages in a flurry of bracelets and painted nails. "Sorry. I know I shouldn't say anything, but you deserved that promotion."

"It was my choice to take leave." Cydney struggled to keep her face blank as the usual startled expression appeared in Tamera's eyes. The innocence of that look reminded her of happier days. "Things will work out for the best."

Did she really believe that when she might have lost all she had worked for?

Ziggy had shunned any type of work. Cydney applied herself to achieving success. Now, Ziggy was dead and her triplets needed Cydney's time and love. It almost seemed as if her sister was reaching out from the grave to force her to take a different path in life.

"Anything I can do to help?" Tamera perched on the edge of the visitor's chair.

"Thanks, but I'm just checking on a few things. I needed to get out of the hospital for a few minutes." Cydney kept her voice calm, not willing to admit her sleepless nights. Never mind the panic threatening to overwhelm her. Hugging notes for the latest assignment to her chest like a shield, she held Tamera's expectant gaze.

"I can't believe Ziggy had triplets!" Tamera jumped up and rearranged the files on Cydney's desk with fluttering motions. "Are they okay? I can't wait to see them."

Cydney cleared her throat, already exhausted by Tamera's energy. "They were all breathing on their own this morning."

"That's good, right?"

Cydney managed a weak laugh. "According to the doctors, that's very good! They gained a few ounces, too."

"Gosh, I can't believe Ziggy is—"

"Me, either…I appreciated you coming to the funeral." Despite the tension tightening in her chest, Cydney felt better. And that was one of the reasons she decided to come by the office after early visiting hours. She needed to see people she knew and understood, people who spoke *her* language instead of medical jargon. She needed to breathe air that didn't smell like illness and death. Escaping from the NICU for a couple of hours felt like escaping from prison.

Now that she was away from the hospital and back in her normal environment, the smothering sensation in her chest had eased. But she still questioned her decision. Was she over reacting to this situation?

Had losing her sister so suddenly caused her to act impulsively, as Ziggy always did?

She sighed. She could run a major advertising campaign with one hand tied behind her back. But when it came to premature babies, she wasn't sure she could do the right thing, and that worried her. She had always been the one in charge, the older sister Ziggy turned to for help, until this latest incident.

Now, three tiny lives depended on her making the right choices. Had she made the right decision about joint custody? Coming to the office was her way of trying to clear her head. She needed to get back in touch with reality. But questions still pounded in her head.

Since the day of her sister's accident, she lived one minute at a time. Every second centered on checking on the triplets and talking over their condition with Daniel. This sudden dependence on another person wasn't the Cydney Eller she thought she was.

Coming to the office was supposed to get her back on the right track. But…she couldn't focus on work, on clients' needs. Maybe…it was too soon. Maybe she wasn't over the shock of losing Ziggy.

Learning of her sister's death had hit hard. Discovering Ziggy's pregnancy had been a her personal nightmare. That the triplets survived the accident seemed like a miracle, and her emotions were still on a roller coaster.

Everything had changed.

In one day, she had gone from planning million dollar ad campaigns, to needing to rely on medical professionals for every decision. These strangers knew more about premature infants than she did, but she felt responsible. So she second guessed every move she made.

Where was the confident woman she had been a few days ago before the accident? Maybe she wasn't the woman she had thought she was after all, and that possibility unnerved her more than all the rest of the questions pinging around in her head.

She had worked to achieve a goal, but for what end? All she could think about now was the three tiny infants in the NICU. Triplets who needed her and she wasn't prepared. She couldn't control the situation or her reactions to Daniel Prince.

Tamera sidled up to the desk. "I uh, I don't suppose you know what you're going to do?"

"About what?" Cydney jerked her attention back to the conversation.

"You know, work and your clients. Your job."

Tension pooled behind Cydney's eyes. This serious tone wasn't like Tamera. Usually, she was upbeat, cheerful. "Have you heard something I should know?"

"No! No!" Tamera flopped in chair and inspected the polish on her artificial nails. "Well, just the usual, you know, who's getting ahead..."

Color flooded the girl's pixie face.

"So," Cydney twisted a pen on her desk, "the office grapevine had me losing the promotion even if I'd been here?"

"They haven't said anything mean..."

Cydney waved a hand as Tamera stumbled for words. "Don't worry; I know how the office grapevine works." Thumbing through the files in front of her, she paused and glanced at her assistant. "But they're usually right, aren't they?"

Tamera looked ready to burst into tears. Something Cydney had never seen. "Not always!" Then in an obvious effort to cheer up, Tamera jumped out of her chair as she said, "I saw the senior partner leave your office a few minutes ago. Did he mention the promotion?"

"Afraid not." Cydney grinned at her assistant's obvious disappointment. Her first real smile in days felt good. The act she put on with Daniel two nights ago in the hospital cafeteria didn't count.

Tamera plopped on a corner of the desk. "It should be you. Your last ad campaign made all the big magazines." Twirling a strand of hair, and peering through narrow dark glasses that made her eyes look like laser beams, she asked. "Have you had time to work on the new account?"

Tamera's energy made Cydney feel old. Even the bright sunny day and clear sky hadn't eased her mood. Doubt filled her head. Had she done the right thing? Could she take care of three infants? Did this sinking disappointment weighing down her chest mean she regretted missing the chance of earning the promotion?

Cydney sighed. Coming here today had been what she needed, but she was going to disappoint her assistant with her decision. Might as well get it over with, "Tamera, I put in a request to work from home."

"Oh!" Tamera's eyes opened wide. Curls bobbed around her head. "I thought you might take a maturity leave, but I didn't expect this."

"Maybe one of the other contenders for the promotion will ask you to be their assistant."

"It isn't the job." Tamera slipped off the desk. "I'll miss you."

Cydney held up the folders, "Mr. Clark wants me to keep the new client, so I'll see you once in a while."

"This isn't about me." Tamera waltzed toward the door. "I was thinking about you. I know how much you like your work." Turning before she left the room, Tamera said with a wisdom older than her years. "You'll be fine, Cydney. Don't worry."

Would she be fine? Tamera was right about one thing. Cydney felt responsible for this whole situation. *Not the accident.*

She had finally accepted the fact that she couldn't keep her twenty-five year old sister under her thumb. But, maybe Ziggy had been searching for something missing in her life when she got pregnant. Had Ziggy been looking for love? Had becoming involved in a relationship been an expression of need?

Cydney released a sigh. Would she end up the same way, alone and unloved, if she continued to try to shut people out of her life?

❦

Those questions haunted Cydney as she returned to the NICU for the next visiting hour. She had gotten very little work done because she constantly checked her cell phone to make sure she hadn't missed a phone call from the hospital concerning the triplets.

After Tamera left her office, she mulled over her reactions to the morning's events. Taking a leave from her position meant giving up future chances at promotion. She wasn't sure how she felt about that. But her quick trip to the office left her feeling lost because she wasn't connected to the triplets.

Once she was back in the hospital waiting room, the sense of urgency eased. Breathing the medicinal odors filling the air soothed her tension as she rushed to the viewing window. It was twenty minutes before the last visit of the day, but she wouldn't feel safe until she checked on the triplets. What was this protective feeling? Why did she feel as if she couldn't breathe if she was out of sight of the babies?

Then it came to her.

She should have expected it. With each passing day, each touch of the tiny hands, and check of all the tubes running from the little bodies, she felt a connection to the triplets. She had fallen in love with the newborns…and in that instant she realized she had told Daniel the truth.

She would do anything to keep the babies safe.

Even making room in her life for Daniel Prince.

❧

Daniel's steps slowed as he reached the NICU waiting room and saw the woman sitting there. Wearing black slacks and a sky blue sweater, Cydney was slouched in the corner of one of the uncomfortable burgundy chairs, fast asleep. Her head rolled to one shoulder, making her look younger than twenty-nine.

His breath hitched. He didn't want the rush of emotion filling his chest, but she looked so vulnerable something inside him responded, and he felt the urge to cradle her head against his shoulder and keep her safe.

His feet seemed to cling to the carpet as he took measured steps towards her. His jaw ached from clenching his teeth to hold back any sign of warmth from his expression. Finally, when he had a grip on his emotions, he nudged her shoulder.

She straightened with a jerk, and stared at him with eyes as wide as saucers. "The babies?"

"They're fine." Daniel backed away from the temptation of her sleepy gaze, and didn't bother to explain he'd rescheduled his late appointments so he could be here for visiting time. "I managed to get away from the office early."

Cydney stared from his face to the big clock on the wall. Finally, her shoulders eased back against the chair, and ran her fingers through tousled dark hair. "I must have dozed off."

Not liking the surge of tenderness making him want to comfort her fears, Daniel looked away. Since their first meeting, he had learned she didn't react well any offer of comfort. "What time did you see the triplets?"

"Two o'clock." Cydney looked at the clock on the wall, again.

It was three o'clock, so she had only been back in the waiting room for a few minutes. She must be tired to fall asleep so quickly. He shouldn't have awakened her. "How are they?"

Cydney's chest heaved, drawing his attention to the curve of her breasts covered by the soft blue sweater, but he forced his gaze to her face. He didn't need a reminder that she was a desirable woman.

Her lips tilted as she leaned toward him. "They're improving. I held Big…um, Zachary, again. His fever is down a little. He seems so big compared to Cece." Her smile faded as she glanced around the waiting room. "We're so lucky, Daniel. One of the families left today."

Daniel watched emotion cloud her eyes, noted her lowered voice, and grasped her meaning. In the days since the accident, they had followed the routine in the waiting area outside NICU. So he knew Cydney didn't mean one of the patients had been discharged to go home.

She was telling him that one of the families had lost the battle with life and death. This was the hard part. The waiting and wondering if there was more you could do for the tiny infants in the NICU.

Greg should have been here.

This situation would have taught Greg to curb his impulsive streak. Missing his brother more than ever, Daniel forced air past the pain constricting his chest. If he had lived, Greg would be here beside them, but even in this serious situation, he would have found a way to make them laugh.

He missed Greg's enthusiasm and the sharing that defined his life. Expelling a breath, Daniel realized he wanted that sharing back in his life. He needed to share and have someone to protect so he would feel complete, again. He turned to Cydney. "Did you have anything to eat?"

"I grabbed a sandwich." She stared at her fingers as she smoothed the crease of her slacks.

Daniel followed the path of her slender fingers, but his thoughts focused on her long slenderness legs. Needing a distraction, he glanced at the schedule. "You can't get back in to see the babies until seven."

"I know, I guess that's why I dozed off."

"And you said they're okay?"

Cydney smiled. "This is their best day, so far. The boys are breathing on their own, and Cece might be by morning."

"I thought they were off oxygen this morning?" Daniel fought back a surge of alarm.

"Cece was restless so the nurses put her back on oxygen. They're going to try taking her off again, tomorrow."

Daniel's shoulders slumped in reaction to the news. The infants wouldn't be listed as stable until they could eat, maintain their body temperature, and breathe on their own. "This calls for a celebration. Let's go out for some real food."

Cydney frowned as she leaned back in the corner of the chair. Her body language said she would leave this waiting room, only in an emergency. "I—no, I don't think that's such a good idea."

"What aren't you telling me? You said they were improving."

"Yes-s, they are. But they aren't out of the woods yet."

Daniel studied her flushed face. From two chairs over, he could almost feel heat from her rosy cheeks. What was she up to now? "Dr. Morgan said things could happen fast after they started breathing on their own."

Cydney sent him a frowning glance, then looked around the room. "I know."

He could almost read her mind. She was thinking about the

family that left.

"I didn't mean bad news." Daniel frowned. She had deliberately misunderstood him. But why? What was she hiding? She wasn't happy to see him…and it was more than just because he had startled her awake.

Well, he had news for Cydney Eller. This was his niece and nephews she was drooling over, and she better not forget it. "If they continue to improve at this rate, they'll be home before you know it." Daniel waited for his words to sink in. "Are you prepared for triplets to go home with you?"

⁂

"I forgot about this class." Daniel led the way to one of the hospital's smaller meeting rooms on the maternity floor. Hand on her arm, he urged her toward chairs arranged in a semicircle around a table.

"I wish we could skip this." Back straight, Cydney pulled her arms close to her body, not touching him.

"Think of this as one more trick in the arsenal of knowledge you need to be a parent." He settled in the folding chair beside her.

His leg touched hers. His scent filled her every breath. Cydney leaned close to his shoulder and whispered. "That's the problem. What if I don't know enough to be a parent?"

His laugh turned heads in their direction. "Don't worry. Babies come with their own *How-To* manual." He shrugged. "Mothers tell me instinct kicks in after the babies are born."

Staring at him as if he were from another planet, Cydney fought the urge to give him a sharp kick in the shin. Had he used those words on purpose? Had it not occurred to him that she lacked the maternal instinct because her body hadn't been exposed to nine months of pregnancy hormones? Or was he trying to put her in her place. Trying to make her admit she needed him.

"Daniel," a soft feminine voice cooed from his opposite shoulder. "It's a surprise seeing you here. You should be teaching the class, instead of me."

Cydney gazed at the beautiful, thirty something blonde staring at Daniel and groaned. *Great.* Could things get any worse? Now the whole hospital would hear about Daniel taking parenting classes with a strange woman.

"Not true, Lois. This is your territory. I'm just observing. This is my…Cydney Eller, meet Lois Clark."

"You have a child?" Lois stared from Cydney to Daniel and Cydney was certain she saw green lights flash in the woman's eyes. "I didn't know."

Why should this woman know about Daniel's private life? Warmth flamed in Cydney's face as she considered the possibilities. Had Daniel dated this woman? Then a more personal angle flared in her head. This instructor thought she'd given birth to Daniel's child.

Oh, help!

Images flashed in her head. Intimate scenes of Daniel with his chest bare leaning over her naked body as they lay on stark white sheets. Her panicked glance darted to Daniel.

Where had that thought come from? She needed air.

But taking a deep breath didn't help because she inhaled scents a lover would know intimately. The clean smell of his aftershave and soap made her head spin.

Daniel leaned over and asked in a low voice. "What's wrong?"

Cydney peeped at him through her lashes, "Trying to stop a sneeze."

Daniel's arm draped around the back of her chair, "You're sure?"

He clasped her bare arm. His touch sent the images replaying in her head. Need twisted her insides. How had this happened? How had her awareness of him reached this level? Searching for an explanation, her gaze swept the room. The instructor was still staring at them and Cydney forced words past her lips. "W-we're not…we're just guardians."

"Oh. I see." Lois Clark turned to answer another parent's question.

"Clearly, she doesn't," Cydney whispered for Daniel's ears only. "Why didn't you explain?"

"Why should I? My life doesn't have to be an open book just because I'm on the staff here."

Ouch! Touched a nerve, had she?

"She seems interested in you. Don't you want her to know you're unattached?" Her lips twitched and she felt the sudden urge to snicker.

"Am I unattached?" Daniel leaned toward her, his brown eyes melted over her face warm as hot fudge. "We have triplets to take care of, you know."

"But, she'll think—"

"There you go, again. Acting as if you're ashamed to be with me," Daniel sighed on the words and leaned close. "What have I done to offend you, Ms. Eller?"

"Class, let's get started." Lois Clark's glance glittered with speculation as she turned to Daniel and arched her brows high. "Introductions first, I think. Daniel, why don't you start?"

"I'm Daniel. This is Cydney." Daniel's tone made it obvious he wasn't sharing any other comments.

"Fine. Next," Lois snapped, unable to hide her frustration at being cheated of details.

"Ted and Alice."

"Ed and Jane."

"Tim and Candace." Daniel jerked his head in a quick nod to the couple.

"John and Suzie."

"Brent and Sally."

Cydney lost track of the introductions as she stared at the man beside her. Daniel was an odd combination of caring and aloofness. She expected a doctor to be caring, but his detached interaction with his colleague was puzzling. He had given the instructor a cool reception, but he exchanged warm smiles with a couple he obviously recognized. What would he be like in his personal life? Aloof? Or fun loving as he described his brother?

But she wasn't anything like her sister.

Far from it, actually. She and Ziggy shared parents, but that was all they had in common. Was that how it had been for

Daniel and his brother? Or had he and Greg shared stronger ties?

From what she had learned about Daniel in the past few days, he was capable of deep emotion. Was that why he had rebuffed the instructor? Had he been involved with Lois Clark? Cydney clenched her fist so tight her knuckle popped, bringing her back to alert.

A large warm hand covered hers. Daniel's whisper tickled her ear. "Relax. This isn't so bad. Pretend you like me and everything will be fine."

Cydney turned her head and stared at him. Could he read her mind? Liking him was part of the problem. She liked Daniel, but she couldn't allow those feeling if she wanted to maintain control of her life. Acting on emotions had been her mother's downfall.

Daniel's warm gaze held hers, turning her insides to mush. His lips spread in a smile that turned his solemn, doctor expression to a seductive look worthy of a candidate in the hunk-of-the month club.

Feeling as if the eyes of every female in the room focused on them, Cydney pursed her lips in an imitation of her third grade teacher's stern expression, and turned her eyes on the instructor.

Lois Clark was sending Daniel admiring glances, same as every other female in the room, making Cydney want to stomp her foot. It was bad enough that she had to work with Daniel. Did he have to turn on the charm when she was trying so hard to keep her distance?

CHAPTER 6

"Do you remember the rules for infant CPR? Two breaths. Thirty compressions?"

"Yes." Cydney forced the word through clenched teeth.

In the last twenty-four hours, she had relived every moment of that CPR class repeatedly. Including the parts with the beautiful instructor hanging on Daniel's every move. She'd been especially attentive when Daniel took his turn practicing on the infant doll the instructor used to illustrate the CPR technique.

Tonight, they were in another class, thanks to the insistence of the nurse in NICU. Cydney didn't dare skip the class and bring Dr. Morgan's wrath down on her head. She liked the NICU doctor and wanted to prove she could care for the triplets.

Releasing a pent up sigh, she tried to remain calm, but she kept remembering things about the class last night. Images danced through her head all night long. Little things like the warmth of Daniel's hand on hers as he guided her through the steps of infant CPR.

She couldn't forget how cute he looked with his hair sticking out in spikes after he and the other men moved the extra tables needed for the practice session. Or his encouragement when she wanted to take one last minute with the triplets, even with the unit nurse calling the end of the last visiting hour of the evening.

Then the nurse informed them, "Parenting classes for new parents start tomorrow night. Three sessions in lecture room three. Be there at seven."

Cydney had rolled her eyes. *Not again?*

Not another night spent huddled in a folding chair trying not to notice how close Daniel was, or how wide his shoulders were. And pretending she wasn't aware that the other women in the room were aware of Daniel, as well. These classes were for new parents, for crying out-loud. Did these women have an overdose of hormones or something?

She remembered one of the thick books she'd read on pregnancy while she sat in the waiting room between visiting hours. Reactions of these women were excusable. Their bodies were overrun with hormones, but she didn't have that excuse. And it didn't explain why the instructor paid more attention to Daniel's technique than to any other new father in the class. Or why any of this grated on Cydney's nerves.

Plopping down on the folding chair, she released a gusty sign. The seat was cold. The metal bottom was hard. Then Daniel sat down next to her. Their elbows brushed. Her face warmed. His leg touched her thigh, making her heart race. His arm settled on the back of her chair, enfolding her in a cocoon of safety...and she stopped breathing.

Any other woman might settle back and enjoy the closeness and warmth radiating off her partner's body. Most women would love the scent of his aftershave instead of the constant hospital odors in the air. But the closeness of their situation scared her to death.

Daniel wasn't her partner and being this close to him was driving her mad. How could she take care of the triplets when Daniel's presence threatened all she had fought to prove? If she took the triplets home with her, would he visit? Would he demand equal time with them? How could she keep her distance from Daniel and work with him to take care of the babies?

"Is this your partner, Dr. Prince?"

Cydney looked up to see a stunning redhead put a hand on Daniel's shoulder as she smiled down at him. *Daniel must be high on the list of eligible males at the hospital.* Angling her chin high, Cydney answered before Daniel could open his mouth. "Hello, I'm Cydney Eller. We're sharing guardianship."

"Oh, I see." The redhead fluttered her lashes. "Well, Daniel, I hope you won't be bored with my class."

"Cydney, Sharon Vance is head nurse in pediatrics." Daniel explained.

"I'm looking forward to your instruction," Cydney managed, but even as the words left her mouth, she wanted to take them back. Had she lost her mind? How could she learn in one class what pregnant women learned during nine months of pregnancy?

The nurse nodded her head and turned to speak to the rest of the parents gathered in the room. "Okay, class, let's get started. Most of you met in the CPR class last night, so we will skip introductions. This is a three-part class. The title of tonight's session is Romance and The Newborn."

Groans and claps followed Sharon Vance's introduction of the class. Cydney understood why the new mothers groaned. Who could feel romantic when they were worried sick about their new infant? But a glance at Daniel's face, to see his reaction to the topic, made her rethink her opinion.

If…and that was a monster-size IF…if Daniel were the father of her child, wouldn't she love him even more after giving birth to the baby they created together? Would the infant grow tall like his dad? And have curls and chocolate brown eyes like Daniel?

Feeling guilt wash over her from her wayward imaginings, Cydney forced her attention to what the instructor was saying. Thinking about Daniel in personal terms put her at risk.

Daniel nudged her with his elbow, sending and electrical shock through her body when he whispered. "Are you going to sleep? That's not very romantic. Sharon says we need to spend quality time together. Just the two of us. I think she's right." His eyes crinkled at the corners, his laughter daring her to object to the instructor's comments.

Her breath hitching in her chest, Cydney considered his words. Spending quality time with Daniel would be so easy, but how would she survive? "What about three squalling babies? How does that fit in with romance?"

"I could hold the baby while you get dressed...or undressed." Daniel winked.

Broadsided by his teasing, she snapped. "And if the baby's diaper leaks all over you? Or one of the other babies starts crying?"

Daniel's face crumpled in pretended disappointment. "There you go, sucking all the romance out of our evening together."

"Daniel, may I repeat that comment?" Sharon paused by his side and turned to the class. "Dr. Prince just made a comment that many new fathers will agree with. Women often find it difficult to shed the responsibility of being a new mother long enough to have a romantic interlude with their husband. You must guard against this mistake. The love you shared in making this infant needs constant attention, just as the baby does."

Daniel's arm tightened around Cydney's shoulders and leaned so close their cheeks touched as he whispered in her ear. "See, I was right. You need to show that you love me, too."

Lips twitching, Cydney rolled her eyes and jabbed him in the side with her elbow. He was joking, but her insides churned with emotion. Her cheeks were hot. Her heart thumped against her ribs. She considered her *fight or flight* options. How could she deal with this side of Daniel? The teasing light flickering in his eyes and his grin begged for her response. The more time she spent with him, the harder it was to remember she was in this alone.

Daniel's humor and charm wouldn't change things. The triplets came first. Acknowledging that fact in her head was easy, but forcing her heart to cooperate was a different matter. By the time the class ended, she was on the verge of melting in a puddle at Daniel's feet.

"Let's go to dinner."

Her heart raced as his breath tickled her cheek. Or was it a reaction to his suggestion? Did he have any idea how her body reacted to him? Or was he playing a game? Was he trying to gain her co-operation, trying to win her over, so he could get custody of the triplets?

Her father had used charm to get his way. Why wouldn't Daniel? Not that she blamed Daniel for trying. It wasn't his fault women fell over themselves when he turned those dark eyes on them and smiled. It was up to her to resist his charm and make logical decisions. She had responsibilities and she had choices, thanks to her career.

Hearts told lies, heads didn't.

Trying to decide on a response, she checked her watch. But her show of bravery was only half the battle. *Did he suspect her mind was filled with images of him in her bed?* When she tried to speak, she struggled to keep her voice from quivering.

"Sorry, I can't. It's time for late visiting hours." She turned on her heel and took off for the elevator.

Daniel trailed behind and watched as Cydney rushed to the baby girl's incubator. He watched as she inspected the baby and felt a tightening in his chest. He couldn't imagine his mother or Cydney's sister acting any more protective.

"Look, she's not as yellow tonight. And there's less tape on her body." Cydney whirled to meet his gaze. "Some of the IVs are gone. That must mean she's better."

"Let's hope so." He heard the excitement in her voice and cast a professional eye over the infant. From all he could see, the smallest triplet seemed to be improving and some of his tension eased.

Cydney checked each baby boy in turn. She held their little hands and mumbled words and sounds of encouragement.

Daniel hung back, listening to the tone of her voice. She

couldn't be more caring if she had given birth to these infants. Reluctantly his admiration grew, because he knew she could fight him for custody of these tiny members of his family.

Cydney was one of those rare individuals who cared about other people. Yet she kept guard of her deepest emotions. It wasn't easy to tell what she was thinking, but instinct told him her heart was in the right place. Watching her with the triplets the past few days, made he want to learn more about her. But Cydney locked her feeling away. Even with all the time they had spent in NICU together, he knew little about her that didn't concern the triplets.

Memory of Phil's investigative report flashed through his head.

He winced as he followed Cydney to the next infant. As she leaned over the incubator to greet Gregory, he looked at the smallest infant boy, and searched for any resemblance to his brother.

Was that a dimple in the baby's chin? Were the baby's eyes shaped like Greg's? They were still a deep dark blue, too soon to tell if they would turn brown like his brother's or remain blue like the mother's? Facing the truth, Daniel expelled a breath.

He wanted these infants to be Greg's children.

He wanted a connection to the brother he'd lost. That admission filled him with guilt because he wasn't just thinking of the triplets. It was time he admitted the truth to himself even if it wasn't the best motive for his actions. He wanted Greg to be the father because he wanted a reason to connect with Cydney.

She ignored attempts to get her attention. Teasing her and offers to help just earned him one of her strained smiles and calm acceptance. He wanted more. With each passing day, his increasing interest in connecting with Cydney on a personal basis brought questions he had to face.

Was he reaching out to Cydney because they shared a responsibility for the triplets, or was his interest personal? Did he want to assume the care of the triplets, whether they were his blood relations or not?

Cydney brushed a hand along Zackary's legs and arms. The

largest triplet wiggled under her touch. Daniel watched as a smile brightened her face. If the baby's jaundice continued to clear up, he suspected the largest triplet might be released from the hospital soon.

What would he do then? He was on call twenty-four-seven, how could he take care of an infant? Yet, how could he allow a stranger to assume care of Greg's children? What did he really know about Cydney Eller? How could he keep these children safe and deal with Cydney until they heard from the DNA tests?

He had considered making an attempt to convince the judge that Cydney wasn't related to the infants, but instinct told him the triplets were her sister's children. How could he overcome that obstacle and gain custody? He had formed a bond with the triplets. That had never happened in any other delivery in his career. Yet, he couldn't claim them as his own.

"Someone is putting on weight." He nodded toward Zackary's little legs.

Cydney beamed at him over top of the incubator. "He is growing, isn't he? His stomach looks normal. Is the swelling gone?" She glanced back at the baby girl. "They all look healthier tonight, don't you think?"

Brows arched, Daniel studied the infants. "I think it time we made some plans."

"What plans?"

"We need to talk about taking the babies home." Daniel glanced around. "I think it might happen soon. I doubt they will be discharged at the same time, but the boys are definitely on track from the looks of things."

"Really," Cydney breathed, then her wide gaze returned to the infants.

Daniel's chest tightened at the note of amazement in her voice. With that one breathy word, she made him want to perform magic. He couldn't walk away and leave her to handle the burden of three infants alone, even if he wanted to.

Whether DNA proved he was related to the infants, or not, he owed Cydney Eller his support. His brother had been driving the vehicle when the triplets' mother was killed. He had a responsibility to the infants and to Cydney.

"Really," he confirmed, his emotions bouncing all over the place.

"I can't wait."

"Things will be harder to deal with when they're separated."

"You mean—"

"Think about it. Will you bring a newborn to a hospital every day when you visit and expose him to germs? Who will keep him if you don't bring him along? How will you visit if two babies go home and one stays?"

"I hadn't thought that far." Cydney stared at the infants.

"Cece isn't close to being discharged." Daniel held up a hand when Cydney gave a startled gasp. He saw the terror in her eyes and wished he could take the words back. "I'm not saying it won't happen. She seems fine. She appears to be making good progress. But she weighed less than her brothers at birth. She needs time to gain weight."

"And she had the heart monitor the whole time." Cydney's eyes filled with tears as she stared down at the infant. "Daniel, what if they have to keep her?"

"Don't do this." He took her shoulders in his hands and gave her a little shake. "Don't fall apart now. You cannot show distress while you are in this unit. Look around you. Look at all the infants who aren't as well as Cece."

"I'm sorry. I wasn't thinking." Cydney tilted her chin and sniffed.

"No harm done. Say good night. Visiting time is over, and I'm taking you to dinner. We need to talk."

❧

"Cydney, I want to be part of their lives." Daniel gave her a pointed stare and picked up the menu.

"You don't even know if you're related. The DNA results aren't back yet." Cydney hoped the noise in the restaurant would cover her weak objection. Hiding her head behind the menu, she struggled to regain her composure. Being around Daniel turned her senses up side down.

So far, she had managed to convince herself that her concern was all for the triplets, but fate was playing tricks on her. Daniel's brother may have been responsible for her sister's death. Yet every nerve in her body seemed to short circuit when they were together. If she allowed her reaction to him to turn personal, it would seem like a betrayal of her own sister. She needed to keep their involvement focused on the triplets...and only the triplets.

And she liked his involvement. Liked it a lot. She liked watching his medically trained gaze scan over the babies. Liked her sense of relief when he seemed satisfied with the infants' progress. She liked having Daniel in the babies' lives. Liked the way his dark eyes softened when he touched a tiny hand. Liked the sense of being safe when he was near.

But she shouldn't like his presence as much as she did, because that meant allowing him in her life, as well. And getting close to Daniel would risk her peace of mind, if it hadn't already.

Daniel's insistence on being involved in the triplets' care reassured her. He wouldn't make the effort if he didn't care about them. But a little voice in her head warned that his interest had nothing to do with her. Just because he wanted to be part of the babies' lives didn't mean he cared about her.

All the emotional turmoil of her parents' divorce came rushing back and filled her heart with remembered pain. She tried to be the perfect child and take care of her baby sister, but it hadn't kept her family together. *What if she failed this time as well? What if she couldn't manage three newborns on her own?*

As an adult, she realized she hadn't been at fault with her parents' failed relationship, but she couldn't shake the feeling she had failed Ziggy.

Would she fail the triplets, too?

"I have a responsibility to those babies whether they or related to me or not. My brother was driving the car. His actions left them without parents." Daniel muttered behind the menu.

The rough sound of his voice put Cydney on alert. Her back stiffened. The truth of his words and his tone, warned her of his inner turmoil. *Responsibility motivated Daniel's actions.* She needed to remember that.

She swallowed a gasp and tried to keep the menu from shaking. But her hands trembled as the truth exposed her growing hopes. She'd imagined caring and love behind his need to provide for infants, but reality forced her to accept facts. His actions hadn't come from an emotional involvement. A guilty conscience motivated him to insist on taking charge of the triplets.

Great, just great. She'd let her guard down and reacted to a man just as her mother always had. Well, so much for her silly daydreams. "I don't hold your brother's actions against you."

"I know. But I do."

There it was. All the proof she needed. He had said the words as clear as day. He felt responsible. "Was he a good driver?"

"Greg drove too fast, but this was his first accident. It only takes one. I told him to slow down."

Cydney recalled the times she cautioned Ziggy about her driving. She understood Daniel's frustration better than he knew. Regardless of how this accident happened, they were both suffering. Seeing the dark emotions in his eyes, she swallowed a lump of regret and fought to hold her voice steady.

"Ziggy was involved in fender benders every few months. She expected other drivers to get out of *her* way, now matter what." Cydney blinked rapidly as the image of her sister's face filled her head.

"You said she loved parties and people. What she was like as a person?"

"Too trusting," Cydney almost choked on the words. "Tender hearted and caring." Her lips trembled as she attempted a smile. "She would have been a great kindergarten teacher, but she wouldn't make the effort to get a degree."

The server appeared at Daniel's side to take their order.

She hadn't wanted to leave NICU, but Daniel over-ruled her objections and insisted they go out for a real meal. So they compromised and ended up at a steakhouse two blocks from the hospital. She could run back to the NICU if she needed too.

"We'll have two specials, cooked medium, salads with house dressing, and iced tea." Daniel made fast work of the order.

Cydney glared at him as the server walked away. "Are you always this bossy? I told you I wasn't hungry."

Daniel settled back in his chair. "You need to keep your energy up. Taking care of three infants is a big job."

His tone was calm. There was no criticism of her efforts to this point. She appreciated that, even if he had ignored her insistence they eat in the hospital. "I don't expect it to be easy, but I'll find a way to cope."

"I know," Daniel nodded thanks as the server returned with glasses of iced tea and deftly changed the subject. "Were you and your sister alike?"

"Not in the least. Ziggy lived in a dream. I deal with reality. She expected life to turn out the way she wanted. I work for what I want. We shared the same parents. That's about the only thing we had in common." Cydney sighed. "But I loved her, dearly."

Daniel's mouth twisted in a half-grin. "Greg and I were like that. Our father concentrated on his political career, so mother turned her attention to spoiling Greg. I was old enough to escape the coddling."

"You don't think boys need love and attention?"

"Of course, but they need a dose of reality in their lives, too."

Bristling at the unfeeling sound of his words, Cydney snapped. "Don't you dare try to deny the twins of all the cuddling I can give?"

"Are you going to spend every waking moment trying to protect the triplets?" Brow arched, his glare locked with hers.

"I'm not going to prevent them from being exposed to the world around them, if that's what you're implying."

Daniel toyed with his fork as he studied her. "My mother ruined Greg with her constant mothering."

Heat filled Cydney's face. The neglect she and Ziggy had

faced flashed through her head, causing a sharp tone to her voice. "There is no such thing as too much mothering for small infants."

Daniel's brow arched. "You sound very certain for someone who just a few days ago, said she didn't want kids of her own."

Glaring at him, she gulped half the glass of tea to cool her emotions. Suddenly, in the dim light of the upscale restaurant, she found him less charming. But one point was clear. When Daniel wanted something, he didn't pull punches. But this time, she had too much at stake to let him win.

"I didn't plan to have kids of my own, but I won't turn my back on my sister's babies." Clearing the lump from her throat, Cydney added. "And I've been around you enough to know you won't either, so I suggest we call a truce."

Emotions chased across his face like words on a ticker tape. This strong man hid his feelings. He said the right words and took care of others, but who took care of him?

The urge to break through Daniel's protective shell hit hard. Her breath shuddering, Cydney faced reality. She needed to concentrate on her own problems and forget his. But discovering the man inside his protective armor tempted the part of her that wanted more than she ever had in her life. *She wanted love, respect...*

"You're right," Daniel lifted a shoulder, "I want the best for the triplets."

And I'll do whatever it takes to make sure they have it.

He didn't actually say the words, but his dark eyes bored into hers with an intensity that sent pain searing through her chest. His level stare and the angle of his squared chin said more than words.

Daniel Prince would protect the triplets with his life.

Cydney felt a wave of longing so powerful it threatened to drown her. What would it be like to be loved by this man? If he cared...really cared, there wouldn't be any worries, or quick looks behind her to check for safety. *You would know you were safe. Authority radiated off Daniel like rays off the sun.* "What kind of father would your brother have been?"

"Indulgent." Daniel stared in his glass of tea. "He would have spoiled his kids rotten, and ignored them when he was bored. But he'd be back for fun and games before the kids noticed his absence."

"Ummm, sounds like he would have enjoyed having triplets."

"Greg loved kids. He was still a kid himself. It's too bad he won't be around to play with his children. He would have had a ball with them."

"Ziggy would dress them up like dolls."

"Greg would be fine with that. How would she be on discipline?" Daniel arched a brow.

Glad they were keeping the conversation away from personal issues, Cydney shrugged. His mellow mood did strange things to her heart rate. "I can't imagine Ziggy enforcing rules. She would turn a blind eye to any misbehavior, or try to guilt them into behaving."

Hearing her sad tone, she sighed. Talking about their siblings in the past tense seemed strange. And so wrong. It had been less than two weeks since Ziggy died. How could things get so mixed up?

One minute, she was asking her assistant to watch for Ziggy at the nightclubs, and the next instant, Dr. Prince was telling her Ziggy had been DOA. She still hadn't adjusted to the shock. Still couldn't believe the accident happened.

But one thing she had learned since they entered this restaurant. Daniel Prince was the same person every time they met. He was aloof and in control. Whether she saw him in surgical scrubs or wearing a casual shirt and pants, Daniel was always in protective mode. He was honest, down to earth, and responsible. *And she trusted him.*

"I think the triplets are lucky." Daniel peered at her in the dim light.

Cydney almost choked on a swallow of iced tea. "Lucky? They are improving, but their parents are dead. How can you say they're lucky?"

"They have you to step in and take care of them."

Cydney stared at him across the table. "Do you mean that? You're not just saying the words to get me to agree for you to take custody?"

"Why would you think that? I made it clear from the first day. I want custody of Greg's triplets."

The server put their plates in front of them, stopping any conversation. Cydney waited until the server refilled their glasses and walked away. "I expected—"

"Eat, then we'll talk."

"I just—"

"You haven't had a decent meal in days." Daniel motioned toward her plate. "I'll answer your questions after you clean your plate."

Cydney smothered a smile as she picked at her salad. He was a good man. Could she bend her long held beliefs enough to allow him to share infants' lives? On the other hand, did she have any right to refuse since the judge didn't believe she was their aunt?

The aroma of yeast rolls and steak tickled her appetite. The food smelled heavenly, but her brain insisted she check on the triplets. Mouth open, hands on the arms of the chair, she glanced across the table.

Daniel's brows arched high. He held her gaze for long seconds then dropped his eyes to her plate of untouched food. Lifting a questioning gaze to meet hers, he waited. After long seconds and a silent battle of wills, she eased back in her seat and picked up her fork.

Okay, she needed strength so she could take care of the babies, but did he always have to be right? Couldn't she make up her own mind without his interference?

Her stomach growled. Okay, she needed food. She tasted the steaming baked potato and flavor burst in her mouth. She swallowed. Her stomach revolted. *What if the triplets needed her?* Peeping through her lashes, she checked on Daniel.

He was watching her with the eagle-eyed stare of parent with a misbehaving child.

Well, she wasn't a child. That was Ziggy's role.
Had been her sister's role.

An overwhelming sense of loss rose up and almost choked her. How could she eat? How could she pretend life was normal? Her only sister had died. All she had left was three tiny babies needing her care. *And she wouldn't have them if she didn't take a stand against Daniel Prince.*

Responding to the rebellion going on in her head, she ignored Daniel's piercing gaze and focused on the food in front of her. One bite, chew, swallow, and then another. Finally, the steak on her plate was half finished. She felt better, but pride kept her from admitting it. "How many regular meals do you eat, Daniel?"

Lips quirking in a lopsided smile, Daniel opened his mouth, but his beeper went off before he could say a word.

Cydney's cell phone rang the next second.

Then Daniel's cell phone buzzed.

They exchanged startled looks of horror.

"The triplets." They said at the same time, bursting into action.

Daniel grabbed his phone and started talking. Cydney grabbed the check and rushed to the check out to pay. They rushed through the exit so fast, their legs almost tangled. Daniel reached for her arm, and steered her toward the car, while he continued talking on the phone.

🚑

"We had a Code Blue on Baby Girl." Dr. Morgan announced as they stood in front of her, gasping for breath. After their frantic ringing of the buzzer, Dr. Morgan stepped out the metal doors. "Sorry to interrupt your evening."

"What happened?" Cydney's voice quavered with the fear building inside her. All the way back to the hospital, she imagined the worst had happened. Even she, a total non-medical person, knew a Code Blue meant absence of vitals. But Daniel hadn't received any more information than she had.

"How is she now?" Daniel's calm tone skipped over Cydney's panic filled words and zeroed in on the pertinent de-

111

tails of the baby's condition.

Clenching her hand against the pounding in her chest, Cydney tried to copy his levelheaded manner. "Can we see her?"

"Just for a minute," Dr. Morgan motioned them through the metal doors, "to ease your mind. But don't excite her. She needs rest after her ordeal. We gave her some medication. I don't want her disturbed."

Baby Girl...*No! Daniel was right about that, too. The babies needed an identity. Needed to be treated like real people.*

Cydney eyes filled with moisture. Her gaze clung to the infant. Cece was lying on her back. One tiny hand curled in a fist at her cheek. New patches of tape covered her chest. Needles were sticking in her tiny feet and in her head.

Cydney swiped tears off her cheeks and tried to keep her voice calm. "What happened? I thought she was getting better."

"She's had breathing difficulties all along, but we noticed improvement. Tonight, for some unexplained reason, her heart stopped."

Cydney gasped as the words registered in her brain. Her knees wobbled. Daniel put his arm around her shoulders. "How long did the incident last?"

"Not long," Dr. Morgan checked the baby's chart. "But we are concerned it could happen again, or last longer. That's the danger we're facing now." She searched their faces, then turned back to study the infant. "We can do surgery, but most pre-term infants grow out of this whether it's Apnea or RDS. Notice she's hooked up to another monitor. We labeled her with Apnea."

"Will it happen again?" Cydney couldn't hold back the words. These medical professionals knew the answer, but she didn't have a clue. If she understood the risk the baby faced, maybe, she could deal with the situation.

"It can happen again at any time with this condition. If the pattern is repeated, we need to revisit the surgery option." Dr. Morgan checked the gadgets connected to the baby. "Her blood levels are fine for now. You can stay ten more minutes. Touch her. Let her know you're here." With a slight nod, she walked away, and then turned back. "We should start kangaroo care, soon. That usually helps."

"What is she talking about?"

"Kangaroo care refers to cuddling preemies."

"Right, I forgot. Why did she say we need to start soon?" Cydney whispered as she held Cece's tiny hand. "Is she worried—"

"Don't even think such a thing." Daniel touched a tiny yellow tinted foot. "You can't do this to yourself. And don't forget, babies have built in radar. They sense tension. When you're in this room, you have to think positive. Dr. Morgan meant the triplets have improved enough to start the kangaroo care."

Cydney tore her gaze from Cece's tiny body and stared at him. But Daniel kept his eyes focused on the infant. She watched as he checked one monitor after another, and then reached for the baby's chart.

Her heart slowed to a painful thud in her chest as she sighed. Daniel was checking to make sure the baby was safe. He had the training and experience to deal with the infant's emergencies.

A new thought caused her heart to clench in pain. How could she keep him out of the infants' lives when he could protect them? Breath shuddering as new fears filled her head, she turned to check the infant boys so Daniel couldn't see her trembling hands.

Both boys were lying quietly in their incubators. Were they sleeping naturally? Or had they been given medication to make them sleep as Baby Girl had?

Cydney held one tiny hand and then the other, but soon turned back to Cece's incubator. Daniel stood beside the infant, staring down at her. Wishing she could read his mind, Cydney reached for the baby girl's hand. It was warm. A pulse throbbed visually in her tiny wrist. How long had her heart stopped? What if it stopped again? Would she survive? Could her delicate little body endure surgery?

"Daniel?" His name quivered past her dry lips.

"Let's get out of here. Our time is up." He checked the boys, then steered Cydney toward the door.

"Dr. Prince," Dr. Morgan stopped them at the exit. "Results of the DNA tests came back. Your brother is definitely the father of the triplets."

"I knew it." Daniel's worried expression eased into a wide smile.

"What about my results?" Cydney choked past the fear blocking her throat.

"Your test results weren't what we expected, Ms. Eller. I'm sorry, the test is inconclusive as to your relationship to the infants."

"Inconclusive?" Cydney repeated in a voice high and screechy as a robot. *What did that mean? Inconclusive?* She pointed a trembling finger toward the incubators holding the triplets. "Those are my sister's babies. Dr. Prince delivered them himself."

"Don't worry." Daniel put a reassuring hand on her arm and steered her out the metal doors, into the NICU waiting room. "We'll do another test."

Cydney pulled away from his touch and raced toward the viewing window. Why would he allow another test when he wanted custody of the triplets? She had learned since the accident, Daniel needed to protect those he loved. His need was as strong as her need for independence. This was his chance to take the triplets away from her. Would he use it?

"I don't understand." She whirled away from the closed curtain blocking any view of the infants and faced Daniel. "The test was wrong. I know those babies are Ziggy's. Why didn't the test show I'm related?"

Cydney was conscious of the increasing volume of her voice, but she couldn't stop the words spilling out in anguish. She felt Daniel's hand tighten on her arm and slumped against the glass. His touch was warm on her skin, but nothing stopped the fear escalating inside her. How could she lose this last fragile link to Ziggy? And lose the infants she loved at first sight?

What did she do now? Then a little voice shouted in her head. *Run! This is your chance. Let Daniel take over the worry, the fear, and the responsibility.* But she couldn't listen. *She could not fail Ziggy again.*

She had tried to be perfect to keep her parents together and failed. She tried to be a good role model for Ziggy and failed. She could not fail this time. Three strikes would mean she was a definite failure. She had worked too hard to avoid that label to allow it to happen now.

She could not stop trying. Her need to have choices wouldn't allow her to stop. The triplets needed her.

⚏

"Let's go for coffee." Daniel urged her toward the elevators and out of sight of staring eyes of other people in the waiting room.

"I'm not leaving." Eyes blazing, Cydney jerked to a stop and stared at him. Her chin tilted, daring him to try to put distance between her and the infant. "Baby Girl might need us."

"Her name is Cece," Daniel growled, but even before he looked into her bruised eyes, he regretted losing control of his emotions. They were both reacting to the shock of Cece's narrow escape, and Cydney was upset about results of the DNA test. He didn't blame her. If Greg hadn't been identified as the father, he would on edge. Forcing back his worries, he struggled for a level tone. "You can't stay in this waiting room every second."

Cydney whirled to face him. Eyes blazing, she stared at him as if he had grown two heads.

Daniel expelled a noisy breath and raked his fingers through his hair. "You need fresh air and something to calm your nerves. You've had two shocks in the past few minutes.

The emotions churning inside Cydney, showed on her face. Her voice trembled and tears streamed down her cheeks. "Those babies are my family, Daniel. You know they are. You delivered them yourself. They're Ziggy's babies."

Daniel pulled her in his arms and let her sob against his shoulder. Pitying glances from other families touched on them and bounced away.

"Let's go for a walk. Fresh air will do you good."

"I'm not leaving." Her voice muffled against his collar. She shuddered in reaction to the events of the last few minutes. "I can't." She pushed back from his chest and looked at him with tears in her eyes. "What am I going to do, Daniel? All this time, I was so sure the triplets were my family. I spent time with them and fell in love with them. What do I do now? Your test was the connection in question. Not mine."

"Take another DNA test, that's all you can do."

"All?" Her voice rose to a screech. "Getting test results from the lab will take time. What if one of the triplets has an emergency while I'm waiting for confirmation?"

"That's not likely. The babies are stable—"

"We thought Cece was okay when we left the hospital." Cydney glared at him. "Don't talk to me about stable. I've heard enough medical mumbo jumbo in the last two weeks to last me a lifetime."

Daniel steered her toward a sofa as far from the other parents as possible. "Sit here and try to calm down. I'll go get you something to drink."

"I am calm. I shouldn't have left the hospital," she clenched her fists as she stared in his eyes, "but I won't make that mistake again."

"You're overwrought." Daniel saw the fierce emotions burning in her eyes. Did she blame him? Had he been wrong to insist she needed a real meal? "If anything happens in that room, you couldn't get in to help. Try to take deep breaths and calm down."

Cydney dropped down on the sofa as the worry in his eyes registered. Forcing air in her lungs, she inhaled deeply and tried to calm her jitters. What was she thinking? She couldn't fall apart like this in front of Daniel. Not now, when she didn't have proof her connection to the triplets. Losing control of her emotions wouldn't help her case at all. Daniel would think she was unfit to take custody of the babies.

Custody?

After the judge learned the results of the DNA tests, there wouldn't be a battle for custody of the triplets. She couldn't claim the babies she knew in her heart belonged to Ziggy. Her breath shuddered in her chest. The heat of her cheeks dried her tears. She focused on her clenched fists, and tried to think of a new plan.

"Will you be all right on your own for a few minutes?" Daniel whispered the words against her cheek.

He was sitting beside her, offering his warmth and strength. Always the protector, his brown eyes studied her with warm compassion. The hand on her arm offered his support. Chewing her lip, she managed to nod, and suddenly realized what she had done.

"I'm sorry. I never fall apart like this, Daniel." Her eyes filled with a silent plea for him not take the triplets away from her.

"You had a shock. Sit here and rest. I'm going to the canteen for coffee. I won't be long." Daniel stood and paused in front of her.

Feeling the warmth of his stare, she gave a nod but avoided meeting his gaze. How much damage had she done to her chances of being the triplets' guardian? Would Daniel think she couldn't be trusted with the infants now that he'd seen her distress?

"Are you sure you're okay?"

Cydney moved her head. *Okay? How could she be okay?* Baby Girl had almost died. Had been Coded Blue, and the DNA test didn't show she was related to the triplets? How could she be okay?

She watched Daniel walk away. Head high, shoulders back, he looked ready to take on the world. She pitied anyone who got in his way. And that included her. He wanted custody of his brother's children and nothing would stop him.

When he was out of sight, she slumped against the back of the sofa like a deflated balloon. *Was this what Daniel had been waiting for, some sign of weakness on her part? Was he on the phone right now, calling his attorney to assert his rights as guardian of the triplets?*

Had her weak moment ruined her chances of having the triplets in her life? Daniel's DNA matched the triplets. No court in the land would dispute the fact that he was the babies' uncle. He could request custody, and she wouldn't have a hope. But he hadn't given any hints. What did Daniel want? What role did he intend to play with the triplets? Air shuddered from her lungs. Feeling numb, she stared vacantly around the waiting room. What happened now? Daniel said get another test. But time wasn't on her side.

Baby Girl might Code out again.

Big Brother's fever could escalate without warning and she would be helpless…voiceless. She pressed a fist to her lips to hold back a sob. Daniel hadn't seemed concerned. Did that mean he wanted her out of the infants' lives? She couldn't believe he did. He needed her. Taking care of the triplets would take two people. He had said so himself.

He needed her.

That was it. That was her trump card.

Daniel needed her help, just as she would need his assistance if she had custody. But it took every ounce of strength left in her body to admit that fact. The reality left her deflated, but relieved as well. All this time she denied needing Daniel's assistance, but reality forced her to admit the truth. If she took charge of the infants, she would need Daniel's help.

Just as Daniel would need her help. He was a medical professional, but she could get maternity leave from work to take care of the infants. She had found a secret weapon. Why hadn't she thought of that argument before?

DNA results forced her to face reality. She had assumed Daniel was showing compassion because he was a good person, but she should have questioned his motives for sticking so close to her. Why hadn't she?

"I wasn't sure if you wanted coffee or tea. I brought both." Daniel put a cardboard tray on the table in front of the sofa and sat down beside her. "Are you feeling better?"

She was feeling empowered, but that was a long way from

feeling better. "I'll have coffee, thanks."

Daniel passed her the cup, took the other coffee and leaned back against the sofa.

Cydney gripped the cup until her knuckles showed white. A nerve twitched in the corner of her eye. Her heart thumped against her ribs. Those babies were her family. Unwanted tears pooled in her eyes as she turned to him. "Daniel—"

"Don't talk. Drink your coffee. Give your body time to adjust to the shock."

She lifted the cup to her lips and sipped. She swallowed and lifted the cup again, like a puppet. The coffee was hot, the caffeine strong and effective. By the time she reached the bottom of the cup, she felt stronger, ready to face her enemy.

"You can't get rid of me, you know." Her words were clipped and raspy sounding.

"Why would I want to get rid of you?"

"Why indeed," She put her cup down on the tray and willed her hand steady as she answered his question with one of her own. "How serious was this incident with Baby Girl?"

"Cece."

"Okay," she huffed, "with Cece."

"On a scale of one to ten?"

Teeth sinking into her bottom lip, Cydney gave a nod.

"Anytime an infant stops breathing, it's serious. With this incident, I'd say a five."

"Why five?" Cydney gasped.

"I should rephrase that. Baby Girl's heart stopped from the Apnea. It's serious and more common than you think. Without monitors, Apnea can be fatal. But… I'm going on gut instinct here as much as medical training, but I don't think surgery is the answer at this point. Not with one incident and considering the other problems she has. Given time, I think she will grow out of the condition. Most infants do."

"What if this happens again?"

"Then she couldn't be in a better place. If she had an incident after she went home, she would need to be rushed to the hospital. She's already in NICU. I say let nature take its course and give her body time to mature."

"You called her Baby Girl." Cydney managed a wobbly smile, causing the tearstains on her cheeks to crack.

"Habit." Daniel offered a weak grin and settled back in the corner of the sofa. Lifting his feet to rest on the coffee table, he expelled a long breath. "You had me worried there for a few minutes."

"I worried you?"

"When you heard the test results, you turned all shades of white." He nodded toward the NICU. "Those incubators aren't large enough for an adult. Where would I put you if you fainted?"

Cydney lifted a brow. "I've never fainted in my life."

"Oh, really?" His eyes bored into hers as they recalled earlier incidents. She had almost passed out when he told her Ziggy had died, and again at the gravesite.

"You don't look so great yourself. Did we pay for dinner?" Cydney tried to recall their rush back to the hospital.

"I think so." Daniel rubbed his chin. "You paid the bill while I called the hospital."

"You drive like a maniac. Are you a former racecar driver or what?"

"Doctor's privilege," Daniel wagged his brows. "And don't you forget it."

"I'm not likely to ever forget that ride back to the hospital."

"We could have walked."

"Are you sure our feet would have touched ground?" Cydney shivered. "I was so scared. What if this happens again?"

"There's no assurance it won't, but Cece's on medication. There are monitors attached to her, and she's in NICU. Cece is as safe as we can make her."

"Maybe she should have the surgery—"

"Not until her condition gets worse than it is now."

Cydney reached out a tentative hand to touch his arm. "You're sure?"

Daniel covered her hand in a warm grip and tilted his head.

"I'd stake my career on it."

Air whooshed from Cydney's lungs. Her shoulders slumped against the sofa. Heat from his grip warmed her chilled skin. She had never been so frightened in her whole life. Not even when Ziggy...

"I need to do another DNA test."

"We'll check on that first thing in the morning."

"They're mine, you know. I love those babies."

"I know. We will resolve this, I promise."

"Daniel, you...wouldn't take them away from me, would you?"

"What would I gain by doing that?"

"I don't know. Custody of Greg's infants? Control of your family? Authority to protect the triplets? It's a long list."

"You've given this some thought haven't you? But since you included positive points, you don't think I'm all bad."

"You? Bad?" Cydney leaned her head against the back of the sofa and stared in his face. "Bossy and determined I agree, but not bad."

"Then why are you afraid I'll take the triplets away from you?" Daniel whispered.

Cydney leaned close to hear his soft words. The warmth radiating off his body chased away the chills of fear and made her feel safe. His soft tone soothed her, and filled her with a longing she hadn't dared admit. She was attracted to him. She wanted to be close to him, trust him. Worse, she wanted him to kiss away her fears. But most of all, she wanted to connect with another human.

And contact with just any person wouldn't do. She wanted Daniel's strength. Wanted him with a need so deep it tugged at her heart. Fear and hope filled her eyes as she stared at him.

When Daniel lowered his head and brushed his lips against hers, she almost cried in relief. Desire flared inside her like a raging flame. And Daniel kissed her again.

She wiggled close, needing more contact with him. His thigh pressed into her midsection as she leaned toward him. Images of them on her sofa, in the privacy of her apartment, filled her head. The craving to feel every inch of his body against her skin heated her from head to toe.

He made a sound against her lips.

She twisted closer.

His lips pressed against hers, claiming all she was willing to give. With desire clouding her judgment, the truth hit like a blow to the side of her head. She wanted Daniel more than she had wanted any man she'd ever met. She trusted him enough to respond to his kisses. Daniel fit her dream of the perfect man. He held her as if he would never let her go, and kissed her with a desire as great as her own. She had never felt so safe.

Could this be real? Had she found the one man she could trust? The one man she could believe in and share her dreams with.

Daniel pulled away from their kiss, but his arm held her tight against his side.

She snuggled close, feeling confident for the first time in days. Daniel cared about the triplets as much as she did. He wouldn't let her down. She had found a man she could rely on.

Fear and uncertainty from Cece's emergency left her drained. Her eyes closed. Daniel's strength and warmth wrapped her in a safe cocoon at his side. And finally, she slept.

CHAPTER 7

"**W**hy don't you two get a room?" The teasing words rang loud in the pre-dawn stillness of the waiting room.

"Phil," Daniel jerked awake at the sound of the familiar voice and groaned. "Why didn't you bring coffee?"

Easing back, he pulled a numb arm from under Cydney's head as she pushed away from him. Cold air shivered over his side where her body had warmed him while she slept next to him on the sofa. He liked having her close. Liked the way she fit perfectly in his arms. Liked the way her lips melted under his.

"I brought coffee." Phil pointed to tall cups with a familiar logo sitting on the table at Daniel's elbow.

"What's going on?" Daniel squinted at his watch. Five in the morning. Something was wrong. "You never get up before six."

"Why are you sleeping in the waiting room?" Phil asked.

"We had an emergency call with Baby Girl last night. What's up?"

"How is she?" Phil passed Cydney and Daniel cups of steaming coffee. "What's with this baby stuff? I thought you decided on names."

"Cece's fine, this time." Daniel sipped the scalding liquid, hoping Cydney hadn't noticed the cautious warning in his words. After some reviving swallows, he eyed his friend. "Thanks for the coffee. This is great."

"Yes, thank you," Cydney sighed after her first taste. "We have named the babies, but—"

"We decided it was prudent to wait on filling out the birth certificates until we heard from the DNA tests.

Phil fell in the chair opposite Daniel and lifted his coffee cup. "The judge knows the test results are back."

"How?" Daniel bolted upright, almost spilling the rest of his coffee in his lap.

Phil shrugged, not wasting time by explaining the speed and effectiveness of the judicial gossip chain. "He's making noises about assigning custody as soon as possible. We have to move fast."

"Cydney's test was inconclusive. She has to do another one."

Phil glanced around the dimly lit room. His sharp legal eye touched on slumbering parents in various stages of waking up, before he turned back to Daniel. "Are you willing to risk the delay another test will require?"

"What risk?" Cydney demanded and holding the coffee cup in front of her like a shield.

"The judge can decide to send the triplets to different foster homes. Frankly," Phil blew out an impatient sigh and avoided meeting their eyes, "it's the decision I expect him to make. No, wait." He held up a staying hand when both of them voiced objections at the same time. "Think about it from his view. No foster parent wants three preemies to care for." He stared at them for long seconds. "Do you want to risk the judge making that decision?"

"Separate the babies?" Cydney gasped.

"How common is that?" Daniel asked.

"What are the options?" Cydney demanded in a quivering voice. "What choices do we have?"

Daniel opened his mouth, but the stark white of her face

blocked his words. One thing he admired about her in the past days was her willingness to consider alternatives. But he feared they were both in for a shock.

"Our best bet? You agree for Daniel to have custody."

"No," she gasped. She struggled upright, and put distance between her and Daniel. "I can't give up Ziggy's babies."

"I understand what you're thinking. But consider this option for a minute. If Daniel is awarded custody, that takes the triplets out of the court system. As their uncle, they have a family member in control of their lives."

Cydney stared at the attorney and shook her head. "I can't reject them, even for a second."

"Listen," Phil insisted in a patient tone, "when the new DNA results come back, we can go back to court and apply for joint custody. But in the meantime, a family member takes charge of the triplets, not the state."

Cydney blinked. Emotions flickered in her eyes. Daniel could almost see wheels turning in her head. She didn't trust anyone to make decisions for her. He respected that. But this was about three innocent babies. His brother's children needed his protection. Didn't she realize she could trust him?

"Cydney, you should listen to Phil. I know you're worried, but if we delay—"

"Save your breath, Daniel." Cydney sighed and concentrated on wrapping a napkin around her cup. "You don't have to talk me into agreeing. I trust you."

"You trust me?" Something inside him coiled tight in his chest. Her searing green gaze bored into him causing a burning sensation in his gut.

She trusted him.

That concept was so startling he almost dropped his coffee cup. The idea shouldn't seem so strange. He had worked with hundreds of patients. They trusted him to deliver their babies. His staff worked beside him and depended on his judgment. Medical colleagues asked his opinion. Why was he shocked to hear Cydney say those three magic words?

Because, as far back as he could remember, trust had been missing from his personal life.

He had lost faith in his parents long before his father's phi-landering had been revealed by his death in traffic accident with a young female assistant. His mother's dependence on the social status of his father's position hadn't earned his respect. As an adult, he could see where Greg's life choices were taking him, and tried to help. But his brother's refusal to change and accept responsibility had hit hard.

Now the results of one of Greg's worst decisions was hanging over his head, and hearing Cydney say she trusted him left him speechless. He rubbed a hand along his jaw scraping his morning stubble. Would Cydney trust him when she discovered he'd had her investigated?

Having trust in another person and giving trust in return, was a wondrous thing. How long had it been since he had trusted anyone? How long before Cydney learned the truth and withdrew her confidence in him?

"Strange for me to say I trust you," Cydney's voice was flat but her gaze held his, "when you consider the fact that your brother got my sister pregnant, and his reckless driving killed them both." She lifted a shoulder. "But you're not like your brother anymore than I'm like Ziggy. And I trust you."

Daniel swallowed a lump of regret so huge it almost choked him and stared in her eyes. Her words hung in the quiet, coffee scented air, taunting him. Challenging him. Why should she trust him?

Because he wasn't Greg.

He didn't shirk responsibility. "True, my brother didn't use good judgment, but accidents can happen to anybody. Greg didn't intend to wreck his car and hurt your sister."

"I-I'm sorry, Daniel. You lost as much as I did in that accident. I shouldn't blame him. I'm just tired." Her eyes filled with regret. Her hand trembled as she ran it through her hair. "Forgive me."

Daniel jerked his head in a nod. She was telling the truth. He could see it in her eyes. He had felt it in her touch the whole night through. They were both exhausted. But she was wrong about one thing. She had no idea how much he had really lost in that traffic accident.

Losing his brother was bad enough, but he had lost part of his self-respect, as well. He tried to set a good example for Greg, but his need to protect his younger brother ended in disaster. Part of him had died along with Greg. Guilt would shadow him for the rest of his days.

He had failed Greg.

He and Cydney had both lost because of that one tragic event. Maybe, if they worked together to save the triplets, they could look forward and not back, because one thing was certain. He had lost Greg, but thanks to medical miracles, he had gained hope with the survival of the triplets. They both had

Daniel's heart filled with wonder when he thought about the tiny triplets in NICU. By some miracle, he helped save his brother's babies. He had a second chance to help Greg, and nothing would stop him from protecting his brother's tiny infants. He would not fail Greg again. That decision meant taking risks with Cydney's trust.

If he hadn't already destroyed it by having her investigated.

"Okay, Phil," he blew out a long sigh, "what now?"

"I'll file for a special hearing." Phil stood, eyeing each of them. "Keep strong."

"You trust me?" Daniel turned to Cydney as Phil departed. "How can you?"

"Is there any reason I shouldn't?" Her face flamed with heat as she recalled events of the previous night. Memory Daniel's lips still warmed her blood.

Her trust in him was evident. She had slept in his arms. Actually, slept. No man had ever held her, protected her all night long, except Daniel. Scary as it was to admit, her actions added to only one thing. She trusted him. He could soon have complete control of the triplets, but she couldn't deny she trusted him.

"I didn't expect you to admit such a thing, considering all that's happened." Daniel lifted a shoulder. "I wasn't aware you had that much confidence in me."

"I'm here, aren't I?" Her chin angled high. "Do you want me to drool over you like those instructors? Or bow at your feet like your staff does when you speak?" She made a snorting sound and lifted her cup for another sip.

"When did you reach this decision?"

"When was the last time you checked on the triplets?" Cydney bounced back in a quick retort.

"Three a.m. And don't change the subject. I want an answer."

"I checked at four. The curtains were closed." She stared at the clock and rocked on the edge of the sofa. "Could you do your doctoring thing and slip in the unit to check on them?"

Daniel made a snorting sound. "I love how you describe my career. And no, I won't throw my weight around and demand special favor because I happen to be a doctor."

"Why not?" She stared at him. "What if the triplets needed you?"

"I have a cell phone and a beeper." He pointed to the pager on his belt and lifted his chin. "I can reach them in two minutes."

"What if something goes wrong—"

"If there's an emergency…I will do my *doctoring* thing. Okay?"

She rolled her eyes and sniffed. "I guess I'll have to settle for that."

"It's only an hour until visiting hours."

"I know. It just seems so long. After what happened last night, I want to check on them every few minutes." Her reference to the night before brought back the memory of his kisses and her face warmed. But common sense kicked in. She wasn't using her head. She melted at his touch. Why hadn't she raced from the room, screaming for help? Why did his arms make her feel safe when she tried not to depend on him?

"Why don't you run home for a quick shower and change?"

"Not enough time." She shrugged. "And you have rounds. Both of us can't leave."

"You could skip the early visit. I'll be here." He offered. "I can shower in the hospital before I go on rounds."

"You want me to skip a visit? Be absent when I could visit the triplets, and have witnesses say I didn't bother to check on Baby Girl after her incident last night? I don't think so." Crossing her arms on her chest, Cydney leaned back against the sofa and glared at him.

"Not ten minutes ago, you said you trusted me. Is this how you define trust?"

"I…do…trust you." She tried to calm the shivers shaking her body. "I'm having trouble getting used to the idea, that's all."

"You either trust me, or you don't." Daniel leaned forward to rest his arms on his thighs and stared in her eyes. "Make up your mind."

"What about you?"

"What about me?" Frowning, Daniel glare at her.

"I don't see you showing trust in me." Cydney waved a hand toward the windows. "You have hospital rounds. Go check on your patients."

Daniel clenched his teeth. "Ten minutes ago, you said you trusted me. But you won't leave the hospital to take the shower you're longing for. Why is that?"

Why?

Because no one could check on the triplets as good as she could, not even a doctor. No one could love them as much as she did.

Cydney jumped up and rushed to the viewing window. The curtains were closed, but she needed to get away from Daniel. She couldn't think straight when she was close to him. She cringed when she thought about last night, and how she melted in his arms. She had practically thrown herself at him and all he had done was kiss her. True, the kiss sent sparks all the way to her toes, but why had she melted against him?

Okay, so it had been more than one kiss. But she didn't do casual flings, and being close to Daniel made her forget her usual caution. That spelled danger.

Noise caught her attention. The curtain opened. She could see the activity in the NICU. The triplets were visible. She sighed, relief running over her like a soothing balm. As long as she could see them, touch them, she could protect them.

Memory of her failed DNA test flashed in her head sending her emotions scattering for cover. Forget kissing Daniel Prince. Forget the warm gooey feelings that washed over her when she was in his arms. She had a bigger problem. One she couldn't solve by herself.

She had reached a crossroads in more ways than one, but she shoved her confusing reactions to Daniel aside and concentrated on the babies. If she wanted to maintain contact with the triplets, she had to cooperate with Daniel, and that meant controlling her wayward emotions. The inconclusive results from the DNA test gave him the advantages in their tug of war over the triplets.

Worse, she'd given him another advantage when she responded to his kisses. Daniel was worthy of her dreams, and a man she could trust, but in the light of day, did she really dare? With her family's trail of failed personal relationships, should she risk the triplets' future because of her response to Daniel?

She and Ziggy had lived the battles that happened when relationships failed. Custody disputes hurt the children involved more than the adults. If she antagonized Daniel, it would add to the mistakes she had made with Ziggy. The triplets deserved better.

Ziggy cheated her out of the joy of celebrating the pregnancy with her. But she had a second chance. If it meant trusting Daniel Prince, she would find a way to deal with his expectations. For the sake of the three infants, she had no choice.

It was ironic really. She had worked for a career so she would have choices, and not be dependent on a man, but she had come full circle. She had to rely on a man to get what she wanted.

Her gaze roamed over Daniel as she walked slowly back to the sofa. With his hair sticking up in spikes, his clothes rumpled, and his face covered with a day old beard, he was the safest looking man she had ever seen, and her reaction scared her. She wanted to depend on him.

Had she been too hasty in agreeing to his attorney's plan? Should she take back her decision? Tell him she had changed her mind. Back away? "What about you, Daniel? You haven't answered my question."

"What question?" He frowned. "We were talking about whether or not you trust me."

"I said I did, and I asked if you trust me."

Color tinted Daniel's skin. "It's too early in the day for this discussion."

Ah, so he expected her to throw caution aside and trust the triplets to his care. He was asking her to rely on him, but he couldn't do the same.

"Or, maybe it's too late." She sat on the opposite corner of the sofa, leaving distance between them. Noise increased in the room. More parents arrived, some walking like robots from lack of sleep. She understood their shock. She sighed and turned back to Daniel. "I should have asked if you trusted me before I agreed for you to get custody."

"Havre you changed your mind?"

"Why won't you answer my question?"

"Because my mother is on a cruise," Daniel slapped his hands on his thighs and turned glare on her.

"How does that relate to whether or not you trust me?"

"Answer me this. Would you return to your vacation cruise if your youngest son had just been killed in an accident?"

Heart thudding, Cydney stared at him. "She didn't come to the funeral?"

"Oh, she flew back home for the funeral." Daniel raked a hand down his face as if trying to rub away his thoughts, and continued in a weary tone. "But she went straight back to the airport after the ceremony. No, I take that back. She had me stop at her favorite dress shop so she could buy some black designer originals. Then she went to the airport to catch a flight to rejoin her friends on the cruise."

"I don't see—"

"Would a loving mother put her friends and a cruise before the death of her youngest son? That's the mother figure that I had, and I intend for the triplets to have better than that." Daniel shot to his feet. Emotions and exhaustion twisted his face. Hands clenched at his side, voice lifeless, he said. "This isn't about here and now. This is about my life, my role models. And you aren't the only one with trust issues, Ms. Eller."

Chills chased down Cydney's spine as she watched him stalk away. Memories from her childhood raced through her head, but she couldn't imagine the depth of Daniel's pain.

For the first time since the triplets arrived in NICU, Daniel missed Dr. Morgan's morning briefing an hour later. "I expected to see Daniel this morning. I'm sure he has questions."

Cydney swallowed. "He...uh...stayed all night. But he had to leave a few minutes ago."

"That's the life of an obstetrician for you." Dr. Morgan sighed. "No matter what emergency is happening in your own life, you have to run help others."

"I'll keep him posted."

"I'm not concerned." Dr. Morgan waved a hand. "He can check in when he has time. There's nothing pressing. Cece is holding her own."

Cydney listened to the doctor's update on the triplets, but she couldn't get Daniel's words out of her head. Had she pushed too hard to gain his trust? Was she wrong to demand that he admit he trusted her? And if he didn't?

Where did that leave them? Two wounded souls, needing to be able to believe in another person...how in the world could they take care of the triplets.

"Donna, I'm so glad you could meet for lunch." Cydney greeted when her best friend arrived at the restaurant.

"Girlfriend, you look like hell. What's wrong?" Donna blurted as she fell into the chair across the table from Cydney.

"We had a scare last night. Baby Girl, we've named her Cecelia Dawn by the way, had an incident." Cydney opened her menu and tried to appear calm, but her insides were twisted in knots. Donna never minced words and Cydney knew she looked like a zombie, but she had good reason. Daniel hadn't appeared all morning to check on the triplets.

"Is the baby okay? What am I saying? Of course she is, or you wouldn't be here." Donna crossed her arms on the edge of the table and glued her x-ray vision to Cydney's face. "So, why are you here? Last time we tried to have lunch, I could barely pry you away from the hospital."

Cydney cleared her throat. Maybe this wasn't such a good idea after all. She needed to talk to someone she trusted, but Donna said what was on her mind.

"She...Cece's fine. The nurses bragged on how perky she is this morning. She's bright and alert like nothing happened." Cydney's shoulders slumped and her guard slipped. *This was Donna. She didn't have to pretend.*

"You don't sound relieved. What's going on?" Donna frowned.

"I'm just tired. We stayed at the hospital all night. How are you?" Donna's laser-stare always saw through her defenses. Too bad Donna hadn't left her *Mom truth detector vision* at home. She wasn't sure she wanted to share details about last night.

"Same ole stuff." Donna buried her nose in the menu.

"Come off it, Donna. You're not the only one with a built-in truth detector. I had lots of practice with Ziggy." Brow wrinkled, Cydney blurted the question that had bothered her since their last lunch date. "Are you and Charlie having problems?"

The server arrived to take their orders. Donna ordered tuna salad and tea. Cydney chose the grilled chicken salad, and waited until the server walked away. Then she turned to Donna. "This is the second time you avoided that topic."

"Okay, I might as well fess up. Things are...tense at home. But I don't want to talk about it."

"That's not very nice. I thought we were friends."

Donna snorted. "Are you saying it's *not* nice that I don't bore you with my dirty laundry? Girlfriend, you have enough worries on your plate."

"It isn't nice because…I…can't drag out my worries if you don't share what's bothering you." Cydney let her glance skim about the room as if her words weren't important.

"Talk to me. What's worrying you besides the babies? Ah ha, I know." Grinning wide, Donna flung against the back of her chair and grinned. "You've fallen for the hunk, haven't you?"

"Donna. Donna. Donna." Struggling to keep her expression blank, Cydney shook her head. "Have you been a housewife and mother so long you have forgotten the girlfriends' code of ethics?"

"I've been tied to that house so long I've forgotten what having a life means." Donna propped her elbows on the table and glared at the breadstick centerpiece.

"What went wrong?" *If Donna and her dreamboat couldn't make things work, no one could.*

"Who knows," Donna shrugged, "me? Charlie? Three kids? Take your pick." She crossed her arms and chewed the corner of her lip. "I miss work. I miss who I was when I had a career. I loved the pressure of meeting deadlines. It's not…I love my kids. And I…love Charlie."

"But?"

"I'm not sure Charlie feels the same anymore." Donna sniffed and sent a glare across the table. "Are you happy now? You've sliced and diced my emotions and the salads haven't even arrived, yet."

Cydney frowned, trying to determine if Donna was teasing or serious. "I didn't mean to pry."

"Sure, you did. But I'm relieved you dragged it out of me. I wanted to talk last time we had lunch, but we'd just left Ziggy's funeral and it didn't seem like the right time." She sighed. "How are you doing, anyway?"

"I don't know." Cydney rearranged her forks. "I spend so much time worrying about triplets, I don't think much about Ziggy." She shrugged. "Then I remember, and I feel guilty about that."

"Join the club. I think females are programmed to feel guilty."

"So, that day, after the funeral when you questioned me about the babies, you were hinting at problems?"

Donna lifted a hand, palm up. "I'm probably not the best person you should talk to right now. But I admit I regret giving up my career. It would have been hard to work when the kids were babies, but I wish I had tried."

"Why not go back? Your youngest starts school this fall."

Donna snorted. "I'm out of the loop. My creative edge is dull. Who would give me a chance?"

"Why not go back to the firm?"

"And expose my lost skills? Besides, I can't work full time, even with the kids in school."

"Mmmm, you need a job-sharing position."

Donna waited until the server put salads in front of them and left. "Enough about me. What's bothering you?"

"My DNA test came back inconclusive."

"Meaning? You know those triplets are Ziggy's."

"I know. You know. Daniel knows. But the judge doesn't and now Daniel can claim custody and the court will agree." Cydney stabbed the salad with more energy than needed.

"Will he do that? After all, he is a bachelor. He probably has a personal life."

"Oh, I already agreed to sign the papers. At five o'clock this morning his attorney left to ask the judge."

"What on earth? No one is in their right mind at five a.m." Donna slammed her glass down. "Wait a minute. What aren't you telling me? Did you spend the night with the dishy doctor? Did he sweet talk you into this insanity?"

"No…well…we spent the night in the waiting room outside NICU, but that doesn't count."

"Oh, hon, I'm sorry. But why agree to give him custody of Ziggy's babies?"

"I trust him, Donna."

"Oh, my…tell me I did not hear you say that." Donna shook her head. "What has this hunky doctor done to you?"

"I can't explain. I fought against him from day one. He offered support and I pushed back. But he kept pushing. He grew on me. I've seen him at his best and hurting as much as I was. I watched the way he responded to Cece's emergency last night." She lifted a shoulder. "If anything goes wrong with the babies, I want him there."

"Well, good for you." Donna gave a thumbs-up. "I never thought I'd see the day you trusted a man. So, if you agreed to him having custody, what's the problem?"

"I told him...I trusted him...and he just walked away."

⚬

"Ms. Eller, are you ready to start the kangaroo cuddle therapy?" The nurse greeted Cydney as she entered the NICU at the next visiting hour.

Cydney glanced down at her button-up blouse. "Are the infants well enough for me to hold?"

"We think so. Let's get start with Baby Girl first." The staff was having trouble using the babies' real names, Cydney noticed as the nurse led the way to Cece's incubator and began her instructions. "Sit in this chair with your back to the room. Unbutton your blouse so I can place the infant on your bare shoulder. I'll watch for the IVs."

Five minutes later, Cydney snuggled her chin against the tiny infant's body as she held Cece for the first time. The baby felt small as a doll against her shoulder. Her breath hitched. Warmth wrapped around her heart and tangled in knots. Could she ever love another child as much as she loved these triplets?

"Kangrooing I see." A deep voice sounded behind Cydney. *Daniel was here!*

Her pulse raced at lightening speed. Her heart thumped against her ribs. Warmth filled her face. She fumbled to adjust her blouse with her free hand.

"Nurse, I'm ready to hold one of the boys."

Cydney glanced over her shoulder as Daniel stepped over to Big Brother's incubator. Heat pooled in her belly as Daniel unbuttoned his shirt and his chest came into view.

Oh, help! No man she'd ever known would take the time to care for the triplets like this.

Ten minutes later, Daniel's dress shirt hung open as he held the infant boy against his shoulder. With his long sleeves rolled up and the shirt unbuttoned, the vision of Daniel holding the tiny infant to his shoulder was a sight to behold.

Alarm bells blared in Cydney's head.

This was how her mother reacted to a handsome man. All mushy words and gooey feelings and she could not go there.

Smothering a gasp, she straightened her spine. She could not start leaning on Daniel Prince. The baby jumped in response to Cydney's sudden tension and let out a mewling sound that could only be a cry. Panic ripped through Cydney. What had she done?

Disappointment, fear, and feelings of incompetence raced through her. She had made Cece cry the very first time she held her. How could she have been so careless? How could she comfort Cece with all the tubes and IVs? She reached up to pat the baby's back.

Cece cried more.

"Poor baby," the nurse appeared at Cydney's elbow, "you can't jiggle her because of the IVs. Let me put her down for now. It's been forty-five minutes and she's probably tired." The nurse lifted the tiny baby and put her back in the incubator. The crying stopped.

"Contact is new to her and so was her position on your shoulder. She needs time to adjust to being held. Ready to hold Little Brother?"

Cydney chewed her lip and gave a nod. But moving closer to Daniel sent color to her face. She had to stop reacting to the sight of him holding a baby to his bare chest. She would not allow her response to this man cloud her judgment.

She had to prove she wasn't as easy to impress as her mother had been.

The nurse placed Little Brother on Cydney's shoulder. "He still has a low fever, but this is good for him."

Cydney put her hand against the baby's back. He had fewer IVs than his sister did, but he was still very small. Her heart twisted. How could she let Daniel claim custody? How could she work and take care of three preemies? Lifting her head, her gaze collided with Daniel's level stare. In that magic moment of sharing, their unspoken words communicated their commitment to protect these infants.

How could she doubt Daniel's intentions? Every thing he had done since they first met, proved he was a man of honor. A man she could trust. But how could she make the leap from being independent to relying on a man she barely knew for the sake of these infants, when DNA didn't show they were related to her?

She couldn't. No sane person would. She couldn't take that blind leap. She wouldn't. Her decision was as simple as those two words.

Daniel's kisses had set her body on fire. Even now, she remembered the heat racing along her veins as he held her close. But she had to ignore her attraction to him and keep her head clear.

Giving in to her reaction to Daniel would take away her hard-earned freedom.

Daniel held the infant against his shoulder with a steady hand, but his heart thundered against his ribs. Greg's son was his responsibility. One he accepted gladly, but he wished his brother were here to share the joy.

The warmth invading his heart didn't have anything to do with duty. He felt a rush of love as he held the baby close. Nothing had prepared him for the emotions taking control of his heart.

First, warmth washed over him, then chills chased close behind. Fear of making a mistake made him rearrange his grip on the infant. He changed position and held the baby tighter. His glance met Cydney's and heat almost consumed his insides.

He hadn't slept a wink last night. Holding Cydney in his arms had been special. She didn't accept help easily, but after the Code Blue for Cece, she accepted his offer of support. It wasn't much progress, but it was enough to give him hope.

During the long hours of holding her, he discovered what

had been missing from his life. Cydney's warm loving response to the triplets was nothing like his mother's reaction caring for children. In his mother's life, children were to be 'shown off', but not heard.

He had chosen to remain single because he expected women to be as calculating as his mother. Holding Cydney in his arms, he realized his mistake. She wasn't cold or distant. Her panic over news of Baby Girl's health scare proved she was caring and loving.

And he had experienced the same protective urge he felt toward this baby. But he knew Cydney well enough by now to realize that telling her how he felt would chase her away. No matter how much he wanted to take care of her, he couldn't share his feelings until she was ready.

Cydney needed to be in charge of her life. He respected that, and admired her independence, but he couldn't restrain his need to protect. And he couldn't force the issue. Using his medical training to his advantage wouldn't work. Winning Cydney's love would take effort.

Clutching Big Brother against his shoulder, he watched as Cydney held Little Brother in a tender grip. This woman was different. She made him believe in love, but convincing her would be a challenge.

"Do you feel the heat from his fever?"

Daniel blinked.

The nurse stood at his elbow. "The baby's fever increased while you were holding him. I thought you might notice." She reached to take the infant.

Heat rushed to Daniel's face. He had been so busy thinking about Cydney, he hadn't noticed the infant's fever.

Some doctor he was. What kind of parent was he? Big Brother was sick, his fever rising, and he hadn't even noticed.

Fastening the buttons of his shirt, Daniel watched the nurse return the infant to the incubator. The rising fever was not a good sign. Sepsis should have responded to antibiotics by now. Did the baby have other problems?

He watched the nurse check the infant's readings. Fear

raced along his nerves. He could use a scalpel on a patient with confidence, and deliver babies with his eyes closed, but this little boy's rising fever made his knees weak.

"When will Dr. Morgan be in to check him?"

"In about an hour, but don't worry, Dr. Prince. If we see any sign of danger, we'll page her ASAP."

Daniel watched the nurse take Little Brother from Cydney. His glance skated past the bare skin of her shoulder. In the aftermath of this new worry, he didn't pause to appreciate the peeping lace of her bra. His attention focused on the second baby boy. "How is Little Brother?"

The nurse checked the baby's readings. "No change. His temperature is reading about one hundred. That's where he's been for the past few days. He's fine."

Fine? How can he be fine?

A low-grade fever could be more serious than a higher reading in the right circumstances. A virus could cause a child's fever to spike. Then in a few hours, the virus would run its course. That wasn't the case with low-grade fevers. He turned to Cydney. "Zackary's fever is up."

"What's wrong with him?"

"Jaundice and sepsis are enough. I'm sure Dr. Morgan will check him closely." Daniel took hold of her elbow, felt the trembles running through her body. "Come on, visiting hours are over."

Cydney hung back, looking over her shoulder. "I need to check him."

Daniel opened his mouth to object, then snapped his lips shut. Even with his medical training, Cydney still didn't feel safe until she had checked the infant. Warmth filled his chest. That's how a mother should respond to her infant.

He wouldn't allow circumstances to push Cydney away. The triplets needed her. He needed her. He had never said that to a woman before, but this was different. He was attracted to Cydney on a deeper level. The need growing inside him was more that attraction. He wanted...no, he needed Cydney to want him in her life as much as he wanted her.

He wanted her to love him. Whoa...The last time he wanted a woman to love him, his mother said she had a meeting, go find the nanny to bandage his scraped knee.

Recalling that incident, the irony of his currant situation almost made him laugh. *Find the nanny.* But he didn't laugh. There was nothing funny about his current problem. If he told Cydney how he felt, she would think he only claimed to care about her because he wanted her to take care of the triplets. She would think he was using her.

He had to win her confidence and earn her trust. She said she trusted him, but he could read the conflicting emotions in her eyes. He needed time. But how could he take time when issues with the triplets' could explode at any second? He had to try. Now that he had found a woman worthy of loving, he couldn't lose her.

"Ready?" He asked as Cydney turned toward him. Outside the unit, he stopped to check his watch. "I made arrangements for you to get a DNA test at Dr. Morgan's clinic. You should leave now. It won't take long."

CHAPTER 8

"Class, tonight our topic is Work, Play, and Baby," the red-haired instructor announced in a playful tone as a wide smile covered her face.

Cydney tilted her head, listening to the groans from the class of new parents. Play sounded more like her sister, but work worried her. Did this instructor know the secret to keeping your job and taking care of triplets?

Daniel leaned over to whisper in her ear, "Today was so crazy I forgot about the class. Good thing the nurse in NICU reminded me."

Clenching her hands on her purse, Cydney tipped her head in agreement. But every nerve in her body jerked to alert. His murmur tickled her memories of the night in the waiting room. They had spoken in soft voices that night to keep from disturbing parents sleeping in the NICU waiting room. But since that scary event with Cece two nights ago, she had seen little of Daniel except the visits to the nursery. It was a good thing the nurse had reminded him of the class. He hadn't given Cydney a chance.

Was he putting distance between them on purpose? Why avoid her? But the little voice in her head answered the question.

Now that he had custody of the triplets, he doesn't need you.

She grimaced as that thought played in her head. Pain sliced through her making her gasp. She sent a startled glance toward the instructor, hoping the sound hadn't been loud enough to notice. But one look at the expression on Sharon's face told Cydney she needn't worry. She could dance on the table, naked, and the redheaded instructor wouldn't notice.

Sharon focused her attention on Daniel. Had he noticed? Did he return the instructor's interest? Cydney looked at him out of the corner of her eye. Why did it matter to her if Daniel noticed the instructor's flirtatious glances or not?

But it did matter and much as she wanted to deny facts, she couldn't escape. In the short time since they met, Daniel had become important to her. Like it or not, as long as she was involved with the triplets' care, her life was connected to his.

If he dated someone, she would be on call to check on the triplets. If she dated another man and went to visit the triplets, Daniel would know. It wasn't an ideal relationship, and not the stuff that dreams were made of, but it was her new reality. It was a matter of responsibility. And she never believed she would thing such a thing, but their connection was the opposite of what she really wanted.

Daniel's kisses opened her eyes to the truth and made her face emotions roiling inside her when he was near. She worked for achievement so she could make her own decisions, but her life was spinning out of her control.

It had been her choice to take care of Ziggy. She could have let protective services worry about Ziggy. Life would have been easier, but she loved Ziggy. Taking charge of a teenager when she was barely out of her teens hadn't been easy.

Now she faced the results of her decisions and the reality was more sad than funny. All her efforts to be a good role model, to guide her sister and give them both a better life, had meant nothing.

Ziggy's party life and careless choices had sealed Cydney's fate and she couldn't escape. Not if she believed in the rules she had expected Ziggy to live by. She had talked the talk, now she had to walk the walk or her whole life would be a farce.

Reality weighed heavy on her shoulders, and Cydney slumped against the back of the chair as she turned a blank stare on the instructor.

"Tired?" Daniel murmured as he put his arm on the back of her chair.

Her pulse rate kicked into high speed at his touch. Blood pounded in her ears. This wasn't her idea of putting distant between them, but she couldn't force herself to shift away from his arm, but she knew she would pay. Two hours of sitting tucked against Daniel's side, absorbing the heat of his body, would have her begging for his attention.

She needed to stick to her plan to do things for herself. But how? Twisting the handles of her purse, she turned to him and whispered. "No, I'm just worried I'll have a flat rear-end from all this sitting."

Daniel choked back a laugh.

The instructor sent him a brilliant, hundred-watt smile, obviously thinking he agreed with her last comment.

But Cydney had lost focus. Was the instructor still talking about the topic for the evening? *Work. Play. And. Baby?* Did the instructor have children? Cydney didn't believe that was possible. One week of responsibility of the triplets had robbed Cydney of any urge to play.

Daniel shifted in his chair and stretched his legs. His thigh brushed against her leg. Heat filled her cheeks and pooled in her belly.

Oops! She'd spoken too soon. The urge to play with Daniel was raging in her blood. But her protective instincts shouted a warning. Playing with Daniel Prince was not an option.

"I'm not sure I can stay awake for this." His low voice wrapped her in a cocoon of longing. What had she done with her life before she met him? What would her future be like when he took charge of the triplets? He wouldn't want her underfoot. He had the resources to hire nannies to take care of the babies. He wouldn't need her. A deep sigh wracked her body.

Daniel tightened his arm around her shoulders. "Stop worrying. I there is no risk of your bottom getting flat."

"Are you saying I'm fat?" Cydney cut a glance in his direction. *Big mistake. Her heart bashed against her ribs when she saw how close he was.*

Daniel leaned close to whisper to her. If she shifted an inch, their lips would meet... she swallowed a gulp, turned toward the instructor and forced her attention to the lesson.

Sharon Vance was sending dirty looks in her direction so she had noticed her lack of attention. Cydney angled her chin high and prayed her face wouldn't turn red. It wasn't her fault Daniel was acting like a schoolboy cooped up in class too long. She enjoyed his nonsense, and loved being near him. With that admission, dread and anticipation swirled in her blood.

In that instant, Cydney realized she would take more if Daniel offered...

Whoa. More what? Get naked with Daniel Prince?

Uh, yeah.

Well, that was not going to happen. It would ruin everything. Didn't she have a brain cell left in her head? Mixing bodily fluids with Daniel would send thrills to every nerve in her body. But her brain was shouting, *"NO WAY."*

She had to use her head. Why would Daniel need her? She wasn't a medical person, or calm and efficient in emergencies. The sight of blood made her squeamish, and the sound of someone throwing up almost made her hurl. What good was she to Daniel? He needed someone with skills.

Cydney flinched against the tight feeling around her heart. Every muscle in her body clenched. She didn't have answers. Ziggy's choices landed her in this situation, but she had to decide what to do. What happened when the triplets left the hospital?

She knew Daniel didn't need her, but until he said the words she would stay connected to the triplets. Torn by reality and longing, she heaved a sigh.

And stay near Daniel, a voice whispered in her ear.

"I'll rub it for you if it will make you feel better." Daniel whispered.

"Rub what?" Cydney turned toward him. *Another mistake.* Her body shouted with need. Her eyes clung to the five o'clock shadow darkening his jaw.

"If you're worried about your bottom getting flat, I could rub it to make sure you have good circulation."

Shoulders shaking with laughter, Cydney met the wicked twinkle in his eyes and fought the feelings threatening to engulf her. How could she live without this man in her life?

"So, class," the instructor raised her voice, "if I could have your attention, please."

Cydney jerked around to face the instructor and elbowed Daniel in the side, for good measure. She wasn't taking all responsibility for the instructor's displeasure.

"I have assignments for you." Sharon Vance announced.

The class groaned.

"We're going to do some role-playing."

Daniel muttered.

Cydney giggled, but recovered quickly when the instructor glanced their way.

"You have five minutes to plan a two-minute skit. That doesn't seem like a long time, but you'll be surprised how much you can say in that short period of time." Sharon glanced at each couple. "That's one point I want you to take away from this activity. Communicate with your spouse. Use every second available."

"Do we have to act this out in front of class?" A woman asked.

"No," Sharon glanced at her watch. "Just for each other. Use your life, your careers, and your new baby in the skit. Pretend the baby is three months old. Now, move your chairs so you're facing each other, knees touching."

Groans filled the air. Chairs scrapped the floor. Everyone sat back down.

"Okay. The wife's employer calls the wife to come to work on Saturday." Sharon paused. "Discuss what you will cover in the skit. Ready? Go."

Daniel shifted his chair so his knees pressed hard against Cydney's and said, "Just trying to keep you awake. You have dark circles under your eyes."

"You're sporting a two-day beard, so we're even."

"You don't like my scruffy look?" Daniel arched a brow and rubbed his chin. "The nurses think it looks sexy."

Cydney snorted. *Eat your heart out George Clooney. You have competition.*

Daniel chuckled. "How do you think the triplets look to-day?"

He watched as her brow wrinkled. Discussing personal issues with a woman who took things seriously was a new experience for him. He expected that response at work, but found the reaction rare in his personal life. Usually, his dates wanted to be entertained and have fun.

Slouching in his chair, his knee slipped between hers. It was an accident, caused by his lounging slump and long legs. He could have moved back, but he heard her startled gasp and admired the rosy glow in her cheeks. Curiosity…and need kept him from moving away.

He wanted a response from her. Wanted to know what made her tick. She landed in his life and everything turned on end, but from the first moment they met, she filled his head. Intrigued him.

"You can stop worrying, you know." He grinned when her startled gaze met his.

"What?"

"Your bottom," Daniel choked back a laugh. "When we moved the chairs, I took the opportunity to check. Your cute little butt is still round and touchable."

Her eyes filled with laugher and the color in her face deepened. Rewarded for his efforts to cheer her up, Daniel relaxed.

"All three infants look more pink than yellow, today." Cydney ignored his teasing and responded to his earlier question. "But I'm concerned about Big Brother and Baby Girl."

Daniel expelled a noisy breath and crossed his arms over his chest. "When are you going to start calling them by name? The birth certificates have been recorded."

Her throat worked, then she said in a rush. "It's habit. I keep trying—"

"Are you worried about Gregory?"

Shaking her head, she said. "He's the smallest twin, but he seems better than his brother."

"Seems odd, doesn't it?"

"Twenty more seconds," the instructor called in a no nonsense tone.

"We haven't even started." Cydney shifted in her seat and sent the instructor a guilty glance.

Daniel shrugged. "We'll manage."

"But we haven't talked about what we'll say. We don't know the first thing about how the other would react."

"Does it matter?" His shoulders hunched in a shrug. "We're not likely to find ourselves in that situation."

Leaning close, Cydney gritted her teeth. "That woman is your coworker. You need to follow instructions."

"Why? She can't flunk me."

"If anything goes wrong with the triplets she can always say we didn't pay attention in parenting class."

"Time," the instructor called. "You have two minutes to act out your skit." She glanced around the room. "Several of you asked why we do this. Why is it important? There are things you can learn by role-playing." She waited for the groans to stop. "But more importantly, I can't dismiss you an hour early if I don't have cooperation from all class members."

Cheers filled the room.

"Here's your scenario again. Early Saturday morning, the wife's employer calls, insisting she come to work." She paused and looked around the room. "Ready? You must discuss this issue for two minutes. Go."

Cydney glared at Daniel. "We should have planned what we were going to say."

He lifted a shoulder and settled back in his chair. "Checking on the triplets seemed more important."

"Getting out of here an hour early sounds good to me."

"I'll take you to dinner."

"I'm too tired." Cydney sent him a glare loaded with daggers. Had he already forgotten the last time they left the hospital, Cece went to Code Blue?

"I've got it." Daniel snapped his fingers and leaned toward her. His arms pressed into her knees. "We should go shopping. We need supplies."

Cydney rolled her eyes and noticed the instructor headed in their direction. Giving him a stern frown, she said the first words that popped in her head. "I have to go to work. I can't lose this job."

"Fine. Go. I'll take care of the babies by myself." Daniel wagged his eyebrows.

"Y-you can't," Cydney swallowed a lump of fear. Could he dismiss her from his life that easily? "You worked all week. You're tired. And you have chores." Would Daniel be willing to babysit after delivering babies all week? Could she leave him alone with the infants and go to a job?

"If you don't want to go to work, then stay home."

"It's not that, I'm thinking about how tired you are. You work with babies all day."

"This is different. These are our kids. Go to work. We'll be fine."

"You don't need me." Cydney heard the needy note in her voice and winced.

"I need you, babe." Daniel wagged his brows. "But you need this job."

"I'll find a sitter."

"On Saturday morning? Good luck with that. Who wants to spend the weekend babysitting someone else's kids? Just go."

"N-no, I'll call the boss. Tell him I can't work." How could she leave Daniel alone with the triplets when his hours were so crazy? In real life, she would want to spend every minute with him, wouldn't she?

"You don't think I can manage, do you?" Daniel pointed his finger at her. "You don't trust me to take care of our babies. What makes you think I can't take care of them as good as you can?"

"Cut," the instructor called. "Very good. One more activity before we go. An impromptu skit, this time."

The class groaned.

Sharon Vance laughed. "In this skit, the husband wants to take his wife out to dinner. Men, get set, on your mark, go."

Daniel leaned close. "Come on, hon. Let's go out to dinner. You deserve a break."

"I'm too tired." Shivering at his use of the endearment, Cydney repeated the words she used earlier. Would she really refuse to spend time with Daniel if he wanted her company?

Daniel rolled his eyes. "That's been your excuse since the day we brought the babies home from the hospital. Don't you want to spend time with me anymore?"

Cydney gazed into Daniel's eyes. *If only this were real.* She would never refuse Daniel's invitation. "You know I do. But I'm tired. Looking after three babies all day is exhausting. I just want a hot bath and some quiet time."

"Quiet time? Alone? Great. That's just peachy." Daniel snarled. "If I had known having kids was going to be like this—"

"What are you saying?" Cydney put her hands on her hips. "You don't love the babies, do you? You thought we'd pop out a few kids like your friends have and go our merry way." *Were those real tears on her cheeks?* She must be more tired than she thought. "You've been acting strange ever since we brought the babies home from the hospital. Now I know why."

"Cydney—"

"You don't love the babies. And you don't love me. You just wanted them so you could brag to your friends. All you care about is having a good time."

"Cydney—"

"Cut! What I heard was great. Now, take the rest of the night off. Go home and discuss what you said in your skits."

Ten minutes later, Cydney rushed into NICU. "Dr. Morgan, how are they?"

Daniel heard the catch in her voice. Could be from their rush to get here in hopes of seeing the doctor, but he guessed it was from emotions tapped by the class skit.

"Dr. Morgan," Daniel angled his head toward the incubators, "are the babies improving?"

He willed his colleague to say yes, and silently begged her to give them a positive slant after the recent worries. They were due a break. The infants should be improving, and he didn't like the dark circles under Cydney's eyes. She would be exhausted before the triplets left the hospital.

"Zackary's temperature is down. His skin is less yellow. Gregory has more yellow and a low fever. We're continuing light therapy for at least another day." Dr. Morgan moved to the infant girl's incubator. "Baby Girl needs the photo treatment as well. Her blood levels have improved, but she can't go long without oxygen."

"Is she improving?" Concern filled Cydney's voice.

Daniel wanted to put his arm around her and offer reassurance. But outside the parenting class, he didn't dare. He had pushed the limits tonight under the eagle eyes of the instructor.

"She has a fever, but I would say there is a slight improvement. What do you think, Daniel?"

Daniel held up his hands. "I'm the stand-in father in this case. You're the expert."

Sending him a speaking glance, Dr. Morgan continued. "You're just in time for kangaroo care." She nodded toward the approaching nurse and smiled. "Have fun."

Ten minutes later, Gregory snuggled on Daniel's shoulder like a little leech, but much as he loved the triplets, all he could think about was Cydney's words in that skit. He glanced to where she sat with a baby tucked into her shoulder. Zackary looked content, burrowed close under Cydney's chin. Daniel imagined her scent, something with vanilla and fruit. Would the infant remember that scent? Would Zackary associate home and love with Cydney, as Daniel did? His gaze locked with hers over the infant's head. All he saw in her eyes was love.

Love!

He couldn't forget her words in that skit. She said he didn't love the infants. Had she been role-playing? Did she doubt his love for these babies? His throat worked. He tried twice before he could get a word past the lump in his chest.

"Happy?" His brow arched as he waited for her response.

Emotions chased cross her face. She nodded. "I love holding them."

Love.

There was that word again. Except for his brother, he had never loved anyone…until now. He tightened his hold on the infant. Baby-soft skin pressed into his shoulder as if they were one being. Until he these infants…and Cydney Eller appeared in his life, he hadn't experienced the emotions filling him now. How had he reached this stage of his life without knowing this joy?

It seemed fate had been kind to him, after all.

He had lost Greg, but his brother's infants filled him with a sense of contentment. More than anything, he wanted to share that joy with Cydney. Being around her opened his eyes to what a loving mother would do for her children. She missed meals, and went without sleep. She cried when she was worried, and laughed at the tiniest bit of good news. He encountered many new mothers in his work, but never observed their actions as intimately as he had Cydney's. The attraction he felt for her grew by the hour. She intrigued him on all levels.

"I'll take a turn with Cece." He stood up, almost trembling in his shoes under the weight of his new awareness. "You keep Big Brother."

"He seems so tiny. I can't believe we call him Big."

Daniel's eyes met hers for emotion filled seconds. His heart slammed against his ribs. His pulse rate equaled an aerobic workout. Despite the churning inside him, he looked in her eyes and smiled.

"I'm surprised by a lot of things these days." He held her gaze, willing her to believe every word he spoke. "I do love them, you know."

❦

"We're going shopping, now." Daniel's determination sounded in his tone as he ushered her out of the NICU.

"I'm tired."

"There you go again with that tired talk." Daniel winked at her to take the sting out of his words. "How can you keep up with three babies if you can't keep up with their uncle?"

"You're worse than all three babies put together. You're demanding, loud, and you won't take no for an answer."

"Sounds like the triplets. But I'm not a baby."

"Oh, no?" Cydney relaxed under their teasing banter. He was fun to be with when they weren't worried about the triplets. But her conscience nagged at her. Should she be worried? Should she leave the waiting room? Dr. Morgan said all three infants had improved, but shouldn't she stay close in case there was another emergency?

"Get that Mama Bear look off your face, Ms. Eller. We're going shopping. And then dinner."

"I...don't want to leave—"

"Do you trust the doctors?"

"Yes, but—"

"No, buts allowed, Mama Bear." Daniel took her arm and urged her in the elevator. "We need to prepare for taking the babies home."

"Who made you the boss?" Cydney huffed as she stepped out of the elevator on the ground floor and allowed Daniel to steer her toward the parking garage.

"I'm the Daddy person. That gives me rights. Fall in line, or else."

Cydney stopped, propped her hands on her hips and tapped one toe. "I'm not a member of your staff, Daniel Prince."

"I'm well aware of that fact, Ms. Eller." His gaze bored into hers for long heated seconds. "I was trying to lighten the mood, not lay down the law."

"Sorry," Cydney lifted a shoulder, "I'm over reacting, but I can't stop worrying."

"Try." Daniel urged her forward. "Worry is part of being a parent, but you can't allow it to consume your life. How can you enjoy the babies if all you do is worry?"

"You're right." Cydney stopped as he beeped the lock of a sleek black BMW that made her long to get her hands on the wheel. "So, you're one of those men who insists that father knows best?"

Daniel held the door and ushered her in the car. "I'm a member of the new generation." His eyes danced as he leaned close. "I pretend I know best until the Mama Person tells me what to do. Then I jump to obey. Let's go. I'm starving."

One comment after the other, and Cydney found herself laughing all the way to the store. The car's luxurious interior and soft leather seats lived up to her expectations of a dream ride. After the worn cushions in the hospital chairs, she felt she was floating on a cloud.

"Babies-R-Mine? Are you kidding?" She exclaimed as he pulled into the parking lot of the famous name store. "This place is a warehouse of temptation. We cannot go in here. Turn around, let's go—"

"Why can't we shop here? I have a list of supplies we need."

"You can find better deals—"

"Time, Ms. Eller. We don't have time to check out other options. This place has everything at one stop. You can't beat that. Come on, before I change my mind and go without you."

"Fine. Blow your budget on things you don't need. I'll sit in this comfy car and take a nap."

"And let me pick out baby cribs and clothing? Choose the brand of diapers they wear, all by myself?"

Huffing, Cydney climbed out of the car, slammed the door and sent him a glare over the top of the BMW. "Will you stop talking and get moving? We need to shop."

Daniel had never considered shopping fun, until he and Cydney locked horns over their choices of what the triplets needed.

In the first aisle, he picked out racecar beds for the three infants, but Cydney said, "You can't buy those. Babies need regular cribs. Save the racecar beds for when they're toddlers.".

After they finally selected the cribs, they moved to the aisle filled with bedding. He picked the fluffy, comfortable looking sets. "Look these have matching sheets and coverlet."

"That set is too thick for an infant." Cydney said. "You can share your favorite cartoon characters with them when they're older. Put it back. Infants are safer with thin blankets for covering."

"How do you know all this stuff?" Daniel demanded as he pushed a loaded cart down the aisle.

"My friend Donna has three kids. I babysit sometimes."

"I'm a doctor and I didn't know thick covers were dangerous." Daniel hunched a shoulder and frowned.

"It's your job to deliver babies." Her gaze slid over him, noted the worried look in his eyes, and had to fight the urge to smooth the ruffled look of his hair. "Usually, you don't take them home with you."

"True, the triplets are the first." Daniel's smile widened. He stopped in the middle of the aisle and stared in her eyes. "Can you believe they're alive? And they are ours? His voice snagged on a wave of emotion. "I'm the Daddy person." He grabbed Cydney in a hug and swung her feet off the floor. "Can you imagine what that feels like?"

Fighting a wave of emotion, Cydney held back a sob and pounded his shoulders. "Put me down, people are staring."

When he lowered her feet to the floor, she wrapped her arms around his waist and gave him a hug. Daniel's heart thundered against his ribs. Suspicious moisture filled his eyes. Not manly at all, but he would have stood there, blubbering in aisle three, if a cranky female voice behind him hadn't said, "Excuse, me, please."

"Sorry." Grinning at the woman, he let go of Cydney and

pushed their cart out of the way. He wanted to pull Cydney in his arms and hold her tight. But she blinked rapidly and he realized her emotions were as close to the surface as his were. Standing in the aisle of a Babies-R-Mine store was not the place to share his feelings for her.

Still reeling with unrequited emotions, he stared as Cydney paused in front of a wall of pacifiers. Obviously, taking care of an infant wasn't simple. Even something as ordinary as choosing a pacifier offered so many choices it was easy to make a mistake.

Make a mistake...

Heart thudding in his chest, Daniel sucked in a deep breath. Nothing about this situation was simple. He and Cydney were bound to make mistakes. They inherited not one, but three infants, so multiply any bad choice they made by three. Beads of perspiration popped on his brow as he stared at the multiple rows of pacifiers in front of him. Numerous colors, sizes, shapes, and grips were available, and this was just the beginning.

Could he do this? Could he face the future without help? He wanted custody of Greg's kids, but even with his training, the future seemed daunting when he thought of facing nights alone. Should he share his concerns with Cydney, or pretend he was in control? He wanted her in his life. Wanted a future with her, but telling her now would give her reason to doubt his was sincere.

Finally, Cydney made her choice. Three types of pacifiers, with three of each kind and she looked at him and shrugged. "Babies can be picky."

Daniel kept his tumbling emotions to himself as they approached the diaper section.

Cydney paused in front of the mountain of choices and sent him a wide-eyed glance. "This is the biggy."

"Yeah, I guess we'll have lots of baby poop with triplets." He reached for the package with cute printed designs on the diaper.

Cydney slapped his hand and laughed. "Put those back. The

other brand is better for newborns."

Daniel rolled his eyes. "What, it takes a rocket scientist to buy butt-covers for babies?"

She laughed softly. The sound went straight to his heart. Realizing he almost missed meeting this woman nearly ripped the air from his lungs. Even with his loss, Cydney and the triplets filled his heart with joy.

On the next aisle, they found shelves of books on baby advice. To refocus his attention, Daniel pulled out the first book that caught his eye. It was a thick volume with a short title. "This was written by a doctor. He promises the answer to any parenting question you can think of is in this book. Perfect."

"I want this one." Cydney pulled a small volume, with a colorful cover, off the shelf and waved it in his face.

"Baby Steps? Leave it to a woman to go for a cutesy title." Daniel made a snorting sound and shook his head. "That book is half as thick as this one." He hugged the bulging volume like a drowning man clinging to a life preserver.

"You don't need half the information in that book. You're a doctor and you live close to the hospital if you have an emergency." Cydney tossed the smaller volume in the cart. "I'm familiar with this one. I know it's good."

"Your confidence in me is so encouraging." Daniel made a face, causing her laugh to erupt. A flash reaction raced through his veins, warming his blood. He made a mental note to make her laugh more often. "But I'm the Daddy person, now, remember?" He wagged his brows in a teasing manner, "And you didn't sound very confident about my abilities during that skit we did in the parenting class."

And just like that, his one careless comment wiped the smile off her face. With a disgusted sigh, he shook his head. Obviously, he had a lot to learn about babies and working with Cydney Eller.

"Can we check out, now? I'm tired."

Holding his breath, expecting her to demand to go home any second, he decided to risk the odds and added. "Good idea. I'm starving."

Cydney eyed the overflowing cart. "Good thing we aren't in the grocery store. We'd need two carts."

"Save that nightmare for when the triplets start eating table food. We might even need three carts." His smile froze to a mask when a pained expression crossed Cydney's face. What had he said? What was wrong? Was she worried the triplets wouldn't get better? Didn't she know he would do everything in his power to make sure they were safe?

"Thanks for talking me into having dinner, Daniel. This was delicious." Cydney leaned back in the comfort of her chair. The hum of soft music and murmurs of conversation from other diners washed over her. Delicious aromas filled the air. How long had it been since she had enjoyed food this much and all thanks to Daniel. Twice he had forced her to eat a real meal and she had enjoyed every bite.

But remembering the first meal, she still felt tense. With every snippet of conversation or dropped utensil, her insides coiled tighter. The last time they had stolen an hour to eat dinner, Cece had a Code Blue incident. Still, Daniel insisted they try again. In the short time, since she met him he had invaded her life, her thoughts, and her dreams.

"You haven't tasted the cheesecake, yet."

"I don't have room for desert." She smiled for the first time since they checked out the baby supplies.

Daniel had insisted on paying the huge bill. He wanted to do everything for the infants, and never once mentioned her role in their lives. He knew she had taken the DNA test again, and wanted joint custody. So, why did he leave her out of his plans for the babies' future? Was there something he wasn't telling her? Didn't he want her involved with the triplets? Did he plan to ignore their connection to Ziggy?

He laughed when she shivered at the mention of cheesecake. "Never pass up dessert at La Chez. Trust me. Even if you're stuffed, you should make room for this dessert."

Cydney eyed him from lowered lids. "You don't look like a man who indulges in over-eating."

"I strive for moderation in all things," his gaze held hers as if willing her to dig deeper into the meaning behind his words, "but the Chocolate Mousse they serve is out of this world."

Laughter erupted from Cydney's lips and some of her tension eased. "In other words, you can't order dessert if I don't?"

A sheepish smile tilted his lips. His warm hand covered hers. "Something like that, but…I want this to be a treat for you, too."

Her heart tripped, then slammed against her ribs. What was he saying? Daniel didn't waste words. He was up to something, but she couldn't decide what. The touch of his hand sent energy tingling along her arm. Heat filled the cavity around her heart. Need and longing exploded inside her in a giant wave.

Why Daniel? Why now?

At any other time in her life, she would use her brain and worked things out. But with Daniel, her defenses against getting involved melted away. His smile filled her with the need to get closer. His touch turned her body into a mass of desire. And all this without giving her any hint of what he was feeling.

She didn't dare respond. Didn't dare show weakness. The next step meant depending on another person for support and that was her greatest fear.

"I know what you're doing. Go ahead. Say it." She released a dramatic sigh, and moved her hand away from his touch. "You're trying to soften me up so I'll agree to those NASCAR beds, aren't you?"

Emotions flickered over his face…objection, regret, resignation…or a trick of the candle in the middle of the table. He leaned back in his chair and studied her. "You saw right through me, didn't you?"

"Mmmm, maybe," she toyed with the spoon on her saucer, "but after all that shopping, I burned enough energy to make room for extra calories, so you win."

"I wish—"

"Anyone for dessert? Sir? Madam?"

Tearing her gaze from Daniel's, Cydney wished the waiter hadn't arrived until Daniel finished speaking. "I'll have the cheesecake, please."

The waiter turned to Daniel, "And for you, sir?"

"Chocolate Mousse and two coffees, please," Daniel said with his eyes on Cydney. "Where were we?"

"Forget about trying to bribe me, Daniel. It won't work. When the boys are toddlers, you can spoil them with the race-car beds."

"This isn't like our skit at all." Daniel's gaze bored into hers. "If I had known it would be like this, I would have asked you out sooner."

Basking in his smiling glance, her lips tilted. "What makes you think I would have said yes?"

Daniel straightened his tie and threw his shoulders back. "Could you resist?"

Heart thumping so hard it roared in her ears, Cydney tore her gaze from his. "I could...if you didn't love the triplets."

CHAPTER 9

"Do you see a pattern developing here?" Daniel demand-ed an hour later as they stood by Zackary's incubator. They had finished dessert and were waiting for the bill when Dan-iel's beeper alerted them to trouble.

Cydney stared down at the largest triplet. "I'm just glad he's okay. What does GERD stand for, anyway?"

"Gastro esophageal reflux disease," Dr. Morgan answered, coming up behind Cydney in her soft-soled shoes so they hadn't heard her approach. "Sorry to beep you again, but things didn't look good for a few minutes there."

Cydney turned to the neonatologist and blurted. "He seemed fine at our last visit."

"The status of premature infants can turn on a dime." Dr. Morgan said in a weary tone. "His temperature has leveled of, so I gave instructions to proceed with his first bottle feeding." She reached out to touch the infant's foot. "And things didn't go well. Poor little guy."

"What happened?" Cydney resisted the urge to grab Zackary and hide to keep him safe.

"Premature infants often suffer from GERD. Their food comes back up. All infants spit up, but with GERD, it's a more violent reaction when food lodges in their esophagus. As a result, he vomited."

"What happens now?" Daniel touched a tiny toe.

"We treat him for an immature digestive track. Time and medication should help."

"You said that before," Cydney heard her wailing tone over the hum of respirators and tried to reign in her emotions. But she couldn't stop the words and fear from spewing from her lips. After the fun shopping trip, and growing hopes of having the babies home soon, this was a crushing blow. "Now, he has a new problem to face. When does this stop."

"It's unfortunate, but preemies start life at a disadvantage. Complications tend to delay their development." The soft-spoken doctor placed a hand on Cydney's arm. "I assure you, this isn't an uncommon occurrence. But time and growth will improve his situation."

"I wish I could believe—"

"You have to believe." Dr. Morgan insisted. "In this unit, you have to keep faith. These little guys sense emotion. No negative feelings allowed, understand?"

Cydney blinked back tears and focused on the green lines on the monitor. Two hours ago, she had actually enjoyed laughing and teasing with Daniel. Now, they faced this new complication. She should have been here. She should have been the one to give Big Brother his first bottle. "I'm sorry, Dr. Morgan, I—"

"Don't apologize, you're human. This unit is stressful for parents of one infant. You have three babies in here. I'm surprised you're doing as well as you are."

"We don't have a choice, do we?" Daniel put a reassuring hand on Cydney's arm.

"Well, sadly, neither do I," Dr. Morgan sighed. "I may as well prepare you now. We expect this condition to develop in the other two infants when they take their first feeding."

"But, they're so tiny—"

"That's the problem. We'll check on them and keep you posted." She gave a tilt of her head and walked away.

"I should have been here."

"You have to eat." Daniel urged her toward the heavy metal doors, pushed the button on the wall, and waited for the clanging noise as they opened. "You're not superwoman. You need food and rest." The beeper on his belt buzzed. He checked the message. "Sorry, I hate to leave like this, but I have a baby on the way."

Did he?

Cydney plopped down on the sofa where they had spent the night. Did he really have to go? Or was he just so furious with her he wanted to escape? Did he blame her for not being here when Zackary's emergency occurred? She blamed herself. Daniel said she was human, but did he believe that or was he frustrated with her for not being on duty?

Rubbing a hand over her tear filled eyes she stared at the door where he had disappeared. Their evening out had been so much fun. Another reason she felt guilty. Regret filled her with a sense of inadequacy. While she was laughing and feasting on delicious food, poor Zackary was barfing up his first bottle.

A real mother would have been here for him. Unless...that mother was Ziggy.

Cydney bowed her head under the weight of her grief. Thoughts tumbled in her head. Her sister wouldn't have handled NICU very well. She would have said things in here were too sad, too serious.

From the second Daniel walked away from her, Cydney felt flighty as her younger sister. She wanted Daniel close, needed his strength. When had his good opinion started to mean so much to her? How was she going to deal with his displeasure when she applied for custody?

Clutching her arms around her waist, she chewed on her bottom lip. Why did she care what Daniel thought? But she knew why. She had admired his response from the moment he learned of his brother's connection to the triplets.

There were other feelings mixed up with her reaction to Daniel that she couldn't explain. She had guarded against personal relationships to protect herself, so there was no way she would believe in love at first sight. Yet her intense attraction to Daniel was dangerously close to what she thought love would be.

But...what about his feelings? He had teased and flirted with her all during dinner. She started to relax under the effects of his charm. Then his beeper called them to the NICU. Now, Big Brother's emergency was barely over, and Daniel rushed off to respond to his beeper. What if he had been at home with the triplets, who would take care of them while he rushed off to do his *doctoring thing*?

Using the term he disliked gave her a tiny burst of pleasure, but her questions remained. If Daniel retained custody, who would provide care of her precious babies?

Daniel's cell phone rang as he rushed toward the maternity wing.

"Where are you?"

Phil's voice blared in Daniel's ear. "Answering a beep to check on a woman in labor. What's up?"

"We've got problems."

Daniel blew out a sigh. He'd had his fill of trouble over the past three hours. First, the dinner with Cydney went so well he opened his mouth to ask, "*Your place or mine?*" Then his beeper went off, sending them into a frenzy of activity. Just as Zackary leveled off and they were unwinding from the tension, his beeper alerted him to a patient in need of attention.

Was the Zackary's emergency a blessing or a curse? He wanted to be there for the baby, but if his beeper hadn't sounded, Cydney might be in his arms right now. Fingers pinching the bridge of his nose, he blew out a breath. "What's wrong?"

"Your DNA results are back."

"They're Cydney's DNA results. Why are you calling me?"

"To put you on alert. It's confirmed. She is the aunt."

"I knew she was."

"And...she wants custody."

"She wants joint custody. She told me—"

"I warned you." Phil disconnected.

With an impatient sigh, Daniel stuffed the phone in his pocket. Phil was wrong. Cydney trusted him. She told him so. What had changed in the last few hours? Why make waves, now? They needed to stick together to get around this judge. If the beeper hadn't interrupted, things might be different. They might be rolling around on his sheets. The image of Cydney in his bed almost knocked him off his feet. He wanted to hold her in his arms, feel her skin next to his. But he wanted more.

He wanted…his breath escaped in a harsh sound…he wanted Cydney. Not just as a temporary fix to care for the infants. He wanted forever with her. But each time he came close to telling her, some baby duty interrupted.

He felt as exhausted as a real parent might.

His beeper buzzed.

He checked the message, whirled on his heel and headed back to the delivery room. This was his life. It was why he had become a doctor. What had he expected?

"Class, our topic tonight is Family History and The New Infant." Sharon Vance nodded to the power point slide enlarged on the screen behind her. "It's late in the scheme of things to discuss this information after birth, but the sad fact is, most couples don't give family health history a thought until they have a baby in their arms. So, here we go."

After a short presentation, Sharon pulled out her beeper. "Sorry, class. Nursing duty calls. I need to take this. We'll have a short break."

Daniel waited until the instructor left the room before turning to Cydney. Her vanilla scent was very refreshing after hours breathing the odor of antiseptics. "Sorry I missed you in NICU. I had four babies today."

"Poor you," she quipped without meeting his eyes.

The exhaustion, laying heavy on his shoulders seemed to lift. Being with Cydney was like basking in a ray of sunshine. Her teasing words were a shot of springtime. He'd never connected with a woman on this level. Usually, women wanted admiration and a man melting under the heat of their sex appeal. They weren't interested in humor. Intelligence. Caring. The change was refreshing and to him Cydney seemed perfect.

"Four boys. All singles. I'm beat." He added a dramatic slouch to emphasize his words.

"We don't have to stay for the rest of class if you don't want to."

Daniel noted the couples moving in and out of the room and considered her suggestion. Her response was another example of how she cared for others. This time, his sigh came all the way from his aching feet.

"It's my responsibility. I need to set a good example for the rest of the parents. If a doctor can't be bothered to take the classes, why should they?"

"Is that all the triplets mean to you, Daniel? A responsibility?"

He couldn't lie to her. She was too smart. "At first, when I heard of Greg's death, the answer to that question was yes, but not now."

Her stare bored into his face, studying every line, every flicker of his eyes. "I hope you're telling the truth. I need to believe you're here for the sake of the triplets."

Daniel pushed out of his seat, reached for her arm. Lifting her to her feet, he steered her to a corner of the room so they would have privacy. His jaw clenched so hard he could hear his teeth grind, but this had to stop. He sucked in a breath and looked deep in her eyes.

"If I don't care about them, why do you think I'm here? Why did I spend nights sitting in NICU when I could have been at home sleeping in my own bed? I love those babies. And not just because they're Greg's children. That's part of it, of course, but after a few days, they became real. I care what happens to them."

Cydney crossed her arms over her chest and refused to meet his eyes.

"You don't believe me? Ask Phil. I told him to put them in

my will the day after they were born."

"Why?" Hands on her hips, breasts heaving, she glared at him. "Why on earth would you do that? They're not your babies. You didn't even know—"

Daniel's head reared back. As one of the top doctors in a major hospital, he wasn't used to being told he was incompetent. "I knew. I had Phil check." Too late, he heard his admission, but he refused to back down.

"S-so, you didn't believe…that first night…it was all pretend?" she sputtered.

Could her eyebrows arch any higher? Daniel could see the wheels turning in her head. He would regret that slip up before this was over, but she would find out sometime. Lowering his head until his nose almost touched hers, he said. "I used my head. I checked facts. It's my responsibility."

"You checked on Ziggy's background, didn't you?"

"In my shoes, you would have done the same thing. I owed it to those babies to find out the facts. They deserve to know the truth about their real family. They needed a health history, if nothing else. Can't you see that?" His nostrils quivered as he inhaled. He had never seen eyes as green or as beautiful as Cydney's.

"Now you're quoting the instructor." Cydney leaned toward him. If he had been her height, she would butt noses with him. "What's the real reason?"

Knocked back on his heels by her bluntness, Daniel reached the end of his patience. His day had gone downhill from the start. Why expect things to change now? Forcing words through gritted teeth, he said. "I didn't know your sister from Adam…or Eve. What would you expect me to do?"

Rolling her eyes, her toe tapping the floor so hard he eased his foot out of the way, she spewed a response. "Just because you have a lawyer willing to invade my family's privacy, doesn't make it right."

"For all I knew, the mother of Greg's babies could have been on drugs, or been suffering from a serious disease. I had to find out."

"Admit it, Daniel. I know it's what you're thinking. Ziggy might not have been good enough for your precious Greg." Eyes shooting sparks she stepped so close she landed on his toe, but she didn't back away. "What does that say about your brother's choice of companions? Should I have him investigated since he's the father?"

"This was for the triplets—"

"Of course, it was." Cydney sniffed disapproval. "They deserve the truth about their parents. But I don't believe that's the reason you investigated Ziggy. For that matter, I'm surprised you didn't have me checked out, too."

Daniel clenched his jaw and watched deep green sparks shoot from her eyes. "I—"

Cydney expelled a startled gasp and stepped back as if she had just learned he had a deadly communicable disease. "You had me investigated, didn't you?"

Daniel's face froze. "You were a stranger. You wanted custody of the triplets. What did you expect me to do? You would have done the same thing."

Color drained from her face, leaving her skin ghostly white. Her chin lifted at the stubborn angle he found so charming. But she wasn't charmed. Her eyes bored holes through him. "It doesn't matter. I don't have anything to hide."

"You think I was wrong? You're one of those people, who think they never make mistakes, aren't you?" If possible, she lost even more color. Daniel inhaled a deep breath and clenched his teeth. He hadn't meant to come across so strong.

Cydney flinched at hearing the familiar accusation. It was Ziggy's trump card. Anytime she acted irresponsibly, she always wiggled out of the situation by accusing Cydney of trying to be perfect.

"I never said that. My mother took my father back several times. Ziggy used up more second chances than I can count." Her chin angled higher. Her eyes glittered suspiciously. "I understand better than you think, Daniel Prince." She stabbed a finger in his chest with each word. "Pride drove you to find the truth. But what do you have now?"

"Class," pausing in the doorway Sharon Vance clapped her hands to gain their attention, "shall we continue? Please take your seats."

Daniel reached for Cydney's arm to steer her back to their seats. "I am not in the mood for this."

Slouching in the chair beside him Cydney crossed her arms over her chest and sent him a sideway glance. "But you'll stay until class is dismissed."

"What makes you so sure?" He demanded. "Ah, you're referring to what I said earlier."

Shrugging, she stared at him. "You'll stay because you never shirk your duty."

Daniel inhaled a startled breath. *Women. If he had his way...*

"Class, since we're short of time I'm going to condense the last activity." Sharon Vance glanced around the room. "Your new baby needs to feel connected to family from day one. Start while the baby is young. Show them photographs of extended family members. Tell them family stories." She paused until the outburst of laughter ceased. "To get you in practice, turn the chairs until you're facing each other. This time the Dads go first. Tell your partner the worst event you can remember from your past."

Daniel clenched his jaw and pulled in a deep breath. *He'd just had the encounter with Cydney, and now this*? Why had he agreed to attend this class?

"Don't stall, class. You have two minutes."

Fine. He could do this. After all, she was the triplets' aunt.

"My father was a powerful senator. One holiday he couldn't come home because of work." Spine rigid, Daniel inhaled. "Later that night he was killed in a car accident." He forced his gaze to meet hers. "He was miles from D.C. and his beautiful young aide died in the car with him. I was fourteen. I learned the truth about my father when I watched the news. Family time never seemed important to him. We hardly saw him. After learning the truth, I swore I would spend my life restoring honor to my family's name."

"Cut." The instructor called in her perky voice. "Now the ladies, you have two minutes."

Cydney twisted her hands in her lap and stared at the strain on his face. Finally, inhaling a deep breath, she spoke in a low voice that Daniel had to lean close to hear.

"After my parents' divorced," she cleared her throat and forced words past the cotton like dryness in her throat, "my mother chased every man she met. It didn't matter if we liked them or not. She only thought of having fun. I was six, but she left me to look after Ziggy. That's when I realized…if I ever wanted to feel safe…I had to learn to take care of myself."

"This is it, boys and girls." Phil ushered Cydney and Daniel to the defendant's table, and turned his stern, attorney glare on each of them he enunciated each word clearly. "It's today or never."

"My DNA test is positive." Cydney lifted her chin and met his x-ray glare. "We're the triplets' aunt and uncle. Why is there a problem?"

Phil shrugged as he meticulously placed his briefcase on the table. He snapped the locks, lifted the lid and extracted folders and a yellow legal pad. Why is he stalling? Cydney's chest tightened. Endless possibilities raced through her head and she almost missed his response.

"This court is funny about placing children. But don't worry. I have your DNA results right here."

Cydney whirled to Daniel. "You already knew? Why didn't you say something when I told you last night after class?"

Daniel lifted a shoulder and glanced around the courtroom. "Exhaustion, I guess."

And I cried myself to sleep last night thinking about your dad dying in the company of his beautiful aide, and how hurt you must have been.

She sat there, staring as if Daniel had sprouted horns, unsure of how to reply. Had their heated exchange in class put this distance between them? Or was it Zackary's emergency, and her being out to dinner?

"All stand."

Her thoughts muddled from lack of sleep and Daniel's behavior, Cydney pushed to her feet. Would he take the triplets away from her? Should she agree with the custody issue?

Too late. It was obvious the decision was out of her hands. Her butt had barely touched the chair when the judge launched his attack. "These documents clearly state the two people requesting custody of the triplets are strangers to each other. Am I to believe what I read?"

"That's true, Your Honor, but since the accident, Ms. Eller and Dr. Prince have become well acquainted. They are both responsible professionals, determined to take care of these infants."

The judge stared at Cydney and Daniel. "You understand we are not talking about three dolls, here. These infants are premature and demand extra care. My sources inform me that premature infants usually lag behind in developmental issues. Are you both aware of that fact? Can you handle these issues and make the best possible decisions for their care?"

"Your Honor, Dr. Prince is well versed in the development of infants. And no one can dispute Ms. Eller's dedication to her sister's infants."

"That's all well and good, Mr. Lawrence, but I want to hear from the defendants. Bailiff, swear them in at the table."

Cydney and Daniel took turns taking the oath.

"Ms. Eller," the Judge glanced down at his notes, "how do you feel about the infants being slow in their mental and physical development?"

"They survived the accident, Your Honor. I'm just happy they're alive."

"Mmm," the judge mumbled as he rubbed his chin and stared over the top of his glasses. After long seconds, he turned to Daniel. "Dr. Prince, the neonatologist explained that preemies usually catch up by the time they start to school. Are you okay with that rate of development?"

"I agree with Ms. Eller, Your Honor. We are fortunate the triplets didn't die in the crash with their parents. We can handle any developmental issues they might have."

"I call that a politically correct response, but I wonder. The information I have states that you are both single. Is this true?"

"That is correct, Your Honor, both of my clients are unattached at the moment." Phil rushed to respond as he sent them a warning glance. "But that will not be an issue."

"That situation can cause tension. What if one of them becomes interested in a third party, how will that affect the triplets?"

"Your Honor," Daniel's voice rang clear in the rumbling noise of the courtroom. "With three infants to take care of, I don't foresee having the time or energy to connect with a third party."

"Are you speaking for Ms. Eller as well, Dr. Prince?" The judge waved a hand. "What about her biological clock? It's ticking by the minute and Ms. Eller might want children of her own."

Face burning from dozens of scorching eyes aimed at her back, Cydney forced words past dry lips. "Three babies are enough, I'm not concerned about having more children, Your Honor."

"Ummm, you both have careers, I see. Will your jobs allow time to provide the care for three premature infants?"

"Your Honor," Daniel's voice rang with sincerity, "if these were our biological children, we would manage to care for them without the court's involvement. Why is it an issue if the infants in question are our niece and nephews?"

The judge slammed his hand on the desk. "Because these infants are not your biological children, Dr. Prince, and as such, they could be mistreated."

Phil jumped to respond, sending Daniel a warning glare. "Your Honor—"

"It says here neither of you have any experience with children."

"We are currently taking parenting classes at the hospital, Your Honor." Daniel replied in his best authoritative tone.

"I see...so, Ms. Eller...after taking these parenting classes, what kind of father do you think Dr. Prince will make?"

Shocked by the question, Cydney turned to gaze at Daniel. *This was her chance.* If she wanted to appeal for custody, this was perfect timing. Phil had cautioned her against attempting such a move. He insisted they should appear united. But…

Cydney cleared her throat. "I think the triplets are lucky to have Dr. Prince fill the role of father. He loves his brother's children."

"Well. I don't like it." The judge reared back in his chair and glared at them over the top of his glasses. "I see problems cropping up from day one. Dr. Prince, you need a wife."

Cydney, Daniel, and Phil gasped in unison at the bluntness of judge's words.

With a quick glance in their direction, Phil replied, "Your Honor—"

"Two single adults with premature triplets is too much. The strain will cause trouble in no time. In good conscience, I can not give custody of these infants to Dr. Prince—"

"Your Honor—"

"Therefore, considering this is a multiple birth, I'm granting joint custody to Ms. Eller and Dr. Prince. And I had better not see either of you back in this court on the matter of these infants. Next."

⚏

Well, she had her answer. She wouldn't have been granted sole custody if she'd ignored Phil's warning and appealed to the judge. If the judge wouldn't grant custody to a doctor, she didn't have a hope. All she could do now was…

After rushing them out of the courtroom and past reporters filling the hallway, Phil stopped at the top of the courthouse steps. "You won, Daniel. Congratulations."

"I don't call that a win." Daniel shook the hand Phil offered. "What happens next?"

"The documents you sighed gives you joint legal guardianship. If visiting rights become an issue, we have to come back to court. But you heard the judge. Don't let that happen. Gotta run. Happy Parenting, Folks."

"Visiting rights?" Daniel's voice was heavy with dread as he dropped to a park bench at the bottom of the courthouse steps. An enormous oak tree shaded the sidewalks and allowed a clear view of Phil as he darted across the street to the parking garage.

Careful not to touch Daniel, Cydney sat down beside him. She heard the distant sound of traffic as she waited by his side.

"I hadn't thought about visiting rights." Daniel could hardly force words past his lips.

"Why would you? Until now, you've had custody." She glanced at him out of the corner of her eye. "You didn't want joint custody did you?"

Daniel ran a hand through his hair. "It's not about you. I want to take care of my brother's kids. Give them the family name and keep them safe. I didn't think any further than that."

Cydney jumped up and paced on the sidewalk in front of him. "I'm okay with the triplets being named Prince. Family ties are important. But, I am part of their family, Daniel. Don't try to shut me out."

"I wouldn't—"

"You nearly did, maybe not intentionally, but you almost succeeded."

"What are you talking about? From day one, I shared my attorney with you. I even arranged for you get a second DNA test to prove your claims of a family connection."

"Yes, you did but Phil is *your* attorney. If I hadn't paid extra, my DNA results wouldn't have returned in time for this hearing. Then what? Your attorney would have requested the judge give you full custody of the infants."

"We've been through all this, Cydney." His patient tone was almost as maddening as his obvious disappointment. "We planned this together. You agreed for me to have custody" Daniel settled back on the bench and crossed his arms over his chest. "If your test results returned late, we could have gone back to court to ask for a joint agreement."

"You really expect me to believe that, don't you?" Cydney kicked the leg of the bench, then winced at the pain shooting through her foot.

"We're wasting time arguing about this." Daniel motioned for her to sit. "It's time to make plans. We still have to please the judge's representative when he comes to check us out."

"What plans? I thought you and Phil had everything worked out."

"I'm not talking about legal issues. I mean living arrangements. When the triplets are discharged from the hospital they'll need more things than we bought the other night." Daniel whistled tunelessly through his teeth and stared into the distance. "We need to check into hiring a nanny, for starters. And you need to think about moving in before then."

"Move in your house?" Her voice rose to a screech. "Why? I like my apartment."

"I have the space and a housekeeper. And my house is convenient to the hospital in case of emergencies." Daniel noticed her startled expression and rushed on. "You heard the judge. He thinks three infants are too much for one person. So it just makes sense to join forces. We'll make a schedule. This can work."

"I've been thinking about what the judge said." Cydney watched a pigeon approach. "What if you decide to get married? I'm not sure I want another woman taking control of the triplets. They're my family. Not some stranger's guilt trip."

"I could say the same, you know." Daniel leaned closer and forced her to meet his eyes as he spoke. "Look. Together we can make this work. Alone, we're sunk."

"Well, that sure sounds like an emergency plan." She leaned back against the bench and sighed. "I want my life to count for more than a last ditch effort."

"I agree, but I'm playing the cards we were dealt. We both lost our only sibling in that accident. Their kids need us. It makes sense to form a team."

"Everything you say is true." She stared at the ground. "But the judge was right. I hadn't thought about my biological clock, but now that he wiped our faces with the issue, I...think I would like to have children of my own. The triplets make me want to be a real mother."

"Cydney, this isn't the time to panic. We don't have time for games, or talk about biological clocks." Daniel paused at the sound of his beeper.

Cydney shot to her feet, ready to run.

He pulled the beeper out of his pocket and read the alert. "Calm down, it's a patient. A woman in labor, but this discussion is not over. Think about it. How can either of us handle the triplets on our own? What if one baby chokes or has some other health emergency, what happens to the other two when you need to rush to the hospital?" Wouldn't you want another adult around to help?

CHAPTER 10

What had she done?

Thirty minutes later, waiting outside the NICU for the next visiting hours, Daniel's words whirled in head. Cooperating with Daniel since the accident had thrown her off guard. She was so used to having Daniel at her side she had started depending on him. Sharing with him. Wanting to be with him.

Just as the judge said, three infants were too much for one person. But unlike the judge, Cydney didn't want the triplets split up and sent to social services. That meant considering Daniel's suggestion. It made sense. They should move in together for the sake of the triplets.

But, if she moved in with Daniel, her life would be over. Considering her reactions to him, she would never want to leave. She'd be stuck in limbo. A live-in, but not a girlfriend and not hired help. Daniel was right about what he told the judge, as well. With triplets to look after, there would be no time for a personal life for either of them.

Daniel would start to take her for granted. The sparks between them these past few days needed fanning if she wanted a flame. But that couldn't happen if she was under his roof all the time.

She watched Donna go through pregnancies and caring for newborns. Romance took a back seat to the demands of the baby. She had witnessed it with her own eyes and Donna only had one infant at a time.

Spending time in NICU showed her how difficult this stage of adjustment really was. How could romance exist with three babies crying for bottles or clean diapers, or worse, three infants with colic? Choking? Apnea? Nope. She couldn't do it. She liked Daniel too much to end up avoiding him so she could have a few minutes of peace and quiet.

Donna and Charlie were desperately in love but their relationship crumbled under the strain of new babies. She and Daniel barely knew one another. She couldn't ruin their friendship. They owed it to the triplets to stick together.

The judge's comment about Daniel's attraction to a third party, and needing a wife, almost ripped her guts out. If their only connection was going to be caring for the triplets, she needed her own space. That meant keeping her apartment.

Daniel's attitude at the last class said it all. He would do anything to take care of those infants. She admired his attitude, but part of her ached over his decision. Daniel was a rare specimen. He wore responsibility like a suit of armor, and she knew him well enough to realize he would sacrifice his personal life for the triplets.

If that meant welcoming Cydney into his home and into the triplets' lives…he would. To Daniel she was part of the package that came with the babies.

She swallowed the tears running down the back of her throat. That kind of relationship described her life. She was tired of being taken for granted. She wanted more out of life. She wanted…she wanted a man who loved her with his whole heart, a man who wanted to have babies with her.

Daniel couldn't be that man. He wouldn't allow his sense of duty to weaken. Even if he said the words, said he cared for her…she would never know for sure he would feel the same without the triplets. Did that make her selfish?

No, it meant she was using her brain. She loved the triplets, but she was in danger of falling in love with Daniel, too, and he deserved better.

Daniel deserved a woman who could lean on him and appreciate his need to protect. She admired the responsible side of his nature. But she could not let herself depend on another person when she was capable of taking care of herself.

⚙

Daniel stalked through the door to the NICU waiting room and tried to appear calm. He spotted Cydney, sitting rigid and staring at the wall, as she waited for visiting hours. He walked to her side.

"Good, I arrived in time. I was afraid I'd be late." He didn't tell her he had run through the hospital corridors like a madman. More than one nurse had called him down, before noticing he was one of the staff, then asking if he needed help for an emergency.

But Cydney was the only one who could help him. It was almost a joke, him needing help.

"Still a few minutes to go," she replied in a stilted tone.

Daniel covered a sigh of regret and shifted for a more comfortable position in his chair. He hadn't handled their last encounter very well. The judge's comments had thrown him off guard. How had the judge imagined anyone would take custody of three babies if they didn't want the best for them? Then to go as far as to suggest Daniel needed a wife?

"I can't believe that judge doubted our intentions."

Cydney turned her head. "I guess he sees a lot of different situations in his courtroom."

"Yeah, but most custody cases have something to do with a conflict over money."

Brow wrinkled, she met his gaze for the first time. "Not this case."

Daniel noticed her red streaked eyes. A rush of need filled his chest. He wanted to put his arms around her and tell her everything would work out, but he couldn't. Cydney would reject his offer of comfort. After his actions the last twenty-four hours, he couldn't blame her.

"If the triplets had an inheritance, I could understand the judge doubting our intentions. But we aren't asking for anything but a chance to take care for our family. I don't get it."

Cydney turned tired eyes on him. "Maybe the judge really cares about what happens."

"Why are you agreeing with the judge all of a sudden?"

Her shoulders hunched. "His comments about third parties made me wonder if we're fooling ourselves and ignoring reality. He was pretty blunt about you needing a wife."

"No matter what happens, I promise I will put the triplets first."

"Save your promises, Daniel." Cydney said with a resigned sigh as she stood and moved with other visitors toward the nursery door. "I've been a stepchild. I know relationships don't always work."

❧

Daniel held Gregory against his shoulder with one hand. The baby had gained five ounces, but the palm of his hand covered the infant's back. Resting his chin on one little arm, he closed his eyes in silent prayer. He couldn't lose the infants after fighting to pull them through. Some days he was so exhausted from worry, he felt as if he were fighting a physical battle.

How could Cydney believe he wouldn't protect the infants? *Because she didn't know him.* He turned his head just enough to watch her out of the corner of his eye. She held Cece as if the baby girl would break. He wished things were different. Cydney didn't believe him because she didn't know the facts, but she loved the triplets as much as he did. How could he reassure her?

If offering her a home hadn't been such a blunder, he might have had a chance. For the life of him, he couldn't figure out how he had gone wrong by asking Cydney to move in. Having the triplets and Cydney under his roof would make things so much easier. He could check on the babies constantly. Anything they needed, he could provide. When he went to bed at night, he would know where they were. Know they were safe.

If they weren't under his roof, he would worry. Wrinkles creased his brow. Was that his mistake? Did Cydney think he didn't trust her to care for the infants? *Did he?*

Daniel brushed his chin against Gregory's little arm, amazed at the feel of the smooth, soft baby skin. Baby powder and the hint of formula filled his nostrils. He longed to provide a secure home for these infants.

It wouldn't be easy. Babies didn't always emit this sweet odor. They could carry the strong scent of spit-up and dirty diapers. They could scream and cry instead of snuggle under his chin. Even a secure family life couldn't smooth out all the issues.

But the fierce need to protect the infants, held him in a tight grip. He had experienced this feeling since he delivered these infants. But now his instinct was stronger, more urgent. This time, he realized he could lose all he hoped for if he didn't make changes fast. He couldn't take over and ignore Cydney's needs and wishes. He tried that tactic when they left the courthouse.

He asked her to move into his home, but his plan didn't work. She must know he considered her part of the triplets' lives? Expelling a sigh, he examined what he had overlooked. For things to work, he needed to consider Cydney's expectations and dreams.

How in hell was he going to do that?

***

"Kangrooing the big boy, I see." Dr. Morgan appeared at Cydney's shoulder and looked down with a smile. "He's doing better. Almost no yellow tint to his skin and his weight is up a few ounces, even with GERD."

"Is he back to his birth weight?" Cydney looked over what still felt like a tiny body and snuggled Zackary under her chin as the doctor check his chart.

"Almost. With his fever back to normal, I suspect he will take off like a weed. We could be sending him home before long."

"Oh, good," Cydney's voice caught on a sob.

Take the baby home? Where? Who?

Would Daniel insist on taking the infant to his house? Or would he agree for her to take Zackary? And even if he did, how would she manage? Her apartment was perfect for her, but it was too small to add three infants. She called a realtor, but she'd thought she had more time.

"Without added complications, two more weeks should see a vast change in all three infants." Dr. Morgan offered. "That puts them at thirty-six weeks, a reasonable age for preemies to go home."

Cydney was conscious of Daniel standing behind her. The air crackled with new energy. Her body flashed hot, then cold, leaving her weak.

He'd invited her to move into his home!

He was holding Baby Girl, but he loomed large next to all the tiny infants. A whiff of his aftershave sent a jolt of response straight to her mid-section. Her muscles tensed. The heat of Daniel's body mingled with her growing desire and added to her awareness to his presence.

But she forced her attention to the infant in her arms and tried to ignore thoughts and feelings Daniel stirred in her. As if she could ignore him. She felt Daniel's presence even with the warmth of the infant in her arms. Nerves in her abdomen clenched. This had to stop. She couldn't react to every move he made. If they were going to make joint custody work, she had to keep her distance from him as much as possible. *Starting now.*

"I-I've been thinking about the triplets being discharged, Dr. Morgan. I wonder if you could recommend a pediatrician on the other side of town."

Forehead wrinkled, Dr. Morgan glanced at Daniel then looked back at Cydney. She opened mouth. Then closed it.

Cydney heard Daniel's loud intake of breath behind her, and face warm, nerves jangling, she lifted her chin and met the doctor's stare.

"Do you want a second opinion on the babies' condition?" Dr. Morgan sounded confused as she glanced at Daniel again. For long seconds they exchanged looks.

I don't blame her for being shocked, Cydney conceded. With Dr. Morgan's care, the infants were improving. All three had symptoms of GERD, but so far nothing serious, thanks to the doctor's keen watch. But she made the request so she could take care of issues on her own, and not depend on Daniel. Drawing a deep breath, she said. "You're doing great job, but I live on the other side of town."

"Dr. Morgan has a practice near the hospital." Daniel explained in a firm tone. "She can see the babies after they're discharged."

Cydney heard the warning in his words. But she couldn't risk looking at him. The sight of his broad shoulders and melting eyes would cloud her judgment. She had thought about this during the long hours in the waiting room.

"I know it isn't that far, but in an emergency, it might be better to have a doctor close to home. That's why I asked." Cydney watched Dr. Morgan exchange another glance with Daniel.

Great! Just great! They left her out because she didn't speak this silent "doctor" lingo.

Had her question broken some unwritten rule or breeched some doctors' code of honor? All she wanted was a chance to take care of her sister's infants. Much as she respected Daniel, he wouldn't give her that opportunity if he had his way. His protective instinct would interfere. "I'm worried about trying to get through traffic in case of an emergency."

"I want Dr. Morgan to continue as the triplets, physician."

"Of course, I'm happy to recommend someone." Dr. Morgan said, proving she and Daniel were on the same page.

That was part of the problem.

Cydney didn't think like a doctor, or speak the medical language. And Daniel should have noticed by now she had strong protective urges of her own. Obviously, she should have asked Dr. Morgan this question when Daniel wasn't around. But that wouldn't seem right. He needed warning about her intentions. Like him, she took responsibility for the triplets seriously.

"I was thinking about emergencies." Cydney repeated, her face burning.

"If you're sure," Dr. Morgan said, her questioning glance returned to Daniel.

"If we have an emergency, I want Dr. Morgan to take care of the infants." Daniel's insistent tone cut Cydney to the quick. He was good at giving advice, but he wouldn't take it, himself.

"Of course I do, if I can get to her in time." Chin high, Cydney met his glare. "I'm trying to be prepared."

She expected objections from Daniel. But she was already under his influence. All the instructors of the classes they had taken, all the nurses in NICU and Dr. Morgan, turned to Daniel as the one in charge of the infants. As if he were the only person making decisions. It was enough to make her teeth grind. The triplets were her sister's children. She could take care of them.

She would take care of them.

Big Brother started to wiggle and complain. Cydney gulped air in her lungs and tried to calm down. Making the infant cry was going to prove the staff's point, not hers. Did she even know her point?

Was she acting like the guilty dog, barking because someone stepped on her tail, when nothing was wrong? Maybe Daniel wasn't trying to over-rule her opinions. Hadn't she learned anything from dealing with Ziggy? Could she share responsibility with Daniel and make things work?

Of course she could.

Could he? That question blared in her head.

"Time's up. I'll take him, now." The nurse lifted Zackary from Cydney's shoulder, making her feel they were all siding against her. "Have you noticed how he's growing?"

"He still seems small." Cydney stood by the incubator as the nurse placed the largest triplet inside and felt Daniel's glare bore into her back. They were adults. They could work together and share responsibilities. She was sure he would agree if it came down to the line.

But…she…had issues.

She faced problems if she tried to take care of the triplets. Doubts filled her head. She had been fine until the judge mentioned Daniel needing a wife, and the issues they faced getting involved with a third party.

She could handle taking turns with Daniel in caring for the triplets. She trusted Daniel, so depending on him for shared childcare wasn't a big leap. She could deal with a partnership. But when the judge hinted that Daniel might fall in love with another woman, reality had crashed down.

She loved him.

In her way, on her terms, she loved him, and her feelings for him came as a shock. She had thought her reactions were the aftermath of grief over losing her sister. But when the judge said they might find other love interests and put the triplets' care in jeopardy, her heart crashed against her ribs. Reality hit.

Daniel in love with someone else?

How could she deal with seeing him, talking to him, share information about the triplets with him, knowing he loved another woman? Divorced couples did it every day. But divorce usually meant a couple had once loved each other, and had fallen out of love. That wasn't her case at all.

She wanted to love Daniel. Wanted to tell him she cared, but she couldn't let go her need to be independent. Her past, his past, it didn't matter. She was tied in knots over her feelings for him, and the worst part was…she couldn't tell him how confused she felt.

"He's not all that small, are you big boy?" The nurse cooed to the baby. "He'll soon be ready to go home and need clothes."

"How soon do you think?" Daniel asked from near Cydney's shoulder.

She could feel the heat from his body and his anger. The sound of his gruff voice raked her nerves, sending shock waves over her limbs. Fog clouded her brain.

"I'm not sure. You need to ask Dr. Morgan." The nurse returned cautiously.

"We need to talk." Daniel touched Cydney's arm.

It was all she could do the keep from flinching away from his touch. Talk? He wanted to talk? Daniel wanted his way, period. She could not give in to him. The triplets' safety counted on her being strong. Her heart needed protection.

Swallowing, she said. "Okay," and checked her watch, "I have a minute."

🚚

"What's the rush?" Daniel fought to keep his voice calm as he steered Cydney out the metal doors of the NICU. It wasn't easy. Her pinched expression sent pain shooting through his chest. The warmth of her arm under his touch, sent waves of need zinging to parts of his body that didn't care if he was in public or not.

"I have an appointment with a realtor."

"Why? If you're relocating, why not move in with me?" He wouldn't get any sleep at night, knowing she was in a room down the hall. How could he rest when she filled his mind? Did she talk in her sleep? Wear pajamas or slinky gowns, or maybe she slept in the nude. He coughed to hide a choking noise as he punched the elevator button.

"You have time for coffee, don't you?" He needed a cold shower, not more stimulant from caffeine.

Cydney turned eyes as green as jewels on him. "I'm sorry. It's later that I thought. I can't miss this appointment."

"Right, we'll talk later." Was she so desperate to get away from him she couldn't spare time for one cup of coffee? He kept his face expressionless as she walked away.

What? She wouldn't even ride the elevator with him?

A lump of fear the size of a gall bladder clogged his throat. He had done it now. Pushing too hard had sent Cydney fleeing. Her retreat meant he had lost control, not just of the triplets, but his life.

How had this happened?

He was trained to manage emergencies. How had he managed this disaster?

Hadn't he learned anything from his parents?

Daniel stalked off the elevator and headed for the delivery unit. His father put desire before family and honor. That wasn't an option in Daniel's opinion, but his ole man had seen what he wanted and taken the risk. His mother wasn't the traditional mother figure, but she had learned a lesson he could follow. *Don't show you care.*

Daniel stopped at the nurse's station. "How is Mrs. Winters?"

"She's still in pain, Doctor."

"Is she on the IV drip?"

"Yes, we followed your instructions. But she hasn't stopped complaining."

"Low pain threshold or needing attention?"

The nurse shook her head. "Hard to say. We considered both possibilities."

Daniel made a notation in the chart and nodded. "I'll check."

Snapping the ballpoint pen in his fingers repeatedly, he made his way to Janice Winter's room. Something about this patient reminded him of his mother. Ms. Winters had suffered long hours of labor, and a breach birth. But since the delivery, her concerns were about her condition, rather than how her infant was doing.

Flashes of memory from his childhood nagged at Daniel each time he saw this patient. Nothing had stopped his mother from attending functions with his father. If he or Greg were sick, she left their care to the nanny. Her lack of motherly love had bothered him for years. Was his patient the same?

"Ah, Mrs. Winters, how are you today?" Daniel forced a cheerful note to his voice as he approached the bed.

A sad faced man stepped away from the window. Daniel noticed the lack of expression on his patient's face, then turned back to the man and offered his hand. "Sorry, I didn't realize you had company. I'm Dr. Prince."

The man's slim shoulders sagged as he stepped toward Daniel and took his hand. "Rick Winters. My wife says she's not well enough to go home."

Daniel pursed his lips as he studied the patient. Mr. Winters hadn't attended any prenatal appointments with his wife. Nor was he present for the birth of their child. Maybe there was a reason for Ms. Winters' lack of healing, but he wouldn't rule out physical issues. "She had a rough time with the delivery."

When he left ten minutes later, Daniel made a note on his chart for Ms. Winters to remain bedridden. What he had thought was selfishness on his patient's part was something much deeper. *The need to survive.*

In the short time he was in the room, he learned the Winters were taking care of Mr. Winter's elderly mother. Even without being told, Daniel could guess that caring for the elderly woman was exhausting.

Ms. Winters wasn't faking her discomfort. She was struggling to survive. Added to that, he found signs of infection when he examined her. This patient realized the need to be in good shape when she went home so she could protect her new infant.

Suddenly, he stopped writing on the chart and his hand froze midair. As a child, he remembered seeing the same expression in his mother's eyes that he had just seen in his patient's eyes. *Could it be?* Had he missed the clues all this time? His mother hadn't been shirking her motherly duties. She was trying to hold her marriage and her family together. Even that far back she had known about his father's cheating.

Rubbing a thumb across his chin, Daniel recalled the painful events leading up to his father's death. His mother's cool reserve had been her protective shield. She had pushed him and Greg away to protect them from her pain.

New appreciation for his mother's determined nature filled his head as he answered his pager. His mother risked everything to hold on to the husband she loved. She even pushed her children away, and risked losing their affection, in her effort to save her marriage to their father.

All this time, he'd had it wrong. What had he done?

He checked on the new patient while his brain flashed warning signals. All this time he had held on to his mistaken beliefs and his need to be in control.

"You dilated four centimeters, Mrs. Crowder. Things will get exciting when you reach ten. Mr. Crowder, remind her to breathe."

As he left the patient, his thoughts jumped to Cydney. Considering his new insight, did he dare risk everything and tell her how he felt? He took chances on the job and saved patients with his willingness to try new techniques. Did he have the courage to take the same risks with his feelings for Cydney? Could he let go his control and share his worries with her?

❧

"I've changed my mind about the area I'm interested in." Cydney turned to the realtor after rejecting several options. She had made a decision. Since she needed to move anyway, she would meet Daniel halfway. If she found an apartment on his side of town, she wouldn't need to change doctors.

That option posed several disadvantages. Driving to work would take longer. But what troubled her most was moving closer to Daniel. It would be so easy to call on him for help if she lived near him. As the realtor checked listings in the new location, Cydney wondered if she was doing the right thing. If she moved closer, would Daniel take her for granted? Would he second-guess her decisions?

As the realtor drove to a possible site, Cydney fought the urge to change her mind again. But visions of Daniel holding Big Brother played through her head. The memory of one tiny dimpled chin, showing promise of looking identical to Daniel's chin, kept her from losing her courage.

She and Daniel deserved an equal chance to know these babies. If she took the risk and moved near Daniel, their shared custody would be easier. She'd to fight becoming dependent on Daniel.

She inspected four apartments and ticked the scorecard the realtor gave her. "I have to leave. But I want to see number two and four next time."

After arranging another appointment, Cydney hurried to her car. It was twenty minutes before the next visiting hours, but the realtor's office was across town, and traffic was heavy. The drive left her with time to think…when she wasn't growling under her breath. Thank goodness, she had changed her mind at the last minute and decided to relocate to Daniel's side of town. Rushing a sick infant to the doctor's office would be a nightmare in this traffic.

But she arrived at the hospital for visiting hours…*this time.*

"How does Gregory like kangaroo care?"

Startled, Cydney looked up and smiled. "Dr. Morgan, I didn't expect to see you this time of day." Then fear wiped the smile from her face. "I-is anything wrong? Are the triplets—"

"Everything's fine. Sorry, I didn't mean to frighten you." Dr. Morgan checked Gregory's chart. "Actually, I made a point of being here because I wanted to talk to you."

"Oh?" Cydney clutched the infant tighter. "W-what's wrong?"

"I'll be honest. I knew Daniel was on a call and we'd have a chance to talk. I realize I focus on him during updates on the babies because…well, we are associates, and he's very demanding. If I offended you in any way, I want to apologize."

"There's nothing wrong with the triplets?" Cydney waited for the answer before she allowed herself to breathe.

"I assure you, this isn't about the babies." Dr. Morgan smiled. "You gave me a shock when you asked for a recommendation for another doctor, that's all."

"Oh." Cydney swallowed. "I'm the one who needs to apologize. I'm sorry, Dr. Morgan. I shouldn't have said anything. This has nothing to do with your care of the triplets. It's all personal." Heat flared in her face. "I was trying to show Daniel I have a voice in the babies' care. I intended to look for a larger apartment near where I live now, but after we talked, I decided to look for a place closer to the hospital." She winced. "I'm sorry I gave the impression I wasn't happy with your care of the triplets."

Dr. Morgan made a face. "I figured it out. Daniel is a teddy bear under that growl. Don't let him shove you away." She pushed away from the cart and put the chart back on the hook. "Now that we have that cleared up, I'll get back to business. Take care of those babies."

Cydney stared after the doctor. Had she done the right thing? Talking to Dr. Morgan made her feel better. But if the doctor was right, moving closer and spending more time with Daniel, would make it more difficult to hide her feelings for him.

Gregory wiggled on her shoulder and whimpered.

Cydney changed position of her hand. She had noticed in the last few days the triplets made real baby noises. Almost on cue, Cece started crying in her incubator.

The nurse approached and checked Cece. She changed the baby's diaper, and made notes on the chart. "Our little girl is very demanding. This is the third time she's cried in an hour." The nurse smiled and darted to another infant making a demanding noise.

Cydney stared at the baby girl, trying to see if anything appeared wrong. Was Cece's color good? Did she look flushed? Was she having trouble with the GERD? Was she having trouble breathing?

The nurse checked and said Cece is okay.

Forcing herself to remain calm, she held Greg close. Since learning that tension caused infants to cry, she tried to shut out her worries when she was doing kangaroo care. Greg was the only baby she hadn't made cry so far, and she didn't want a perfect record.

How bad was that? She made the babies cry just by holding them.

Listening to the pings and whooshing of the equipment lining the room, she shoved away her unease. Thinking about the triplets' progress, and the machines they didn't need now soothed her tension. Their battle wasn't over, but the triplets had made progress.

Where was Daniel? It wasn't like him to miss visiting hours.

CHAPTER 11

Cydney glanced around the waiting room outside the NICU, but didn't see Daniel. She couldn't miss him. The open seating area made it easy for doctors to find parents at a glance. But Daniel wasn't there.

Relieved, she left the unit to use her cell phone.

After a short conversation with her boss, confirming she could see him in an hour, she closed the phone and drew a shuddering breath. The next step she had in mind would change her career path forever. Did she dare make such a drastic change? But even as the questions raced through her head, images of the triplets chased close behind and confirmed her decision as she turned toward the elevator.

Knees trembling, she fell to a vacant seat in the lobby. She didn't remember riding down on the elevator, but this was a life changing decision. She had to get it right.

Much as she wanted to deny Daniel's influence on her decision, she knew it wasn't true. Thoughts of his involvement in her life made her decision even harder. How would he react when he heard what she'd decided? Would he think she was trying to keep him away from the triplets?

Forcing herself to move and stop stalling, she pushed

through the glass doors exiting the lobby. Her gaze traveled past the landscaping along the sidewalk and down the circle drive in front of the hospital. Crepe Myrtles framed the parking lot with lush pink and white blooms. As she unlocked the car, her glance traveled to the long walkway to the hospital entrance. The view was beautiful, belying the urgency dwelling inside the walls of that building.

A trip to this hospital changed lives forever. Birth, death, illness, influenced everyone who came here. Memory of the past few days flashed through her head. She had learned about other peoples' influence on her life the hard way. Since the accident, every decision she made related to what happened in this building and the people working inside.

After all they had been through in recent days, she couldn't imagine her life without Daniel or the triplets. And that confirmed the decision she had made minutes earlier. Pulling her phone out of her purse, she hit the speed dial button for her best friend. What would Daniel think about her latest decision?

"Donna? Can you meet me at the office in an hour? Sorry, it's short notice, but this is important. I need you."

After a millisecond pause, Donna agreed.

"Okay. My office. Come earlier if you can. Bye." With the rumble of traffic on Wendover Avenue filling her ears, Cydney dropped the phone in her handbag and fell in the driver's seat just as her knees threatened to buckle. Realizing her life had changed forever, she gripped the steering wheel to stop her hands from trembling.

She had made two decisions this morning. Neither of them were something she would have done before Ziggy's accident.

Staring at road in a trance like state, she drove to her office. Who was the real Cydney Eller? Was she the woman making phone calls today or the woman who ignored her personal life to pursue a career?

How would Daniel react to her decision to take time away from her job to care for the triplets? Would he think she expected him to support her and the babies? Would his reaction be more personal? Would he accuse her of trying to take over the infants? Or imagine she was trying to invade his personal life?

By the time she reached the parking lot outside her office, her nerves were in tangled knots.

"Oh, good, Donna, you're early. We need to talk before the meeting." Cydney greeted as she entered the lobby.

"You call ten minutes early? I had to find a sitter, put on my face and dress after you called." Donna fanned herself and looked ready to drop as they waited for the elevator.

"Sorry for the short notice." Cydney stepped off the elevator and led the way to the senior partner's office. Twenty minutes later, when they walked out, they both looked pale. "I hope I didn't push you into something—"

"No, this is great. I think." Donna put a hand on Cydney's arm and stopped in the middle of the corridor. "Did I hear right? We're job sharing?"

"You're coming back?" Tamera squealed when they approached her desk.

"I'm taking official leave." Cydney glanced at her friend. "Donna is coming back for half-days starting next week."

"With half a brain, you mean. I must have lost my mind to agree to this. I have to arrange for a babysitter. Oh, Lord, I've got to talk to Charlie."

Cydney checked her watch. "I need to run. It's nearly time for visiting hours. Check out the office while you're here, Donna. We need to reorganize so we both know where things are."

"How are things—"

"I don't know." She clutched her purse to keep from shaking. "The triplets are improving, but that's causing other issues I haven't worked out. I'll call you later. Tamera will answer your questions about work."

Cydney didn't draw an easy breath until she was back in the NICU waiting room. Her insides were wiggling as if she had eaten a can of fishing worms. Her fingernails ached. She had only been away two and a half hours, and it was still early for visiting hours, but she couldn't calm her nerves. Staring at the observation window, she paced and checked her watch. Where was Daniel? Why had he missed the last visit? Was he so angry with her that he checked the triplets between hours? He could do that since he was a doctor, but before their disagreement he always waited with her.

The metal doors clanged open. Dr. Morgan stepped out. Face rigid, she glanced around the waiting room.

Cydney's breath hitched. Denial filled her head. Dr. Morgan had other patients besides the triplets. Just because she searched the waiting room with jerky motions of her head, didn't mean her urgency involved the triplets.

"Ms. Eller." Dr. Morgan rushed across the room.

Cydney's heart thumped. *It was the triplets.* "What's wrong?"

"I don't want to frighten you, but the infant female had another incident."

Cydney reached out a hand, wanting to grab on to something solid. Not just anything would do. She wanted Daniel, wanted his strength, his support. But Daniel wasn't there. She had chased him away with her refusal to admit she needed him.

She was on her own

All this time, she had claimed she wanted independence. But being independent meant facing emergencies alone as she had all her life, and she had worn out that t-shirt. What she really wanted was someone to share the worry with her. She wanted assurance and the secure feeling of knowing that someone loved her enough to care when things were tough. Really care about what mattered to her.

"Is she okay? How serious is it? What happened?"

"The infant is stable for now," Dr. Morgan replied when Cydney finally ran out of breath and gave her a chance to speak. "But she stopped breathing, again and—"

"Stopped breathing? I thought she had out-grown that problem."

"We thought she had. But that's the thing with preemies. Things can go wrong, fast. We think it's time to do surgery to keep this from happening again."

"We?" Cydney swallowed to stop the roar in her ears. *They had made the decision without asking her?* "You and Daniel decided she needed surgery?"

"No, I haven't seen Daniel. My staff and I came to that conclusion. I need you to sign the approval form. You are the guardian present. You need to make the decision to send the baby to surgery."

"Surgery?" Cydney forced that one word past the boulder blocking her throat. Baby Girl was so small.

How could her tiny body stand the strain? How could they cut on her sweet little body? How could she make that decision without Daniel's approval?

"I know surgery sounds like a drastic step. But I think it's the best answer for the baby's problem. We don't want to risk her going without oxygen and suffering brain damage."

"Brain damage?" Cydney repeated the words as if they were a foreign language. Her brain was racing and she couldn't string two thoughts together. *Brain damage?*

"I don't mean to frighten you. The baby isn't in danger at the moment," Dr. Morgan said, "but each time she goes through one of these episodes, we risk having permanent damage."

"B-but…I-I…thought she was improving."

"She is gaining weight and that's in our favor. Actually, we didn't suggest surgery right after birth because she was so small, but now," Dr. Morgan paused, but her message was clear. The doctor hadn't expected Cece to survive. "I think surgery is the best option. We don't want to send the baby home hooked up to monitors."

Home? Hooked up to monitors? How?

Cydney inhaled in a breath to stop her head from swimming. "W-w-hat does Daniel say?"

"We can't get in touch with Daniel."

But they had tried. Even knowing she spent most days sitting in this waiting room, the staff tried to get Daniel on the phone before stepping out those doors to ask what she thought.

Dr. Morgan held the clipboard toward Cydney. "We only need one guardian's signature. If you would sign on the bottom—"

Swallowing, Cydney took the clipboard in numb fingers. Prying her gaze away from the doctor's somber expression, she stared at the form. But all she saw was a green sheet of paper filled with black squiggles. She blinked but she couldn't read the words.

Drawing a shuddering breath, she stared at the doctor. "Why can't you get hold of Daniel?"

Dr. Morgan frowned. "We're not sure. We paged his beeper and tried his cell phone. We even called his answering service. They're trying to reach him now." She pushed the clipboard toward Cydney. "I don't think we should wait."

Ears buzzing, Cydney stared at the clipboard, then jerked her head up. She tried to focus, but the doctor had two heads and blurred features. She blinked. *How could she make a life and death decision when she couldn't even see straight?*

"I-I," Cydney swallowed and tried to focus. *Okay, it had happened. Her worst fear. The thing she worried about.*

With three premature infants, there were bound to be emergencies, but she expected Daniel to be here to help make decisions. Yet, when she finally admitted she needed him, he was not around.

Just like all the other frightening times in her life, she was alone. Except, this time three babies were in her care. If that wasn't independence, she didn't know what was. But one thing she did know, facing life alone wasn't all it was made out to be. Let the career types rave about their freedom and independence. She would rather have Daniel's strength by her side than face trouble alone.

"I-is she breathing on her own now?" Cydney forced the words past the fear blocking her throat. "Is she at risk?"

"She is stable for the moment, and her breathing is normal. I would say the risk has decreased for the time being. But that's all the more reason why we should go ahead."

What would Daniel do?

But this wasn't about Daniel. This was about her making a decision as the baby's guardian. It was her responsibility. She accepted this duty in court, under a judge's eagle eye. If she intended to take care of her sister's infants, now was the time to start.

What if she made the wrong choice?

"You said she's breathing normally? She's not in any immediate risk?"

"That's correct," Dr. Morgan sent a pointed glance at the clipboard Cydney clutched to her chest, "but if you're waiting for Daniel's opinion—"

"I'm not," Cydney squared her shoulders and tried to ignore the way her heart was pounding, "I know Daniel's opinion. We discussed surgery." She angled her chin and spoke with renewed determination as she passed the clipboard to the doctor. "I want to wait."

"Ms. Eller, I strongly advise you to reconsider that decision. Waiting could be disastrous for the infant if she stops breathing again."

Oh, Cece, you precious baby girl. What if I'm wrong?

"Her condition has leveled off? She's breathing on her own, correct?" Cydney waited for the doctor's nod. For the first time in days, she noticed the strong odor of antiseptic hanging in the air of the waiting room and fought a wave of nausea.

"She has oxygen in the incubator, but she is stable for the time being and I think we should operate."

"Is she in any more danger at this minute than she was this morning? Or last week?"

"Not at the moment, but the fact that she had this second incident shows that a problem still exists." Dr. Morgan's tone was firm and more distant than usual.

But Cece wasn't the doctor's child.

She isn't mine, either.

Cydney stared at the viewing window. *Yes. Yes, she is yours.* Ziggy gave life to this baby, but since birth, Cydney had bonded with the infants. They filled her heart and her head every second of the day.

This was her decision to make.

She had never dreamed she would make this admission, but she wanted Daniel's opinion before agreeing to surgery. "I think we should wait."

"Ms. Eller—"

"I appreciate everything you're doing, Dr. Morgan. But I can't sign that form as long as Cece isn't in immediate danger."

"Very well," Dr. Morgan sighed and turned to leave.

"May I see her?" Cydney reached out a hand to touch the doctor's sleeve, but at the last second, her hand dropped to her side.

She was in this on her own.

"In the circumstances, I think it's better if we let her rest." Dr. Morgan frowned. "The nurses might need to work with her."

In other words…Cece might have another incident.

What had she done?

Whathadshedone?

&⟐

For long minutes, Cydney paced in front of the viewing window. Then, realizing she might cause other parents to be alarmed, she sank into a chair and chewed on her thumbnail.

Where was Daniel? In all the time since they first met, he had only been a phone call away. She had watched him answer beeps the instant his pager sounded. Where was he now? Why hadn't he answered when Dr. Morgan paged him?

Why hadn't he answered when she needed him?

Her breath caught.

It was true.

She was ready to admit she needed Daniel. It was an admission she wouldn't have dreamed of making days earlier. But admitting it now brought new fears.

What if she had made the wrong choice? What if waiting for Daniel's opinion put Cece in danger? He said he wasn't in favor of surgery. But what if...

It was one to finally admit she needed another person in her life, but at what cost? If the baby died…if she had made the wrong decision, and Baby Girl suffered from her choice, Daniel would never forgive her.

She would never forgive herself.

For someone who prided herself on being independent, she had made an odd choice. But the baby's condition was stable. Cece was breathing normally. She hadn't suffered any lasting damage.

Early on, Dr. Morgan warned them this could happen. Why over react to this incident and rush the baby to surgery? Would Daniel change his mind when he heard of this latest event and agree with Dr. Morgan? Or would he approve of Cydney's need for caution?

Wouldn't Cece be better off if she could grow out of this condition on her own without having anesthesia? Dr. Morgan said time and growth could solve the baby's issues. But...what if they ran out of time and she'd made the wrong choice?

What have I done?

Hushed sounds of her surroundings filled her head. Hospital odors made her stomach heave. Where was Daniel? Would he ever speak to her again? Would he rush to court and demand sole custody of the triplets? Would he lift his chin and stare at her as if she were dog pooh stuck on his shoe? Would he lose all faith in her judgment and question her ability to care for the triplets?

Surging to her feet, she marched to the viewing window on legs that trembled. She was here, he wasn't. But Daniel couldn't berate her anymore than she was doing herself.

If anything happened to Cece, she had failed him and the triplets.

He left her in charge and she had kept the infant from having surgery. It was her decision. Her responsibility, but it was Cece's life at risk. Daniel might be furious, but she had weighed her decision carefully. Staring at closed curtains of the viewing window, she sighed.

At work, she made decisions on multi-million dollar ad campaigns. She might have second-guessed those decisions at times, but she had made her choice. What had changed? Why insist on waiting for Daniel's opinion?

Because. His opinion was important to her, and not just because he was a doctor. She knew he loved the triplets as much as she did. She had seen the evidence of his caring with her own eyes.

Trusting him…believing in him, opened the door to falling in love with him. That's why it upset her so much when the judge said Daniel needed a wife. If he fell in love with a third party as the judge suggested, it would break her heart.

She loved him.

Cydney turned away from the window in a daze. There was no doubt she trusted Daniel. Her actions today proved it. Had she risked that precious baby's life to wait for his opinion?

Had she done the right thing? Would Daniel be furious?

Then reality hit, easing her tension.

Daniel's opinion mattered. But so did hers. They shared custody of the triplets. She had made her decision based on previous talks with Daniel and the doctor. Right or wrong, she made a choice. Working with Daniel, depending on him, didn't mean she couldn't use her own mind.

Please, God, please let Baby Girl be okay.

Whispered conversations in the waiting room grew louder. Rustling noise and urgency filled air, signaling time for visiting hours to begin. What condition would Baby Girl be in?

The outer doors whooshed open. Daniel rushed in wearing his surgical blues.

Cydney's heart thudded like a jackhammer in her chest. Would he…

"I thought I would be too late. Why all the pages? What's wrong?" Daniel grabbed her elbow and urged her toward the line of parents entering the unit.

Cydney's tongue stuck to the roof of her mouth. She swallowed. "Why didn't you answer your pager?"

"I was drafted for a Medivac run. Didn't you hear the helicopter land on the roof?"

Cydney shook her head. All the time they had tried to reach him, Daniel had been trying to save lives. "Cece had another breathing incident."

"Did she stop breathing?"

Cydney nodded. "Her monitors went off. Dr. Morgan says she is breathing on her own, but getting oxygen. She tried to page you."

Daniel raked fingers through his hair. "You were here, weren't you?"

Cydney stumbled and turned stunned eyes on his face. If Daniel hadn't caught her arm and pulled her to his side she would have fallen. Realizing she was lightheaded, she inhaled, deeply, his words echoing inside her head.

You were here, weren't you? He trusted her. He trusted her!

❧

"Daniel, I tried to page you." Dr. Morgan met them at the metal doors.

"I heard. How is she?"

"Leveled off for now. Her color is back to normal." Dr. Morgan led them to Cece's incubator. "Looking at her now, it's hard to imagine she had serious issues a couple hours ago."

"How bad was it?"

"She stopped breathing." Dr. Morgan glanced at Cydney, then met Daniel's gaze. "Have you had time to talk?"

"I just arrived."

Dr. Morgan hugged the chart to her chest. "We suggested immediate surgery, but Ms. Eller refused to sign the form until we got your opinion."

Daniel glanced at Cydney and turned back to study the infant. After staring at the baby for long seconds, he crossed his arms over his chest. "What are her blood levels? How long was she in distress?"

Daniel forced his attention to the doctor and kept his eyes off Cydney.

How could he tell her what he was feeling? He didn't have the words. He left her in anger. But while he was gone, she had stepped in and taken charge when the triplets needed her. Why had he thought he could do this alone? When Cydney was at his side, things went smoother.

202

Did he need a wallop up the side of his head to make him see the truth?

⚏

Somehow, Daniel held it together until they left the NICU. But the instant they stepped through the clanging metal doors, he steered Cydney toward the elevators. "Come on, I need a drink."

"I'm not leaving." Cydney pulled back and dug her heels in the commercial gray carpet. "The triplets might need me."

"I need you." He swallowed and tried to lower his voice. "I need you to fill me in."

He needed more. He wanted to take Cydney in his arms and kiss her until they both needed air, but an elevator full of parents prevented him from doing more than pulling her close to his side.

When they stepped out of the elevator on the first floor, leading to the cafeteria, the hall was empty. Daniel glanced toward a huge potted plant standing beside the door and made a split second decision. Reaching for Cydney's hand, he pulled her to the other side of the greenery, and turned her to face him so he could look deep in her eyes. "Are you okay?"

She looked up at him and shrugged. "After being half scared out of my head? Yes, I think so. Are you?"

Daniel held her arms in a tender grip and pulled her close as he whispered. "I don't know." He touched his forehead to hers and stood there, breathing in her scent. "I'm still trying to analyze the issues."

"I was so worried something would go wrong. And you didn't answer your phone."

Daniel pulled her against his chest and finally found the comfort he needed. Resting his chin on her head, he held her close and sighed. "While I was trying to save someone else's infant, we almost lost Cece. I've been so blind."

"I-I was afraid you would be angry when you heard my decision." She wrapped her arms around his waist and leaned against his chest.

Daniel's blood warmed. This is what he needed, her com-

203

fort, her caring "Why? You were here. You saved Cece from unnecessary surgery."

"You agree with my decision?" Cydney pushed away from his chest to stare in his eyes. "You think I made the right choice?"

"I do. She's gaining weight and breathing better. This is only the second incident. I don't want to put her through surgery if we can avoid it."

"Dr. Morgan seems to think—"

"We're the parents. It's our decision." Daniel hugged her tighter. "You rescued Cece from going under the scalpel. I admire you for making that decision."

Cydney put her head on his chest. "I was so scared. So lost."

"The triplets are lucky to have you." Daniel lowered his head and kissed her eyelids. His lips feathered down her cheek. Finally, when the heat inside him felt ready to explode, he kissed her lips.

Heat zinged through his body, warming his blood and feeding his need to keep her close. He never expected this. Never knew this sense of belonging to another could take control of him after he fought so hard to deny his need for love.

"So am I, if you'll have me." His chest heaved with a shuddering sigh. "I thought I could take care of the triplets on my own. Be the responsible uncle and dad all wrapped into one, but I can't. You taught me that with your constant vigilance on their behalf."

"Three infants are too much for one person." Cydney agreed. "The judge was right about that."

"Ummm," Daniel rubbed his nose against hers in a teasing, motion, "it could be done, but I don't want to try. I learned that lesson." He leaned down and kissed her with all the emotions inside him. "I take risks on the job all the time. At home I want stability." He laughed at his own words. "I've met my match. I need you in my life, Cydney Eller."

"I need you, too, Daniel. I risked Cece's life by insisting we wait, but I—needed your opinion. I don't know what's happened to me."

Daniel kissed her again, this time tasting her lips, and making her body melt against his. "I do. The same thing happened to me. I discovered I want you in my life. It's true I need help with the triplets, but this is about loving you. Needing you. Just you. Now that I've found you, I can't imagine life without you."

"You don't have to worry about losing me. After I talked to Dr. Morgan this morning, I decided you were right. I should move in with you and help you take care of the triplets."

"I'm not asking for temporary, Cydney. I want forever—"

"But what if you fall in love with some—"

"I have fallen in love. That's what I'm trying to tell you."

Sound roared in her head. Heat filled her cheeks. Her heart skipped a beat and for a second, Cydney felt the life drain out of her. The judge's words had come back to haunt her. Daniel had fallen in love. Her knees buckled.

"Let's find a place to sit. You need food."

Cydney clutched at his waist, not wanting to let go. If she did, she could never hold him again. "I-I'm okay."

"You're not okay. You're exhausted and probably starved. You didn't hear a word I said." Daniel kissed her cheek. "When I propose to my future bride, I want her full attention."

Propose?

He was going to propose to his future wife and make her listen. Shaking her head from side to side, she said. "I can't—"

Daniel hugged her close. "I don't want to let go of you. But after the last few hours, I really need coffee. You don't want your future husband to faint at your feet, do you?"

"My future...you love *me*?" Cydney's eyes widened with hope and fear.

"I think I fell in love with you the instant I laid eyes on you. You looked so prim and put together, I wanted to ruffle your feathers. When you think about what was going on at our first meeting, this must be a really powerful attraction."

"Oh, Daniel, I love you, too." She buried her head in his chest. "I need you."

He kissed her soundly. "Please say you'll be my bride."

"What else would I say? I love you, but we can't get married."

"Why not?" He held her away enough to look in her eyes. "If you love me—"

"What about your mother? Isn't she on a cruise?"

Daniel started breathing again, and wrapped her tighter in his arms. "Yeah, she's with her friends, enjoying her period of mourning in the south of France. She says the French understand her moods and her friends think she looks ravishing in black."

"Have you told her about the triplets?"

"No, why spoil her time of mourning?"

"Are you going to tell her about our engagement?"

"How long are you going to make me wait?" Daniel sealed her lips with a lingering kiss.

But Cydney didn't need words. The heat of their embrace was all the response she needed to get her message across. She loved Daniel and never wanted to be apart from him. Why wait? She had found her heart's desire, found a man she loved. And the triples needed them. "I don't want to wait."

Daniel kissed her for long minutes.

"Then I'll tell my mother about our marriage and the triplets when she returns. She'll have a reason to celebrate and so will we." Long minutes later, he lifted his lips from hers. "The judge was right about one thing. I do need a wife, but only if it's you."

Feeling as if her heart would burst, Cydney smiled. "I love you, Daniel Prince."

ABOUT THE AUTHOR

A reader of romance since her early teens, Carol spent many hours doing chores and making up her own romance stories. College brought interesting conflicts, one being whether to major in biology or home economics. Both majors were heavy with science classes but the creative side of home economics won her over.

A teaching career followed, with marriage to her own hero and two wonderful sons. Yet, the stories in her head would not be still. When she retired from teaching, Carol started putting her dreams on paper and this book is one of the results.

See other titles on the next page.

Other Books by Carol Hutchens:

The Redbud Romance Series
THE SUBSTITUTE BRIDE #1
A BRIDE FOR MR. RIGHT #2
WHERE THE HEART IS #3
SO THIS IS CHRISTMAS #5

The Cupid Dog Romance Series
WHEN A DOG PLAYS CUPID #1
HERO'S BALL #2

Other Romances
THE BEST MAN

Medical Romance
DR'S SURPRISE TRIPLETS WIFE NEEDED
HOW CAN THE HEART FORGET

Mystery
FLAMES OF DECEIT
WHO MURDERED MR. WICKHAM [historical]